Dear Reader,

There's a place where life moves a little slower, where a neighborly smile and a friendly hello can still be heard. Where news of a wedding or a baby on the way is a reason to celebrate—and gossip travels faster than a telegram! Where hope lives in the heart, and love's promises last a lifetime.

The year is 1874, and the place is Harmony, Kansas . . .

A TOWN CALLED HARMONY
KEEPING FAITH

Faith Lind is Harmony's new teacher—although she's barely more than a schoolgirl herself . . .

Kincaid Hutton is a traveling salesman who's moved into the boardinghouse with his little girl, Amanda . . .

When Amanda turns out to be Faith's most mischievous student, Faith confronts Kincaid and suggests he settle down and spend more time with his daughter. But Kincaid knows he's running from his past—ever since losing his wife, he's shut out the pain and protected his heart from real love. Realizing that Miss Lind is smarter than he'd like to admit, he vows to change for Amanda's sake. But can he change a heart that's afraid to love—and find a way to keep Faith by his side forever?

Turn the page to meet
the folks of Harmony, Kansas . . .

Welcome to A TOWN CALLED HARMONY . . .

MAISIE HASTINGS & MINNIE PARKER, *proprietors of the boardinghouse . . .* These lively ladies, twins who are both widowed, are competitive to a fault—who bakes the lightest biscuits? Whose husband was worse? Who can say the most eloquent and (to their boarders' chagrin) the longest grace? And who is the better matchmaker? They'll do almost anything to outdo each other—and absolutely everything to bring loving hearts together!

JAKE SUTHERLAND, *the blacksmith . . .* Amidst the workings of his livery stable, he feels right at home. But when it comes to talking to a lady, Jake is awkward, tongue-tied . . . and positively timid!

JANE CARSON, *the dressmaker . . .* She wanted to be a doctor like her grandfather. But the eccentric old man decided that wasn't a ladylike career—and bought her a dress shop. Jane named it in his honor: You Sew and Sew. She can sew anything, but she'd rather stitch a wound than a hem.

ALEXANDER EVANS, *the newspaperman . . .* He runs <u>The Harmony Sentinel</u> with his daughter Samantha, an outspoken, college-educated columnist. Behind his back, she takes out an ad to lure a big city doctor to Harmony—and hopes to catch a husband for herself! Surely an urbane doctor would be more her match than the local bachelors—particularly Cord Spencer, who winks every time she walks by his saloon . . .

JAMES AND LILLIAN TAYLOR, *owners of the mercantile and post office* . . . With their six children, they're Harmony's wealthiest and most prolific family. It was Lillie, as a member of the Beautification Committee, who acquired the paints that brightened the town.

"LUSCIOUS" LOTTIE McGEE, *owner of the First Resort* . . . Lottie's girls sing and dance and even entertain upstairs . . . but Lottie herself is the main attraction at her enticing saloon. And when it comes to taking care of her own cousin, this enticing madam is all maternal instinct.

CORD SPENCER, *owner of the Last Resort* . . . Things sometimes get out of hand at Spencer's rowdy tavern, but he's mostly a good-natured scoundrel who doesn't mean any harm. And when push comes to shove, he'd be the first to put his life on the line for a friend.

SHERIFF TRAVIS MILLER, *the lawman* . . . The townsfolk don't always like the way he bends the law a bit when the saloons need a little straightening up. But Travis Miller listens to only one thing when it comes to deciding on the law: his conscience.

ZEKE GALLAGHER, *the barber and the dentist* . . . When he doesn't have his nose in a dime western, the white-whiskered, blue-eyed Zeke is probably making up stories of his own—or flirting with the ladies . . .

A TOWN CALLED HARMONY

KEEPING FAITH

Kathleen Kane

DIAMOND BOOKS, NEW YORK

This book is a Diamond original edition,
and has never been previously published.

KEEPING FAITH

A Diamond Book / published by arrangement with
the author

PRINTING HISTORY
Diamond edition / July 1994

ISBN: 0-7865-0016-6

Diamond Books are published by The Berkley Publishing Group,
200 Madison Avenue, New York, NY 10016.
DIAMOND and the "D" design
are trademarks belonging to Charter Communications, Inc.

PRINTED IN THE UNITED STATES OF AMERICA

10 9 8 7 6 5 4 3 2 1

CHAPTER

ONE

"Can't you look any meaner than that?"

Faith Lind sighed and glared at her reflection in the wavy glass of the old mirror. Deliberately she forced her full lips into a grim line and lowered her finely arched blond brows over her big hazel eyes. She held the expression for only a second or two before her shoulders slumped in defeat. "It's no use," she said aloud to her empty bedroom. "The children will never see me as stern or forbidding."

She turned away from the mirror and plopped down onto her bed. Her first day as the new school-teacher, and she couldn't even manage to convince *herself* of her new authority. The whole situation was impossible. How could the kids of Harmony be expected to treat her differently than they always had just because she would be sitting at old Mr. MacDougall's desk?

For an instant she let herself remember how she and the other students had always deferred to Mr. Mac's wisdom and solemn, booming voice. She would *never* be able to fill the older man's shoes. Lifting her eyes to the ceiling, Faith whispered plaintively, "Lord, if you were so set on taking Mr. Mac, couldn't you at *least* have waited till the end of the term?"

She blew out another long gust of breath and let

her gaze wander down over the outfit she'd chosen with such care for her first day as teacher. Suddenly the soft pink shirtwaist and gray skirt seemed all wrong.

But then again, maybe it wasn't the clothes. Maybe it was just her. Heaven knew, she was much too short. And though she wouldn't call herself plump by any means, she *did* seem to have a lot of excess . . . *flesh* in certain places. Her nice new clothes, instead of making her appear older, more experienced, only emphasized her well-rounded figure and gave her an air of fresh youthfulness.

Exactly the wrong approach.

Muttering under her breath, Faith pushed herself off the mattress and stood once more before the too honest mirror. No matter how she tried, her blond hair continued to wave and curl gently about her face. For what must have been the hundredth time that morning, she tried again to pull the heavy mass of hair tight against her scalp to the knot of curls at the nape of her neck. When a few ringlets escaped her hands, Faith grumbled in irritation. Then she caught a glimpse of herself in the mirror and laughed out loud. If the kids could see her now, they'd all *leap* to obey her slightest command.

"Faith!"

She jumped, startled at the sound of her own name echoing through the old boardinghouse. Crossing quickly to the door, she pulled it open and called out, "Be right down, Maisie!"

"See that you are, else the hogs'll have your breakfast!"

Faith turned, a grin on her face, and snatched her reticule off the nearby chair. Maisie's threat, as always, was an empty one. She didn't *have* a hog.

*   *   *

The other boarders were already seated at the long, oak table. Their heads bent, hands folded, they waited dutifully for Maisie's sister Minnie to finish saying grace.

Faith paused in the doorway. The two women sitting at either end of the table were as alike as two sisters could be. They'd even lost their husbands within six months of each other! Tall, angular women, they each wore their iron-gray hair in knots on top of their heads. And though they'd be the last to admit it, each of them hid a soft heart beneath sometimes gruff manners.

They took turns cooking for their boarders, each of them striving to be declared the best cook. In fact, they competed in everything, from saying grace before meals to deciding which of their late husbands was the laziest.

Faith smiled and shook her head as she listened to Minnie continue her prayer of thankfulness. Knowing full well how the two sisters tried to outdo each other in the length and depth of their prayers, she leaned against the doorjamb and let her gaze wander over her fellow boarders. Though she'd only been living in town a little over two weeks, she already felt as though the small group of people were family.

She smiled again when she heard Minnie proclaim loudly, "And, Lord, thank you for letting my Sunday cake turn out so nice and fluffy when Maisie's fell flatter than a poor man's dreams. It was good of ya not to let our guests here have to do without dessert altogether. . . ."

Shaking her head, Faith let Minnie's voice and Maisie's outraged snort fade into the background. Instead, she watched the others at the table.

To Maisie's right, Jake Sutherland, the blacksmith, shifted in his chair. In the five years Jake had lived in

Harmony, the huge, silent man had created quite a name for himself as an honest hard worker. But he didn't have many friends.

He looked up suddenly to find Faith's eyes on him. She was almost sure he blushed before he quickly lowered his gaze again.

Travis Miller, the sheriff, hid a yawn behind his folded hands. His blond hair was rumpled, his shirt wrinkled, even his *badge* was pinned on at a lazy tilt. Idly, Faith wondered what was so important that it kept a town sheriff up all night.

Directly across from Travis, his back to her, sat the latest addition to the boardinghouse: Maisie's nephew by marriage. Faith didn't even have to see Kincaid Hutton's face to know that it would be carefully blank. His deep green eyes held a wealth of secrets, and he made it clear with his polite but cool behavior that he didn't want anyone getting too close.

And yet, there was something about the man that drew Faith's attention. It wasn't just his elegant manners or the well-cut clothes he wore so well. It was . . .

A loud, rhythmic pounding shattered her thoughts. Straightening, she noted absently that the sound had also cut Minnie's prayer short.

"Amen, Lord," Minnie said hastily, then added, "What in the devil is that noise?"

After only a moment or two everyone at the table turned to look at the little girl sitting beside Kincaid Hutton. Amanda Hutton, eight years old and full of vinegar, was deliberately kicking her heels against the legs of her chair.

"Here now, child," Maisie demanded, waving one hand at the other end of the table, "stop that at once."

Minnie raised her fingertips to her temples. Her ever present smile nearly gone, she muttered, "For heaven's sake, Kincaid. Make the child stop. It's much too early for all that racket."

"Amanda," her father said gently, his patient tone speaking louder than his words, "that will do."

Faith walked to her place beside the little girl and saw Amanda's small features take on the stubborn expression she wore so often. Glancing quickly at Kincaid, Faith watched him suck in a gulp of air and close his eyes momentarily. When he opened them again, she saw the sad frustration he usually managed to hide shining in their green depths.

And still the girl went on pounding. Obviously, the man hadn't been able to reach his child, despite the gentle understanding he lavished on her. Faith slipped into her chair quietly, leaned over, and whispered something into Amanda's ear.

The kicking stopped immediately.

All eyes fixed on Faith, but she serenely ignored them all and reached for the coffeepot. From the corner of her eye she saw Maisie's sharp blue eyes narrow thoughtfully and knew without looking that a matching set watched her from the other end of the table. Instead of looking at either of the sisters, though, Faith glanced back at Amanda and smiled.

The little girl cocked her head and stared at her warily.

Slowly Kincaid nodded his thanks. Faith ignored him. She'd already noticed how difficult it was for the man to accept help, or even *friendship*, from anyone.

Slowly the others around the table began reaching for the platters of food, and the little incident with Amanda was pushed aside.

Faith poured herself a cup of coffee and spread

some fresh-churned butter onto a still-steaming biscuit. Before she had a bite, though, Minnie asked, "So how are you today, dear? A little nervous?"

Maisie snorted. "Now, why on earth would she be nervous? Don't she know each one of those kids like they were her own?"

"Hush up, Mrs. Know Everything!" Minnie shook one finger at her frowning sister. "Doesn't matter one little bit if she knows 'em or not. This is different, isn't it, Faith?"

Faith nodded and bit into the warm buttermilk biscuit.

"Nervous about what?" A deep voice rumbled into the discussion.

Faith glanced up at Kincaid Hutton and found his clear green eyes fastened on her with interest. It was as though he were staring right through her into her soul. Desperately she fought to swallow the suddenly too big mouthful of biscuit. Before she could, though, Maisie piped up with the answer to his question.

"Kincaid, I thought I told you. Faith here is the new schoolteacher!"

His face remained impassive, but his eyes reflected his surprise. Slowly, measuringly, he looked her over. Faith fought down the urge to curl into a ball.

"Aren't you a little *young* to be in such a position?" he finally asked.

Deliberately she straightened up in her chair. Throwing her shoulders back and lifting her chin, Faith retorted, "I'm old enough to have learned some manners, *Mr.* Hutton."

Minnie cackled delightedly and clapped her hands. "Well said, Faith dear." Shaking her head, she added, "Kincaid, you know better than to question a lady's age."

Hutton's mouth worked furiously, but all he said was "My apologies, *ma'am*."

"Don't you worry, Faith," Travis cut in, and she looked at him gratefully. "You'll do fine. You just keep a wary eye on Harry Taylor, mind."

Grinning, Faith nodded. Yes, she thought, Harry *would* be the one to watch. Between falling madly in love with someone different nearly every week and the outlandish pranks for which he was fast becoming legendary . . . why, she shuddered just to think of it. It was only a year ago, she remembered, that Harry actually took a rope from his father's mercantile and wrapped it tight around the school's outhouse. Poor Mr. MacDougall had been trapped inside for a couple of hours before Travis heard the man yelling for help.

The sheriff must have been remembering the same incident, because he said with a smile, "You see that boy with any rope, you call me right away, all right?"

Faith laughed. "I'll watch him, Travis. Thanks." Turning to face Kincaid Hutton again, she asked, "Will you be bringing Amanda to school today? It *is* her first full day, you know." She heard the little girl beside her pull in a deep breath, as if she was waiting for her father's answer, too.

"No."

Amanda exhaled on a sigh as he continued.

"I'll be leaving right after breakfast. Have to go into Ellsworth . . ."

He didn't even finish his sentence. He didn't have to. It was clear to Faith that Ellsworth was simply an excuse. He and Amanda had been in the boardinghouse a week or so, and despite his gentleness with his daughter, he almost seemed *afraid* to be alone with her.

She spared a quick look at Amanda and saw the

sad acceptance on the child's delicate features. For one infuriating moment Faith wanted to pull Amanda to her with one hand and smack Kincaid Hutton with the other.

But at almost the same instant she realized that her anger wouldn't solve any problems. It would only create more. The thing to do, she knew, was to find out the reasons behind Kincaid Hutton's distance from his daughter and somehow remedy the situation.

She wouldn't be doing it for *his* sake, anyway. No matter how annoying the man, Faith couldn't bear to see a child so downhearted.

Just then, Hutton inclined his head toward her, and she saw the closed, guarded look in his eyes. It wouldn't be easy, dealing with a man as obviously hardheaded as this one. But wasn't her father always saying, "Once Faith sets her mind to something . . . come hell or high water, it gets done?"

Besides, she told herself, as the new schoolteacher, wasn't it her job to look out for the children in her charge? Faith forced a smile to her lips, and she was pleased to read the confusion on Kincaid Hutton's face.

The early morning air was chilly, but it felt good after the close warmth of the boardinghouse. Faith stood on the boardwalk and pulled in a deep breath in an attempt to steady her nerves.

It didn't make any sense, she knew. Maisie was right. She'd known all the children in Harmony for years. There was no reason to be nervous. And yet . . . she wanted so badly for everything to go well.

Absently she smiled and waved to Zeke Gallagher, the barber. He sat in his favorite chair outside his shop next door to the boardinghouse, his feet propped up on the hitch rail. After greeting Faith, he turned his eyes back to the dime novel he'd been reading. One hand absently stroking his full white beard, he gave himself over to the thrilling deeds of bandits, lawmen, and shady ladies.

Across the street Jane Carson was just opening up her dress shop. A quiet, pleasant woman, Jane was equally at home sewing up a hem or taking a few stitches in torn flesh. And with no doctor in town, she'd come in handy more than a few times.

Faith suddenly shook herself mentally. She was wasting time and she knew it. Trying to put off going to the schoolhouse. Imagine a grown woman afraid to face a few children!

"Good morning, Faith!"

"Sam!" Faith jumped and turned around quickly, delighted to see her friend standing right behind her. Then, her eyes widening in appreciation, she walked a slow circle around Samantha Evans, shaking her head in admiration. "Your new dress is beautiful!"

Only two inches taller than Faith's five feet, Sam always dressed at the height of fashion. And, although she *looked* the image of a prim, cultured lady, there was no hiding the flash of deviltry in her blue eyes. But the pale lavender gown she wore today was by far the loveliest Faith had seen yet.

"Isn't it wonderful?" Sam ran one hand down the smooth silk skirt. "I swear, Jane Carson is a magician with a needle and thread. No one in Boston could touch the work Jane does! And in *this* dress, if I stand very still against the wall," she added with a laugh, "I'll disappear and be able to listen in on everyone in town! Just think of all the information I could gather for the paper then!"

Faith chuckled softly and realized Samantha was quite right. Her dress was almost the exact shade of the newspaper office, where Sam and her father, Alexander Evans, published *The Harmony Sentinel*. And whoever heard of a purple building?

Smiling, Faith silently acknowledged that no one but Lillie Taylor would have thought painting every building in town a different color was enough to "beautify" Harmony.

Although, Faith admitted silently with a furtive glance at the boardinghouse's bright pink walls, one short walk down Main Street was all it took to wake a body up. With its jumble of buildings crouched tightly together behind boardwalks that rose and fell unevenly, Harmony would have been no different than any other Kansas town but for Lillie Taylor.

Instead, the loud, cheerful colors greeted each day defiantly, giving the folks in town just a touch more pride and determination.

"Faith!" Samantha said on a laugh. "Are you coming back anytime soon? You're not listening."

"Hmmm? What?" Faith shook her head and smiled an apology at her friend. "What did you say?"

"Nothing important, really." Samantha inhaled sharply, then blew her breath out again. "I was wondering if the sheriff had anything interesting to say this morning."

"No. But then, Travis doesn't say much. What were you hoping to hear, Sam?"

"Oh, nothing really, I suppose."

"Hunting up gossip for Billy's column?"

Samantha grimaced. "Faith, you know how I feel about that...."

"Uh-huh." Faith grinned at her friend. "No one will admit to actually *liking* gossip, Sam. But you can bet everyone in town reads Billy's column. Including *you!*"

"Well, of course I read it, I do the typesetting and . . ."

Faith's eyebrows quirked.

"Oh, you're impossible!" Laughing, Samantha pulled the door to the newspaper office open. "I have to get back to work. And teacher"—she checked her pendant watch—"if I'm not mistaken, you're about to be late for your first day of school."

"Good Lord!" Faith snatched the hem of her skirt up, raced around the end of the building, jumped off the boardwalk, and ran across the yard and up the steps of the bright yellow schoolhouse.

CHAPTER

TWO

KINCAID DROPPED the plank of wood and let his head fall back on his neck. Sweat rolled down his face and under the collar of his blue cotton work shirt. Hands on hips, he stared blankly at the ceiling.

He'd been in the workshop behind the boarding-house since breakfast. And even after spending the day swinging a hammer and wielding a saw in a futile attempt at venting his frustration, his whole body screamed with tension.

Shaking his head wearily, he straightened up and pulled at the buttons of his shirt. After shrugging out of the sweat-soaked material, he balled it up and wiped his chest dry. Tossing the shirt into the corner, he bent, picked up the fallen plank, and carried it to the workbench. Even if nothing else was accomplished, he told himself wryly, at least Maisie's back door and leaky roof would be fixed.

Measuring carefully, Kincaid began to move the saw back and forth against the wood, losing himself in the steady, repetitive motions. But while his body worked, his mind was free to wander. And as it had all day, his brain conjured up Faith Lind's image.

He saw her clearly. Her disapproval . . . no, he corrected mentally, her *disappointment* in him. Why the hell should she be *disappointed* in him? She didn't even know him! Why was what he did or didn't do any of her business?

The saw stilled. And why did he give a damn what she thought?

"Keep your mind on what you're doin', Kincaid," he mumbled. "The one thing you don't need is another woman in your life."

Good Lord, no. Not after the mess he'd made of his life with Amanda's mother, Mary Alice. If you couldn't make a woman who *adored* you happy, he told himself, you have no business trying again with someone else.

A familiar stab of guilt slashed through him at the mere thought of Mary Alice, and he pushed it away quickly. But in its place came thoughts of Amanda, and these, he couldn't ignore.

Sighing, he set the saw down and leaned his hip against the edge of the table. Amanda.

What the hell was he going to do about Amanda? Oh, sure, he'd moved to Harmony, hoping that Maisie and Minnie could give the child more of a sense of family. But if he was honest with himself, he would have to admit that it was more than that. He'd gone running to Maisie like a frightened child.

He'd seen the changes in Amanda and known that he was to blame.

He never should have taken that traveling salesman job. But at the time, a few weeks after Mary Alice's death, it had seemed like a godsend.

Wearily he let himself remember that silent time after his wife died. The memories were always near, as if part of him refused to let him forget. More than a year had passed, but the images of his dead wife were still so clear it might as well have been yesterday.

He saw again the empty house, dust slowly collecting on Mary Alice's prized possessions, and the china she'd valued so highly, stacked dirty in the sink. But mostly he remembered Amanda. The way she watched him as if afraid to look away lest he die and leave her, too.

Even then, he'd understood her loss and her need to be with him. And yet, at the same time, he'd felt strangled by the quiet. When helpful neighbors finally stopped coming by with food and offers of sympathy, it had been just him and Amanda in the suddenly too big house.

Kincaid couldn't stand it. Maybe it would have been different if he'd loved Mary Alice the way she'd deserved to be loved. But he hadn't. Instead, he'd felt a comfortable, companionable affection for the woman who made no secret of the fact that she loved him to distraction.

And when she died, guilt overwhelmed him to the point of suffocation. He'd had to get away. If only for a while.

He took a job as a whiskey drummer, left Amanda in the care of the preacher and his wife, and began long months of traipsing over the countryside. Every week or so he would get back to town and visit with his daughter in a strained, awkward fashion. But during the week he visited saloon after saloon in the course of business. And between sampling his own wares and dallying with the "ladies" he encountered, Kincaid tried desperately to forget his own failures.

The aimless drifting might have gone on forever, too, if he hadn't begun noticing changes in Amanda. Small things at first. She stopped clinging to his hand when he arrived for a visit. And as the weeks passed, she seemed more and more distant to him. Almost as though she were deliberately cutting him out of her life. She didn't answer him when he spoke to her, and when it was time for him to leave again, she simply turned and went into the preacher's house, hardly sparing her father a second glance.

Not until then did Kincaid realize how close he was to losing Amanda as well as Mary Alice. And he wouldn't allow that to happen.

But it wasn't easy. Mary Alice's features lived again in his daughter's face, and he had to fight down the guilt that gripped him every time he looked at the child.

He sighed, shook his head to banish old memories, and told himself that really not much had changed, despite his efforts. Even though he no longer traveled, Amanda remained as distant as ever. If anything, her behavior had worsened. As if to test him, she deliberately misbehaved to judge his reaction. And usually, like that morning at the breakfast table, he knew he failed her tests.

Kincaid could still see Amanda's brilliant green eyes staring at him, waiting for his response while she continued to bang her heels against that goddamned chair. And then Miss Faith Lind sticks *her* nose into things, and immediately Amanda stops and behaves herself.

Though he'd *love* to know exactly what Miss Lind had said to the girl, he couldn't bring himself to ask.

He picked up the saw again and ran his fingertips gently over the serrated edge. No matter what, it seemed his mind was determined to taunt him with images of Faith. It wasn't enough that he be driven to distraction by her alone. No, he must also live with the fact that his daughter was bemused by the young woman as well.

As he positioned the saw to start work again, a childish squeal shattered the afternoon's quiet. He glanced up in time to see two of the Lind kids race past the workroom's open door.

School was out.

Faith smiled and didn't bother to hide her relief at the close of her first official day as schoolteacher. All in all, it had gone well, she thought. Once she'd set a few things straight.

And wouldn't you know it would be her own little brothers who would cause her first problem? They hadn't even waited for class to begin! Ben, at eight, and Gary, just a year behind him, had informed the class that *they* would be helping their older sister run the schoolhouse now. In fact, before she'd even reached her desk, two of the other children had come to her demanding to know if they really had to do Gary and Ben's homework as well as their own!

A few well-chosen words in private were enough to convince her brothers to give up their quest for power.

She only wished that Amanda Hutton's problem could be solved as easily.

"Afternoon, Faith, I mean . . . Miss Lind."

"Hmmm?" Her thoughts interrupted, Faith looked up quickly to find nine-year-old Harry Taylor staring at her with the same round-eyed fascination he'd focused on her all day. "Oh. Goodbye, Harry. See you tomorrow."

The little boy grinned. His wild red hair bushed out around his head, and his green eyes sparkled mischievously. One front tooth was missing, freckles danced across his nose and cheeks, and a slingshot poked from the pocket of his well-worn overalls. To look at him, no one would guess that *Harry* was Harmony's romantic! "You bet," he went on. Leaning closer, he winked and asked, "You want me to come in early like? You know, so's I could help you get set up for all them children?"

It was all Faith could do not to laugh outright. The boy said *children* like it was a race of people he had nothing in common with! It was no wonder that after giving birth to Harry, Lillie Taylor had never had another!

On a sigh Faith told herself that clearly *she* was the lucky object of Harry's affections this week. And knowing the boy as she did, she knew she had to be careful in handling him. Otherwise, she just might find herself tied inside an outhouse.

"That's very sweet of you, Harry," Faith said cautiously, and tried not to be nervous when the boy swaggered at her praise. "But, I think I'll be able to manage by myself."

His face fell, but only momentarily. "Well, if you're sure . . ." Brightening again, he asked, "How 'bout if I bring ya some chalk from the store? Bet you could use some more, couldn't ya?"

"Well, yes . . ."

Harry nodded and raced off.

Faith called after him, "But only if your father says it's all right!" The boy didn't even slow down. "For heaven's sake," Faith muttered, staring after him. Now she'd probably end up using chalk pilfered from the counter of Taylor's Mercantile!

"Faith?"

A small voice shook her, and she looked down at her younger sister Sarah. At ten the girl was already showing signs of becoming the beauty in the family. "What is it, Sarah?" Faith smiled and waited.

"Mama said to tell you you should come home for supper this Saturday."

Home. Thoughts of the Lind farmhouse rose up in her mind, and Faith had to fight down a sigh. Even with all of her brothers and sisters, and all the confusion they created, she really missed being at home every night for supper.

But it only made sense for her to live in town as long as she was teaching. The ride back and forth from the farm was much too long to make every day, though the kids didn't seem to mind it any. Still, as teacher she had to stay late with extra work, and come winter, there might be days she wouldn't be able to get into town at all for the snow!

Besides, she told herself, summer would soon be here and she could go back to the farm then. But for now she'd have to make do with the occasional visit.

"All right." She reached out and tugged one of Sarah's long blond braids. "Tell Mama I'll be there." Before she could say anything else, though, Amanda Hutton stepped outside. Head down, mumbling, she walked to Faith's side and stopped. "Did you want something, Amanda?"

The girl shook her head but didn't budge.

"Maybe she wants to push me off the steps like she pushed me off my chair earlier."

Faith shot a glance at her sister. She couldn't really blame Sarah for being upset, but it was so unusual to see a frown on the girl's normally smiling face! "All right, Sarah, you'd better go on home now."

"Yes, Faith." Sarah stuck out her tongue at Amanda's still-bowed head, then jumped off the last step and skipped off toward Main Street.

When Sissy and Billy Taylor hurried off, Faith sat down on the top step and pulled Amanda to a seat beside her. The girl was still mumbling, and unsure what to do next, Faith instinctively smoothed her hand down the length of the child's silky black hair. After a few minutes she asked quietly, "Who are you talking to, Amanda?"

The little girl picked idly at an embroidered rosette on the skirt of her soft green dress and ignored the question.

Faith stifled a sigh. As she continued to stroke the girl's hair, she let her mind go back over the day's events.

All morning Amanda had sulked in the corner of the room. When Faith moved her to the front row, the girl had insisted that she needed a two-seat desk all to herself and promptly shoved Sarah Lind out of her seat. With Sarah soothed, the rest of the day had crawled by. But Faith had noticed something peculiar. Amanda Hutton talked to the empty seat beside her. Not once or twice. The child did it all day.

At recess she hadn't played with any of the children. Instead, she'd sat beneath the oak tree behind the school, muttering the whole time.

It broke Faith's heart to watch. The child looked so lost, so . . . lonely. Whatever the reason for Amanda's solitude, Faith was determined that it not continue. Besides, she had a feeling that Amanda wasn't entirely happy with it, either. Every once in a while she would catch the girl looking at the other children with an almost fierce longing on her features.

But, Faith thought cautiously, trying to help Amanda wasn't going to be easy. There was a stubborn set to her jaw that told Faith she was in for a battle of wills.

She almost smiled when she realized that it would be Amanda, not Harry Taylor, claiming the honor of being her "problem" pupil. Now that she'd made up her mind to get to the bottom of Amanda's withdrawal, Faith decided there was no time like the present to begin.

"Can you tell me who it is you've been talking to all day?"

A long pause and finally a soft voice answered, "Boom."

"Boom?"

Sharp green eyes looked up at her, and Faith swept Amanda's too-long hair aside. "Who is Boom?"

"My friend."

"Oh." Frowning slightly, Faith asked, "Where is he now?"

"Right here. And she's not a boy. She's a girl."

"I beg your pardon." Invisible friends. Well, Faith told herself, at least the girl was talking. And, if she remembered correctly, Faith was pretty sure that her sister Suzanna had had an invisible puppy when she was very little. "You say Boom is right here?"

Amanda nodded.

Before she could stop herself, Faith glanced around, then mentally chided herself for her foolishness. "Well, uh . . . where does she live?"

"At the boardinghouse."

"I see. Does your father know?"

"No." Amanda's lips twisted mutinously. "He never sees Boom. Boom doesn't like Papa much."

"Hmmm. Why not, I wonder?"

" 'Cause he left us." The girl ran her palm over her skirt and cocked her head. "And Boom says I shouldn't get to likin' him, 'cause he'll just go away again. Maybe forever this time. Like mama did."

Faith's throat closed, and she had to struggle to keep her voice low and soothing when what she wanted to do was to snatch the girl up and hold her close. "When did Boom first come to live with you, Amanda? Do you remember?"

"Uh-huh." With one foot Amanda rubbed at the wrinkled stocking on her other leg. "After Papa left me at the preacher's and he was gone a awful long time."

"That must have been lonely."

The girl chewed at her thumbnail and nodded. "But then Boom came and it was all right. 'Cept sometimes, Boom does bad things and I get in trouble."

"Really?" Faith struggled to keep her rising emotions in check. She was so torn between sympathy for this child and rage against a father too oblivious to care that her head began to pound furiously.

"Uh-huh." Amanda turned suddenly and stared up at Faith. "Like this morning? It was Boom told me to kick that chair." She leaned in closer and confided, "And she didn't want me to stop when Papa told me to."

"You're right. That wasn't a very nice thing for Boom to tell you to do. A friend shouldn't try to get you into trouble."

"She didn't mean to. . . ." Amanda looked away again. "But since it wasn't really my fault," she whispered, "do I still have to scrub off the marks my shoes made, like you said?"

A tiny smile curved Faith's lips, but she let it fade away before she answered softly, "I think it would be best, don't you? After all, it wouldn't be fair to make Maisie or Minnie have to clean up after Boom when they don't even know her, would it?"

A long thoughtful minute passed before Amanda sighed heavily. "No, ma'am."

Snaking her arm around the girl's shoulders, Faith gave her a brief, tight squeeze and forced a bright note into her voice. "Good girl. Now, why don't you go on home, and I'll see you there later."

"Yes'm."

Faith didn't move from her seat on the school steps. She sat quietly and watched the lonely little girl plod across the schoolyard, her toes scuffing at the dirt. But when Amanda turned her head to one side, obviously listening to "Boom," a grim determination settled over Faith.

Jumping to her feet, she turned and raced back into the school. She had to pick up her books and reticule first. *Then* she would march straight to Kincaid Hutton and lay the problem of "Boom" at his feet. Where it belonged.

The minute she walked into the workshop, Kincaid knew he was in trouble.

She stood in the open doorway, silhouetted against the afternoon sun. Soft tendrils of her shining golden hair fell against her neck, lending her a delicate look at odds with her rigid posture. As he stared, he imagined he could actually *see* the air around her bristle with the force of her obvious anger.

Good, he told himself. Better that she be angry with him. In defending himself from whatever accusation she was about to deliver, perhaps he'd be able to ignore the tremendous attraction he felt toward her.

He stepped away from the worktable, wiping his palms on his jean-clad thighs. Then, hands on hips, he faced her, waiting.

It didn't take long.

"I've come to talk to you about Amanda," she said. "Your daughter?"

"I *know* who she is." He crossed his arms over his bare chest.

"I'm relieved to hear it." Faith stepped farther into the workshop. "Perhaps you also know her 'friend'?"

He frowned. "Who do you mean?"

"Boom."

"*Boom?*" He cocked his head and stared at her. No,

it wasn't a joke, he told himself. She was perfectly serious. "Who or *what* in the hell is Boom?"

"There is no reason for profanity, Mr. Hutton."

"Kincaid."

"What?"

"I said, call me Kincaid." He pushed one hand through his hair and called himself every kind of fool. Hadn't he just determined to keep her at arm's length? Then he heard himself add, "I don't answer to Mr. Hutton."

"For heaven's sake, why not? It's your name, isn't it?"

He blew out a rush of air and said more harshly than he'd intended, "Did you come over here to argue with me about my name?"

"No." She swallowed heavily, shifted the weight of books and papers in her arms, and lifted her chin slightly. "I came to discuss your daughter. As I told you."

"And this Boom person."

"Yes, and Boom."

"All right, *Miss* Lind. Suppose we start there?" He took a half step toward her and was pleased to note she backed up just a pace. She was nervous. "*Who* is Boom? I haven't heard his name before. What's he look like?"

"Boom, Mr. Hutton, is a girl. And I'm not sure what she looks like."

Faith smiled and Kincaid braced himself, sure he wouldn't like what was coming next.

"You see, Boom is invisible. The only one who can see her is Amanda."

Hell.

CHAPTER

THREE

INVISIBLE FRIENDS? Kincaid stepped back, away from Faith, and turned around. One hand rubbed his jaw while he tried to think. Instead, his mind quickly darted from one wild thought to another.

His own child, forced to create a playmate! Good Lord, had he really botched fatherhood *that* badly?

In the next instant he reassured himself. No, by heaven, he had not! There wasn't anything wrong with Amanda!

For God's sake, the child was only eight years old, and in the last year or so she'd lost her mother, seen her father run off to lick his wounds, and been up-rooted from the only home she'd ever known. Of *course* she was having "difficulties."

Hell, most *adults* would have trouble dealing with all that! Let alone a child!

"You *do* see why I felt I had to speak to you about this?"

He'd almost forgotten Faith's existence. Slowly he turned back around. His gaze reluctantly slipped up to her features, and the sympathetic expression on her face slapped him back to the present in a heart-beat. He didn't want her *pity*! And he didn't need her concern! A hot, irrational anger swept through him as she moved toward him.

Before he could stop himself, he said, "No, Teacher. Why don't you tell me why you're so *concerned*?"

She stopped, cocked her head, and stared at him, clearly baffled. "I *told* you. Amanda is talking to—"

"I know. An invisible friend." He nodded and turned back to the worktable. "Kids do things like that, *Miss* Lind."

She took a step toward him again. "Mr. Hutton—"

"Look . . ." He raised his gaze to hers and tried not to notice that her soft hazel eyes had suddenly darkened to a deep green. "I appreciate your concern and—"

"I'm sure, with a little time, Amanda will be fine," Faith interrupted.

Kincaid struggled to listen to her over the roaring in his ears. In all the times he'd thought about the two of them being alone together, never once had he pictured her as an angel of mercy tending to him as the father of a troubled child!

"She simply needs to get used to being part of the town. Soon she'll make *real* friends." Faith smiled. "Until then, though, perhaps if you were to spend a little more time with her—"

Advice. More well-meant advice. The last thing he wanted from *anyone*, let alone Faith!

"Thank you, Miss Lind." His voice sounded hoarse, even to him. But at least he wasn't shouting. Silently he congratulated himself on his control. For however long it lasted. "Like I said, I appreciate your concern. But I can take care of Amanda."

"I didn't mean to imply that—"

"I've got some work to do here, and it'd be best if you went along now." He picked up the saw.

"Mr. Hutton . . . *Kincaid*." Her voice dropped, and his gaze met hers.

She stared at him uncertainly. The pulse in her

throat sped up, and she licked her lips, clearly nervous. A long denied hunger gripped Kincaid's body.
Stunned by the strength of his own desire, he struggled to compose himself. Clenching his hands into
fists to keep from reaching out and drawing her to
him, he closed his eyes briefly in a futile attempt at
ignoring her.

It didn't work. Suddenly all he could think of was
kissing her, tasting her. He wanted to pull the pins
out of her hair and feel its soft weight tumble down
over him.

"If we could just . . . talk," she whispered, her
voice as shaky as if she were reading his mind.

His eyes flew open. Talk! Hah! The last thing on
his mind at that moment was *talk*! Abruptly he knew
that he *had* to get Faith Lind out of that workshop.
Quick. Taking a deep breath, he said the one thing he
knew would make her angry enough to storm out
and leave him to whatever peace he could find.

"I'll take care of Amanda my way. Besides, what
advice can you give me about children?" He looked
her up and down slowly, then added, "You're little
more than a child yourself."

Her cheeks flushed red. She pulled in a great gulp
of air and held it, clamped her lips together tightly,
and spun about on one heel. In a few furious strides
she was again in the doorway. Before she left, she
turned for one last look at him.

Even with her eyes in shadow, Kincaid felt her
gaze move over him contemptuously. When she left,
he kicked the workbench and watched his carefully
measured plans fall to the floor.

"Of all the simple-minded, insulting, know-it-all
men . . ." Faith's tirade wore down slowly as she

stomped across the yard, around the newspaper office, and into the street.

On impulse she continued on, toward the bright sunshine-yellow mercantile. She couldn't go straight to the boardinghouse as upset as she was. Maisie and Minnie would no doubt meet her at the front door with mountains of questions about her first day of school—and she was in no mood to answer them civilly.

The hem of her skirt flapped wildly with her hurried strides until it wrapped itself around her legs, and she tripped and fell to her knees in the middle of Main Street. Her papers and books scattered all around her in the dust, Faith sat back on her heels and ground her teeth together in exasperation. What she wouldn't give right now to be able to curse and swear and scream like a heathen!

In the next instant she admitted silently that swearing wouldn't do any good. The only thing that might help would be wiping out her entire day. As if it had never happened.

At least, she thought grimly as she reached for a paper about to flutter away down the street, she would like to erase Kincaid Hutton from her mind. Grumbling, she picked up her history book and shook out the dirt, telling herself that she should have known from the moment she walked into the workroom that her little meeting wouldn't go well.

After all, how could she be expected to keep her mind on business when Kincaid Hutton stood there just inches from her, his broad expanse of chest as naked as the day he was born!

And suddenly, as if seeing him once wasn't enough, her traitorous brain conjured up the image of Kincaid's strong, lean body, and she felt her heart race just as it had before.

Then the memory of his cutting words shattered the image. No wonder the child talks to imaginary friends, she told herself. It would certainly be better than speaking to her father!

"Need some help, Faith?"

A low, train rumble of a voice sounded nearby, and she looked up into a handsome, smiling, coffee-colored face.

Charlie Thompson, the bartender at the Last Resort, stood beside her, waiting.

"Thank you, Charlie," she said with a half laugh. "I guess I could, at that."

The tall, thin man pulled her to her feet, then dropped to one knee and scooped together the last of her belongings. Standing again, he brushed most of the dirt off the loose papers before handing them over to Faith.

"Not very clean, I'm afraid, but"—he swept a quick glance over the street—"I think I got everything."

"Thank you, Charlie. I guess that'll teach me to keep my mind on my walking." She reached out and brushed fine, pale dirt off the deep scarlet vest he wore to work every night. "Oh, no, now I've gone and gotten you all dirtied up just before work."

His gaze followed her movement, and quickly he ran his long, thin fingers over the silky material. "Don't concern yourself, Faith. Cord's always got me digging around in that storeroom of his." He grinned at her. "And I'd be willing to bet that it's *much* dirtier than this street!"

Slowly Faith returned his smile and felt her dark mood lift just a bit. Charlie Thompson had a way with people. Effortlessly, it seemed, he could soothe a hurt child or calm two drunks bent on destroying each other *and* the Last Resort. Maybe it was his easy smile. Maybe it was his deep voice speaking slowly and distinctly in a crisp Philadelphia accent.

But whatever the reason, Faith was glad she'd run into him. She already felt better.

"All right then," she said finally. "I won't feel too bad about dirtying up your vest. But if Cora gives you any grief over it, you tell her it's my fault."

He laughed out loud and turned for the saloon. Over his shoulder he said, "Now, *that* I just might do! My wife feels about dirt the same as Southerners feel about General Grant."

Still smiling, Faith glanced back at the boarding-house, then turned determinedly toward the mercantile. Just because her mood was a little brighter didn't mean she was any more ready to face Maisie and Minnie.

She stepped up onto the high boardwalk and crossed to the door. Distractedly going through her papers, Faith didn't hear the raised voices until she was inside the store and it was too late to get away.

"Faith!" Maisie called out imperiously. "Good! You can settle this here and now!"

"For heaven's sake," Minnie scolded. "Let the child get in the door before you start jumpin' at her!" She smiled and added, "Hello, Faith dear, how was school?"

She inhaled sharply, drawing in the mingled scents of fresh-ground coffee, tobacco, and just a hint of cin-namon. Lillie must have done her baking that morn-ing, she thought absently.

For the first time the jam-packed shelves and friendly clutter of the mercantile did nothing to soothe Faith's jagged nerves. She'd hoped for a little peace and quiet to compose herself before having to face anyone.

She sighed heavily and stared at the cluster of people at the front of the store. What *else* could go wrong today? she thought glumly. The very women she'd hoped to avoid for a while were lying in wait for her—*and* they weren't alone.

With dismay Faith's gaze swept the small crowd quickly. In addition to Maisie and Minnie, James and Lillie Taylor were there, of course, standing behind their well-stocked counter. Their eighteen-year-old daughter Mary stood off to one side, a smile hovering around the corners of her mouth. Zeke, the barber, stood in between Maisie and Minnie, smiling at first one, then the other of them.

No doubt, Faith told herself on a silent chuckle, to ensure that his supply of baked goods from the sisters competing for his attentions would continue.

At the far end of the counter, in front of several glass jars filled with penny candy, the two Englishmen stood side by side. As unlikely a pair as you'd ever want to see in Kansas, the two men owned the Double B farm, just outside town.

Faith smiled at the older of the two as he dipped one hand into the nearby barrel and pulled out a couple of crackers. Frederick Winchester, known locally as Fred, was nearly bald save for the gray fringe that ringed the back of his head from ear to ear. His rounded belly and sparkling gray eyes were the perfect complement to his ever present smile. He seemed to enjoy the easygoing way of life in Harmony and had already made a lot of friends.

His nephew, however . . . Faith's gaze moved over the younger man quickly. Stiff and stern, Edward Winchester spent most of his time sniffing elegantly and curling his lips in distaste. Faith reminded herself that he *was* royalty of some kind, and perhaps that explained his pompous behavior.

And, she thought with a smile, perhaps it also explained why the Americans had done such a splendid job during the Revolution!

But whatever the reasons behind his puffed-up, self-important airs, Faith dearly loved to watch the man's face whenever someone called him "Ed."

She shook her head slightly. For the life of her, she couldn't understand why two such *refined* gentlemen wanted to be *farmers*, of all things!"

"Faith. Faith!"

Startled, she jumped and turned to Maisie. "I'm sorry, what?"

The older woman's eyebrows lifted slightly. "Goodness' sakes, child. Didn't you hear a word I said?"

"No, Maisie. I'm sorry."

"Hmmph! Well, it's no matter. I'll say it again." Sweeping one arm over the small crowd, Maisie went on. "*We* have been *discussing* a difference of opinion. . . ."

"She means arguing." Mr. Taylor observed dryly.

"I do not!" She turned a fiery glare at the man before adressing Faith again. "*You* know I don't argue, dear."

"Course not." Faith bit the inside of her cheek to swallow a smile.

"Thunderation!"

Everyone turned to look at Minnie.

"For the love of—" The woman pulled in a gulp of air and shook one finger at her sister. "It's only April, Sister. And the way you're pussyfootin' around this little story here, by the time you finish, we'll have to dig a tunnel through the snowdrifts to get back home!" Frowning, she added, "You never could get to the point of a story!"

"Fine. *You* tell her."

"Plan to." Minnie turned to Faith and smiled. "We were arguing over how to spell the word *favor*."

"What?"

"That's right. Don't recall how it got started, but James over there"—she jerked her thumb at Mr. Taylor—"insists you spell it fav-*Er*." She wagged her head sadly as if thinking how terrible it must be to be that ignorant. "*I* say—"

"*We* say," Maisie prodded.

"Yes, yes. *We* say it's fav-*Or*." Minnie nodded firmly, agreeing with herself.

"Well, that's easy," Faith said in a rush, relieved to be able to bring the situation to an end so quickly.

"I ain't finished." Minnie held up one finger to silence the young woman, then slowly moved that index finger to point at Edward Winchester accusingly. "Then His Worship—His Royal Somebody or Other . . . oh, for heaven's sake, *Ed* over there—"

Faith glanced at him and was in time to see his face freeze and his eyes roll up. Hiding a smile, she looked back at Minnie.

"Keeps tryin' to tell us it's spelled f-a-v-o-*u*-r!" She shook her head again and squared her shoulders. Giving the young man a look that would quell an Indian uprising, she finished by saying, "Now, Faith. *You* tell 'em *I'm* right."

"*We're* right," Maisie amended.

Everyone was quiet. Waiting for Faith to deliver the verdict.

"Actually, Minnie, I think you and *Ed*"—she stressed the name on purpose—"are *both* right." Shooting a glance at Mr. Taylor, she shrugged. "Sorry, Mr. Taylor. But in America *favor* is spelled the ladies' way." Her gaze went back to a triumphant Minnie. "And in England it's spelled Ed's way."

Ed snapped a sharp bow toward Minnie, and it

didn't bother him a bit when the woman shot back, "This ain't England. So *I'm* right."

"*We're* right."

"Yes, yes . . ."

"Actually," Ed pronounced in his stilted tone, "I'm right. America is wrong."

"The whole country's wrong and *you're* right, Your Lordliness?" James Taylor's brow wrinkled thoughtfully.

Ed cringed visibly at the title Mr. Taylor had given him, but still he went on.

"Correct." He ran his thumbs under the lapels of his well-cut brown coat. "English, and I hesitate to use the word, when spoken in this benighted country, is simply a bastardized version of the proper usage."

Gasps sounded in the room. Lillie Taylor's right hand splayed over her bosom, Maisie's jaw dropped before snapping shut again, and Minnie's eyes narrowed.

"Did he say what I think he said?" Minnie hissed.

Fred, somehow sensing that his nephew was about to start another revolution, stepped into the breach.

"Ladies, ladies. I apologize for my nephew's unfortunate choice of words . . ."

"Now, Fred," Maisie said quickly, waving one hand at her sister, "before you start spoutin' off, I want to say that what that boy of yours had to say sounded like a challenge to me!"

"A challenge?"

"Yes." Maisie stepped away from Zeke's side and looked down the length of the counter to Ed. "And for myself, young man, I accept!"

"Accept what?" Fred looked from Maisie to Ed and back again.

"A spelling bee."

"Spelling *what*?" Ed's face was a mask of confusion.

"Bee, boy. Bee," Minnie repeated, then grabbed her sister's elbow. "That's a wonderful idea, Sister! We'll have teams. Faith can be the judge."

"Now, just a minute ..." But Faith's voice was drowned out in the hubbub.

"Ladies, ladies," Zeke said smoothly, obviously concerned that an argument might slow down his supply of baked goods, "let's not get into a lather over this now."

"Hush a minute, Zeke." Minnie snapped and looked at her sister.

"Let's see." Maisie tapped her forefinger against her rather pointed chin. "We'll each captain a team, Sister. Fair's fair. This is our idea after all."

"True, true," Minnie agreed eagerly.

"Maisie, *I* think ..." Faith still tried to interrupt but was ignored again.

"Now," Maisie pointed out, "today's Monday.... We'll have the first meet Thursday night. At the school. That all right with everybody?"

"The first?" Faith whispered.

Minnie nodded. "Fair enough. And we pick our own team members." Her hand shot out and grabbed hold of Zeke's shirtfront. "I choose Zeke."

"You can't—" Maisie started, then stopped at the victorious grin on her sister's face. "Fine. I'll take Fred. Anybody that can spout poetry like he does *must* be a good speller."

Frederick Winchester grinned proudly and rocked on his heels. "A pleasure, madam, a pleasure."

"You just keep in mind we're playin' *American* rules, you hear?"

Fred nodded.

"Well, I ain't takin' Ed, that's for dang sure!" Minnie snorted.

Edward stiffened and managed to look down his aristocratic nose at the lot of them.

"I don't want him, either." Maisie agreed.

"Perhaps I can spare either of you good 'ladies' any further torment." A pained smile crossed his face. "I regret to say that I will not be able to join in the festivities." He bowed stiffly and left the store without another word.

As he passed her, Faith would have sworn he looked just a little embarrassed and disappointed . . . if she hadn't known better.

"The hunt is on, Minnie," Maisie crowed. "And come Thursday night, me and my team are gonna give you what for!"

"Talk is cheap, Maisie. The proof is in the doin'."

"I'll wager a month of washin' dishes on my team winnin', Sister."

After a long moment, Minnie shook her sister's hand. "Done."

They gave each other an adversarial grin, then, as one, turned for the door. No one in town would be safe from the two sisters.

Faith jumped out of their way and tried to understand how she'd managed to lose control of both her talk with Kincaid *and* the ladies.

CHAPTER

FOUR

"I AIN'T gonna let no durn *girl* hit me! I don't care what Pa says 'bout not hittin' womenfolks!"

Faith grabbed her little brother as he raced past her headed for Amanda. He kicked and squirmed in her arms, shaking a fist at the little girl standing just out of reach.

This was *not* how she'd imagined her first week of teaching! Faith sighed and tightened her grip. Only Tuesday afternoon. She'd only been in charge of the schoolhouse two days, and each of those days had brought its own disasters.

The noise was deafening! Every child in the schoolhouse was shouting at the top of his lungs, and no one was listening to Faith. For heaven's sake, she asked herself as she struggled to keep a hold on Gary, how had this gotten so out of hand?

"Durn you anyways!" Gary screamed and lunged again for Amanda. "Why'd ya wanta hit *me*? What'd *I* do?"

"You stepped on Boom, and you did it on purpose!" Amanda yelled right back at him.

"Amanda, take your seat," Faith ordered and blew a long strand of hair out of her eyes. Gary's swinging foot smashed into her shin, and she grimaced and lifted him off the floor. "Gary," she warned, her voice low, "you be still now, or so help me, I'll tell Pa you tried to hit a girl."

Immediately the boy slowed down, but then he said plaintively, "Faith, I didn't do *nothin'*!"

"Anything," she corrected without thinking.

"Anything," he amended. " 'Sides, how's a body not s'posed to step on somethin' he can't even *see*?"

"Yeah, Faith, I mean Miss Lind," Harry tossed in. "Gary didn't do nothin'. That ol' Amanda's just loco is all."

"Harry!" Faith set her brother back down and frowned at the other boy.

"She is not loco, Harry Taylor!" Sarah Lind stepped up. "Gary stepped on Boom. I saw him! Near killed ol' Boom with those big feet of his!"

Faith sighed. Sarah clearly enjoyed seeing her pesky little brother in trouble. But the shy, pleased smile on Amanda's face at the unexpected support touched her heart.

Still, the last thing she needed in this already too crowded classroom was one more student playing with invisible friends! If she wasn't careful, *all* of them would start bringing in imaginary classmates.

Then where would she be?

"All right now." Faith clapped her hands and shouted in the voice she used to use on the farm when it was time to bring the kids in from the fields for supper. "That will do! Amanda, Gary, Harry . . ." The children stared at her, waiting. "Each of you go to a corner of the room and stand there, facing the wall until I tell you to move."

"What'd *I* do?" Harry piped up.

"Would you like to stand a little longer than anyone else, Harry?"

"No'm," the boy whispered and shot her a look

that convinced Faith his crush on her was over. But it was a small price to pay for peace.

"Serves you right, Harry Taylor!"

"Sarah!" Faith glared at her little sister. "Take your seat *now*!"

"The rest of you, too." She added with a sweep of her arm. As everyone reluctantly moved to do as they were told, Faith said softly, "Boom, you stand in a corner, too."

The class stopped. She felt the children's stares, but she didn't react. Even if she did feel a little foolish ordering an invisible child to take her punishment, she wasn't about to let it show.

"You want *Boom* in the corner?" Amanda finally asked in an astonished whisper.

"That's right." Faith met the little girl's gaze squarely. "If Boom is going to insist on coming to school with you, then she is going to have to abide by the rules, just as the rest of you have to."

The little girl swallowed and bit at her bottom lip. Her big green eyes even bigger than usual, she finally mumbled, "Yes, ma'am."

"And Amanda," Faith went on, "I think from now on Boom should sit in a chair at the front of the room. That way no one will accidentally step on her again. Will that be all right with Boom?"

Harry snorted and called out, "Why don't you just ask Boom, Faith?"

Over the burst of laughter she answered without even looking at the boy. "Corner, Harry. Now."

"Shoot!"

"Amanda?"

After looking uneasily around the room at the interested faces, Amanda lowered her gaze to her shoetops and answered, "I guess she won't mind any."

"Good, then." Faith straightened up and clapped her hands twice for quiet. "That's settled. Now, the . . . *four* of you—to the corners."

Sullen expressions and shuffling feet accompanied the three students Faith could see as they moved off toward the corners of the room. One glance at the empty spot where Boom supposedly stood facing the wall was all Faith allowed herself.

With order restored, the other students were once again reading their primers. She was only half listening to the recitations, though. Instead, she rethought all that had just happened.

Despite the children's argument, Faith felt good. Not only had Amanda stood up to the boys, but she seemed to have made a friend of Sarah. No matter, she told herself wryly, that Sarah's allegiance had more to do with attacking Gary than defending Amanda. What was important, she thought, was that a line had been drawn—and Amanda hadn't been left standing alone. In fact, Faith seemed to remember that a couple of the children had been shouting encouragement to Boom and Amanda.

With another look at the corners of the room, Faith told herself she was making progress.

But an instant later she frowned. Was it progress to go along with the pretense of an invisible student? Wouldn't it be better to make Amanda realize that a *real* friend was much better than an imaginary one?

She shook her head to dispel her doubts. One step at a time, she thought grimly. The look of surprise on the little girl's face when Boom received her punishment flashed through Faith's mind. If including an invisible child in the class discipline was a step toward winning Amanda's trust . . . so be it.

*   *   *

Kincaid sat down in the shade and pulled in a deep breath of the fresh April air. A beautiful day, he thought as he watched the billowing ivory-colored clouds scuttle across the wide expanse of blue sky. Leaning back against the side of the workroom, he stretched his long legs out in front of him and crossed his booted feet at the ankle. A cool breeze blew over him, and Kincaid found himself wishing that the wind could blow *through* him, ridding him of the anger that still held him.

He yanked a tuft of grass out of the ground, crushed it in his fist, then tossed it aside. It seemed to be taking forever for school to let out today, he thought in irritation. But maybe it was just as well. If he'd spoken to Faith earlier, he wasn't at all sure he could've contained his fury.

Lord. Kincaid closed his eyes and leaned his head back against the trunk of the tree. If he hadn't seen it, he never would have believed it. And if he hadn't gone to the school to take Amanda her lunch, he might never have found out just how Harmony's "Teacher" conducted her class! In memory he saw it again. Standing just inside the schoolhouse door, he'd gone unnoticed by everyone, including Faith Lind. Of course, she'd had her hands full.

He was willing to admit that she'd handled the fight very capably. And her punishment was fair, he told himself, remembering that his own child had been one of the children sent to a corner. *But.* When she casually announced that she was also sending an invisible student to a corner, anger flared up in Kincaid with a rush.

It took every ounce of self-control he possessed to leave Amanda's lunch on the coatrack bench and leave the building. But he'd done it. In fact, he'd been so quiet, he was sure that Faith Lind had no idea that someone had witnessed the little scene in class.

His eyes flew open and he glared at the school-house across the way. When he thought about all that young woman had had to say to him about dealing with Amanda ... She'd acted as though she had all the answers.

He snorted. If *that* was her solution to Amanda's so-called problem ... well, he had a few things he wanted to say to the schoolteacher. And none of it could be said in front of the kids.

Dammit, he cursed silently. He should never have left South Dakota. Maybe this whole move was a mistake. Maybe he should have held on to his little store. For all he knew, Amanda would have been just fine if he hadn't dragged her off to live with strangers in an unfamiliar town.

He stopped suddenly and considered that. Maybe that was the answer to all his problems. Perhaps he should just pack Amanda up and go back. The store was still there, waiting for him. Lord knows, he was having a helluva time selling it. He might *never* be able to sell it.

And what if he did stay? He couldn't very well go on being his aunt's handy man. That wasn't a living. He didn't know the first thing about farming, and the one thing a little town like Harmony *didn't* need was another mercantile.

But was running again the right thing to do? He snorted a half laugh. Running is what it would be, too. Only this time, instead of running *to* Maisie ... he would be running *from* Faith! Or at least, from the feelings Faith aroused in him.

A sudden gust of wind whipped past him, and Kincaid straightened abruptly. The schoolhouse doors flew open, and a small flood of children poured out into the late afternoon sunshine. Laughing and talking, they raced across the yard toward Main Street. Most of them, anyway.

Sarah Lind stepped out onto the top step and paused, glancing over her shoulder into the building behind her. Then, almost reluctantly, she walked down the steps and followed the other children.

Kincaid held his breath, waiting. He hadn't seen Amanda yet. His chest tightened as if an unseen hand held him in a giant fist. When his daughter sidled out of the building, he sighed. She looked so small. So alone.

Head bent, her night-black hair hanging down on either side of her face, Amanda drooped down the steps. As she crossed the now empty yard, Kincaid noticed the slouch in her narrow shoulders and her shuffling feet kicking up tiny clouds of dust as she passed.

Teeth clenched, Kincaid swallowed past the knot in his throat and sucked in a great gulp of air as he realized that his daughter was mumbling. No . . . *talking* to nobody.

Boom again.

His hard gaze shifted from the lonesome figure of his daughter to the schoolhouse. Grimly he pushed himself to his feet and brushed his palms over his pants. It was time for him to settle a few things with Faith Lind.

Raised voices caught his attention, and he glanced to his left. Maisie and Minnie, each trying to out-shout the other, were headed for the mercantile. No doubt still trying to round up last-minute teammates for the spelling bee.

Deliberately Kincaid lengthened his stride and made a dash for the schoolhouse.

*   *   *

Faith gathered up her papers, then let her gaze wander over the room one last time to make sure she hadn't forgotten anything. Smiling, she slipped the strings of her reticule over her wrist and stepped off the slightly raised platform that held her desk.

All in all, she thought the day had gone well. Of course, Harry wasn't quite so infatuated with her anymore. But, remembering the dried snakeskin he'd brought her only that morning—before the fight— Faith thought that might not be such a high price to pay.

Besides, after the children had served their punishments in the corner, Faith had caught Amanda's curious gaze on her once or twice. If nothing else, she'd *definitely* surprised the little girl.

"I could use something to smile about." Kincaid Hutton's voice shattered her thoughts. "Would you care to share the good news?"

She hadn't even heard him come in. Faith watched him walk down the center aisle toward her. In the jumble of small desks and chairs, he looked even bigger than he usually did. Her fingers tightened around the papers she clutched to her chest. Her heartbeat sped up, and she felt the first stirrings of anger at herself for letting the man affect her as he did.

For heaven's sake. This was *her* schoolroom. In this building *she* was in charge. Kincaid Hutton was simply the father of one of her students. It was time she remembered that and behaved accordingly.

Still, she thought as he got closer and she had to raise her gaze to meet his, it wouldn't hurt to even think out a bit. Taking a half-step backward, she climbed back onto the platform. He was still taller than she, but at least she didn't feel like one of the students facing a headmaster.

Of course, she'd feel better about their coming talk if he didn't look quite so grim.

"Not willing to share your good humor?" he asked and came to a stop directly in front of her.

Faith shook her head. She should have been paying attention instead of letting her imagination run wild. "I'm sorry, Mr. Hutton. I didn't hear you. What did you say?"

"Nothing." Inhaling sharply, he crossed his arms over his chest, glanced toward the window, then looked back at her. "I stopped by earlier today. Amanda forgot her lunch." One eyebrow quirked slightly when he added quietly, "I didn't want to disturb your class, so I stayed by the door."

"Oh?"

"Normally, I would have intervened, but you appeared to have your little 'problem' well in hand. Is your class *always* so disorganized?" He rocked back on his heels and seemed to be waiting for an answer.

Faith frowned slightly. It was obvious he'd been witness to the children's fight earlier. But for goodness' sake. If he'd seen it, why the devil hadn't he offered his assistance?

"As I said, I would've helped," he continued as if he could read her mind, "but you handled it . . . quite well. All things considered."

"Thank you," she said dryly.

"To a point."

Her eyebrows lifted. Nervousness forgotten, Faith looked him square in the eye. For the first time she noticed a glimmer of what could only be anger flickering in the dark green depths.

What could he *possibly* be angry about? Surely not Amanda being sent to stand in a corner! If he'd really witnessed that scene, then he must realize she'd deserved discipline as much as the others had.

She watched the corners of his well-shaped mouth twitch as though he was aching to say something more. Was he playing some sort of cat-and-mouse game with her? Was she supposed to *guess* what it was that had brought him to the school? He took a half step closer, and Faith straightened her shoulders and lifted her chin. It was time to remind Kincaid Hutton just *who* was the teacher and *who* was the parent.

"If you have something to say, Mr. Hutton, I suggest you say it." She tapped the papers she held. "I have a lot of work to get done before supper tonight."

Clearly taken aback, Kincaid's eyes widened. He gave her a slight nod and said, "Fine, Miss Lind. Since you're so busy, perhaps you wouldn't mind explaining—very *quickly*, mind you—just what you thought you were doing by going along with Amanda's fantasy?"

"What?" She cocked her head and stared at him.

"Don't pretend you don't know what I'm talking about." He pushed one hand through his hair and glared down at her. "I was there. I heard you."

"Heard me what?"

"I *heard* you send *Boom* to a corner, for God's sake!"

Boom? He was this upset over Boom? Slowly, reluctantly, she felt a smile curve her lips despite her best efforts to hide it.

"Frankly I don't see anything funny in this situation, Miss Lind."

"I'm sorry." She shook her head gently and continued to speak softly, slowly. "It's just that the children appeared to have accepted my judgment much better than you have."

"They're *children*." He spun about, took two steps

away from her, then came back just as quickly. "What on earth did you think you were doing, going along with her pretense as you did?"

"Mr. Hutton." Faith took a deep breath and told herself that it was only natural for a child's father to be interested in a teacher's actions. It was up to her to explain her reasoning. "I felt that Amanda should be shown that her imaginary friend would be expected to live by the same rules as any of the other children."

"Why?"

"Why?" She frowned. "I'm afraid I don't understand."

"That's obvious." He clamped his mouth shut, inhaled, then started again. "Amanda is *my* child. You will please remember that."

"Of course. But in school—"

"In school," he interrupted, "I will of course expect her to obey you. But I also expect you to respect my wishes."

"Which are?" Her right foot tapped against the platform.

"There will be no more talk about this . . . Boom. If you continue to coddle Amanda, she'll *never* let go of her imaginings."

"But Mr. Hutton—"

"No." He shook his head and forced a grim smile to his lips. "I'm afraid I insist. I will have a talk with Amanda this evening. I'm going to forbid her to so much as mention Boom again, and that will be the end of that!"

"No, it won't."

He stared at her with all the surprise he would have given a talking rock. Faith took advantage of his silence and plunged in.

"You can't *order* a child to feel safe, loved. You

can't *insist* that she stop being afraid or lonely." One hand on her hip, Faith leaned toward him, speaking quickly. "You have to understand her fear. You have to spend time with her. *Show* her she's loved. And in time Boom will simply fade away. When *Amanda's* ready to let go of her."

His breath came fast and furious. Faith guessed he wasn't used to being contradicted. But to give him his due, he didn't lose the temper that was obviously rising.

For the life of her, she couldn't understand why he was so upset. He'd never seemed a particularly *hard* man. Why should Boom bother him so much?

"You're entitled to your opinion, Miss Lind. But since Amanda is my daughter, we will handle this situation *my* way."

"But—"

"No." He stepped back from her and half turned. The look in his eyes wasn't quite as hostile as when he'd arrived. "Thank you for your concern, but *I* will take care of Amanda my own way."

There wasn't a thing she could say to that. The girl *was* his daughter, after all.

After a long, silent moment Kincaid turned and marched back down the aisle toward the door. But she couldn't just let him leave without telling him one thing more. "I have to tell you," Faith called out, "I think you're wrong, Mr. Hutton."

He stopped suddenly and glanced at her over his shoulder. A grim smile touched his mouth briefly. "It surely wouldn't be the first time, Miss Lind."

CHAPTER

FIVE

HE PULLED the yellow and green flower basket quilt up to her neck and smoothed it gently. Turning to the bedside table, Kincaid turned the lamp wick down low, then let his gaze drift around his daughter's bedroom. Out of habit his eyes went first to the window. Plain white curtain pulled against the night. He'd already checked to make sure the bolt was fastened securely. Her clothes for the morning were stacked neatly on the marble-topped dresser in the corner, and the closet door was closed.

It made no sense, he knew, this ritual he had of checking a perfectly safe room. But still, since Mary Alice's death . . . hell, he was only trying to take care of his little girl.

Shaking his head at his own foolishness, he turned back to his daughter. Amanda lay in the center of the big bed, her cheeks still rosy from her bath. Tenderness washed over Kincaid as he sat down on the edge of the bed. Then he noticed the wariness in her eyes and fought down the stab of pain it brought.

He pulled in a deep, steadying breath, knowing that what he was about to say wouldn't do a thing toward endearing himself to his child. Awkwardly he tugged at the quilt again. He was still getting used to the nightly ceremony of tucking Amanda in, and he wasn't the least bit convinced he was doing it right.

Besides, he never knew what to say to her. Good night didn't seem enough, and he doubted very much if she would care for him singing a lullaby!

"Good night, Papa," she whispered into the strained silence.

Here it was. He couldn't put it off any longer. "Before you go to sleep, Amanda," he started, "I think we should talk about something."

She only stared at him with those big green eyes so much like his own. Obviously, she wasn't going to make this any easier for him.

"It's about Boom." Kincaid waited, hoping for some sort of reaction. Nothing. "I, uh ... saw what happened at school today, Amanda, and—"

"It wasn't my fault, Papa," she said quickly. "Gary stepped on Boom!"

"I know."

"And Faith put Boom in the corner, too." She cocked her head. "That's not fair, is it?"

True, he told himself. It wasn't fair. It was crazy.

"No," he said reluctantly. "I suppose it wasn't. But that's not what I want to talk about."

"Oh. Then what?"

"Amanda ..." He sucked in another gulp of air and rushed on before he could stop himself. "It's time you stopped talking to Boom."

"But—"

"No." He held up one hand for her silence. "I understand how you needed Boom at first—when your mama—"

Her face closed up. Her eyes shuttered.

"Well. I mean, when we moved here, you didn't know anyone. Didn't have any friends ... but now you do. You have Maisie and Minnie and me and Sarah ..."

"And Faith," Amanda reminded him sullenly.

"Yes. And Faith." Kincaid leaned over her and lowered his voice. "What I'm trying to say is, you don't need Boom anymore, Amanda."

"Yes, I do."

Her eyes filled suddenly, and Kincaid panicked. Lord, he hated it when she cried.

"Amanda . . ."

"But I do!" She raised her voice as if a new tone would convince him. "Boom's my bestest friend in the whole world. She *is*!"

"Lower your voice, young lady!" he hissed and cast one quick glance at the closed door behind him. Obviously, being soft and sympathetic wasn't working. The only thing left to do was be firm with her. "Now, Amanda, I want you to listen to me very carefully."

Her lips pursed, eyes narrowed, she stared at him. All wariness was gone from her face. It had been replaced with out-and-out dislike.

Kincaid swallowed. Guilt threatened to swamp him, and his patience was wearing thin. After all, this was an *imaginary* friend they were talking about!

"I absolutely *forbid* you to talk about Boom ever again. Do you understand me?"

Her mouth worked, but she didn't say anything.

"Amanda?"

After a long, painful moment she jerked her head in a nod. Her bottom lip quivered dangerously, and Kincaid stood up. He'd known it would be hard. He just hadn't realized *how* hard.

"All right, then. Now that that's settled." He leaned over, cupped his hand around the lamp chimney, and blew out the flame. Darkness crashed down around them, and he thought he heard her sniffle.

He steeled himself against the sound. Quickly he

bent down, kissed her forehead, and said "good night, dear" with more cheer than he felt.

There was no answer from his daughter, and after waiting only a moment longer, he let himself out of the room and closed the door behind him.

Rubbing one hand across his beard-stubbled jawline, Kincaid wavered uncertainly. He *hated* not knowing if he was doing the right thing or not! He cocked his head toward her door and heard the unmistakable sounds of weeping. Dammit, he thought wildly. Why did she have to *cry*? Didn't she realize that he was doing all this for her own good?

She's not a baby anymore, his brain reminded him. It's time for her to give up living in a pretend world. Once again he told himself that he'd done the right thing. For heaven's sake, he didn't want a twenty-year-old Amanda wandering the countryside talking to herself!

And yet . . .

It broke his heart to hear her cry. Lord knew, she'd had far too much already to cry for in her life. And knowing that he was responsible for this bout of tears only made it that much worse to hear. Straightening up, he stared across the lamplit hallway at Faith Lind's closed door.

She could probably hear Amanda, too. Then he remembered how Faith had played along with Amanda's fantasy, and renewed anger swelled in him. Actually, this whole situation was *her* fault! If she hadn't encouraged the child, perhaps Amanda wouldn't still be so attached to that goddamned Boom!

What the devil did a girl her age know about dealing with an unhappy child? For God's sake! Faith could be Amanda's *sister*! Kincaid frowned and gritted his teeth together against the sound of his daughter's tears. What was wrong with the people of Harmony, anyway? How could they *possibly* have made a *child* the schoolteacher? Didn't anyone in town think? Hadn't they ever noticed that most schoolteachers were at least a thousand years old?

His breath rushed in and out of his chest like a bellows. The longer Amanda cried, the more his temper grew. Until finally he heard her begin to quiet down. Another moment or two passed, and he almost smiled. The crying had stopped.

It would be all right. He'd done well. Amanda would be fine. He was sure of it. And he'd done it without the help of Faith Lind.

Suddenly, as if he'd conjured her up simply by thinking her name, Faith's bedroom door opened.

Through the open wedge, Kincaid saw pretty ruffled curtains, a vase of flowers, and even a painting on the wall. Just a corner of her bed was visible, but he noted the lacy coverlet and embroidered pillow slips. A delicious, flowery scent drifted out to him, and he inhaled sharply, savoring the soft perfume he'd come to associate with Faith.

And then she was there. Standing in the open doorway, drawing the strings of her pale blue dressing gown tight beneath her lush bosom. Unconsciously Kincaid's gaze swept over her, and he felt his blood quicken and his heart begin to pound.

He'd called her a child, but the living proof that she was not stood in front of him.

Her long blond hair was loose, hanging free down her back in a riot of tangled curls. Big hazel eyes wide with curiosity and concern, she stared at him, lips parted as if to speak. But all he could do was think about kissing her. Running his hands through the length of her hair and holding her tight against him.

Dammit. In spite of *everything* he wanted her like he'd never wanted another woman in his life.

"Mr. Hutton?" she said softly. Then, softer still, "Kincaid? Is everything all right?"

His body aching with need, he strangled the wild desire coursing through him. Didn't the fool woman have the slightest idea what kind of effect she could have on a man dressed as she was? Gratefully Kincaid accepted the anger growing in him and let it build until he felt safe again. Safe from emotions he had no business even considering.

"Was that Amanda crying?" Faith stepped into the hall. "Can I help?"

Kincaid moved back a pace quickly. His voice harsh, he said bluntly, "Amanda's fine."

"But I heard—"

"Yes, she *was* crying. I've just forbidden her to ever speak to or about Boom again." He swallowed and tried not to inhale. Her scent surrounded him. "Naturally, she was upset. But she's stopped now."

Faith took a deep breath, and Kincaid tried desperately not to glance at her breasts.

"Mr.—" She stopped, smiled, and said instead, "Kincaid. I really think it's a mistake to try to sweep Boom under the rug, and—"

"Look." He groaned inwardly at the toll her presence was taking on his body. He knew that he had to get away from her. Quick. Or he just might be tempted to do something he *knew* he'd regret. "As I've already told you—Miss Lind. *I* will take care of my own daughter. And I'll thank you to keep out of it." He jerked her a nod. "Good night."

In three long strides he was down the hall and in his own room. But he didn't feel safe until he'd shut and locked the door behind him.

*   *   *

The spelling bee was in full swing by the time Kincaid strolled into the packed schoolhouse. He stood in the back of the room and looked around futilely for a seat. Still not sure why he'd come, he was determined to stay now that he was there.

"All right, everyone!" Faith shouted. "I think we'll take a short break now."

"Good idea, Faith!" Zeke laughed. "I'm about wore out. Ain't done this much thinkin' in too many years!"

Kincaid chuckled along with everyone else, then tried to flatten himself against the wall as people started milling about, heading for the refreshment table along the back wall.

"Isn't this amazing?" a nearby voice shouted.

He staggered as a stranger bumped against him, then looked down into Samantha Evans's laughing eyes.

"I didn't know there were so many people in Harmony," he said loudly.

"Oh, they're from all over the county, practically." She held up her notepad and pencil. "I'm just setting out to talk to some of them. You never know what you'll find out!"

"Always working?"

She grinned. "Yes. A good reporter is always looking for a story! See you later, Mr. Hutton."

He watched as she disappeared into the crowd, her fashionable emerald-green dress fading into a sea of calico. Another determined stranger pushed him as he let his gaze wander over the room. He tried to pretend that he was simply curious about who had shown up. But it was no use. Even *he* didn't believe it. Finally, unerringly it seemed, he found Faith.

Near the teacher's platform she stood talking to several different people, Maisie and Minnie among them. The older ladies waved their hands, shrugged, and never stopped chattering as if they were pleading a case before a disinterested judge. And perhaps, he told himself as he straightened up and looked over the crowd, that's just what they were doing.

Standing beside Faith, a good-looking young cowboy smiled down at her and leaned close to hear what she was saying.

Frederick Winchester's tall form suddenly appeared in Kincaid's line of vision, and Kincaid swayed back and forth on his feet, lifting his chin, trying to see.

Faith, so short she was pretty much hidden by the crowd of people, laid one hand on the cowboy's forearm, and Kincaid sucked in a breath through clenched teeth. The cowboy grinned and leaned down even closer. Sonofabitch, Kincaid thought furiously and glared at Frederick until the man moved.

What the hell did Faith think she was doing, letting that cowboy hang all over her like that? And just who the hell *was* he anyway? Hands balled into helpless fists, Kincaid watched the cowboy drape one arm around Faith's shoulders and was pleased when she slipped just out of reach.

Good girl, he cheered silently. Then she laughed up into the young man's face, and a wave of anger so fierce it threatened to choke him swept over Kincaid. Desperately he looked at the crowd, hoping to find a way to reach the front of the room.

And then what? he asked himself. Oh, he knew what he'd like to do. He'd like to take that damn cowboy out and break his nose for him. But just as quickly reason shot through his brain. What right did he have to do anything? Faith didn't owe him anything. Besides, hadn't he been spending most of his time trying to stay away from her?

Yes, he admitted. But that didn't change the fact that he was furious to know that cowboy was close enough to enjoy Faith's perfume.

As people settled down once more and the two teams took their places at opposite sides of the schoolhouse, Kincaid leaned back against the wall. He couldn't seem to stop staring at her. He didn't even look away when the cowboy left the room, though he was glad enough that he had.

Faith called out a word, and vaguely Kincaid heard the teams begin to take turns spelling. But even with the shouts of encouragement rising up all around him, he only had eyes for Faith.

It was taking longer than she'd thought. Faith looked down at the list in her hand glumly. They'd almost covered every word she'd come prepared with.

Glancing up, she looked first from a triumphant Maisie to a grinning Minnie. Both teams had done well. And despite her earlier objections, she'd enjoyed the contest as much as anyone else. But she was tired.

After the confrontation with Kincaid the night before, she'd lain awake half the night trying to figure out how she'd made him so angry. And she was still no closer to an answer.

She stifled a yawn. Between the lack of sleep the night before and a long day of dealing with children, well, all she really wanted was to go to bed.

"C'mon, Faith girl!" Minnie called out suddenly, startling her back to the moment at hand. "Give us another one."

Smiling her apology, Faith said, "All right, Minnie. The word is *behavior*."

Minnie nodded briefly, then looked down the

length of her team to Mr. Taylor. "Well, go on Jim. Your turn."

Everyone in the room turned to him. James Taylor took a half step forward, wrinkled his brow, and started: "Behavior. B-e-h-a-v . . ." He paused thoughtfully, then rushed on. "Y-o-u-r."

Minnie's eyes screwed up as if she was in great pain. Faith shook her head sadly and tried to ignore Maisie's gleeful cackle. "I'm sorry, Mr. Taylor. That's wrong." Turning, she said, "Maisie?"

"Hmmph!" The older woman looked down the line of her players until her eyes fell on Frederick Winchester. "All right now, Fred. You tell 'em!"

"A pleasure, madam." He bowed, smiled humbly, and said, *"Behaviour.* B-e-h-a-v-i-o-u-r."

Maisie clutched her throat, and Minnie's delighted laughter carried over the crowded room.

"I'm sorry, Fred. That's wrong, too." Faith shrugged.

"Oh, dear," Fred offered quietly. "I'm afraid I—"

"You're durn tootin' you did." Maisie frowned at him, then turned toward Faith. "Now, Faith, if we was in England, we'd have won!"

"But you ain't in England, Sister," Minnie crowed from across the room. "We agreed on American rules!"

And the war was on. Helplessly Faith looked from one side to the other. Everyone was shouting. Jumping up and down. Or so she thought, until her frantic gaze fell on Kincaid Hutton.

Leaning against the far wall, he wasn't moving. He was staring at her with an intensity that seemed to leap across the space separating them. And in his eyes she saw the same anger she'd seen the night before.

Well, good Lord, she thought disgustedly. What

had she done *now*? Nothing. Nor had she done anything the night before to warrant such venomous looks. And she wasn't going to allow him the satisfaction of knowing that it bothered her, either.

Deliberately she looked away, clapped her hands, and shouted in her best farmhand voice, "Quiet! Quiet, everyone!"

Slowly the babble of voices faded off until she had everyone's attention. Like it or not, this session was finished. Smiling bravely, Faith announced, "I think we'll have to call this evening a tie."

"What?" Maisie and Minnie shrieked together.

"It's the only fair thing to do," Faith assured them.

In the rush of mumbled voices, Faith was sure the battle was about to start again. But it never got a chance. Instead, everyone was distracted by a loud, splintering crash followed by a very high, young voice screaming, "Goddammit! Look what you made Boom do!"

CHAPTER

SIX

A MUFFLED titter of laughter shattered the silence. Kincaid was already moving toward his daughter. He hardly noticed the people who jumped to get out of his way. When he finally reached the refreshment table, he stopped dead.

Maisie's crystal punch bowl lay in shards on the floor. Punch-soaked cookies littered the table, and Minnie's best white lace tablecloth looked as if it were bleeding. He slowly pulled in a deep breath and let his gaze travel to Amanda.

At least, he told himself with a silent groan, the girl had the sense to look ashamed of herself. In fact, he noticed as the moments flew past, that she looked as embarrassed as he felt. But that illusion was destroyed when Amanda raised her gaze to her father's.

Kincaid fought down a rising tide of helplessness as he recognized the defiance in his little girl's eyes. It seemed as though his every effort to be closer to Amanda only served to push her farther away.

Shaking his head slowly, he reached for Amanda's hand. As his long fingers curled around her small ones, his gaze swept past all the interested faces and focused only on one. Faith.

Standing on the platform at the head of the room, she was looking directly at him. He found it surprisingly easy to read her expression. Mingled with concern for Amanda, there was definitely an "I told you so" gleam in her eyes.

Sunlight stabbed through his closed eyes and sent needlelike spears into his brain. Kincaid groaned, tried to roll over, and felt his head snap free of his body. Shit! He hadn't know there was this much pain in the world!

Slowly, carefully, he pushed himself to a sitting position. His stomach churned momentarily, then subsided. But the pounding in his head refused to stop.

Well, he asked himself silently, what did you expect? Too much whiskey in too little time. Vaguely he remembered Cord Spencer, the owner of the Last Resort, trying to get him to stop and go home. Kincaid snorted, then groaned again. If only he'd listened to him.

But no. Like an idiot, he'd tried to drown his problems. After getting Amanda cleaned up and in bed, he'd been about at the end of his rope. He closed his eyes and saw the night before in memory.

She'd hardly said a word to him on the walk home. And all through the preparations for bed, she'd kept her lips clamped tightly together, refusing to speak, no matter *what* he said.

Her green eyes followed his every movement, and he felt the sting of her silent accusations. Even knowing it was useless, Kincaid had made one last attempt to reach her.

He tucked the quilt up around her chin and said tiredly, "Amanda, there *is* no Boom."

Her little face twisted into a mutinous frown, and her bottom lip stuck out stubbornly. "Oh, yes, there is," she said flatly. "And Boom says I should tell you that she don't like you much, either!"

Kincaid sighed and opened his eyes wide, closing his mind to any more recollections. He didn't want to remember how she'd turned her head away from his good-night kiss. He didn't want to remember that after closing her bedroom door, he'd heard her talking to Boom again.

And he knew, without hearing her say so directly, that it wasn't *Boom* who didn't like him. It was his own little girl.

Hell, he told himself silently. He hadn't thought it possible for one man to muddle up a situation *that* badly.

He guessed it still wasn't much of an excuse for drinking the town dry and behaving like a jackass. But it was all he had.

Somewhere outside in the early morning air, a bird began singing. Kincaid frowned, swung his legs to the floor, and forced himself to stand. One hand braced against his forehead, he turned resolutely to the full-length mirror in the corner of his room. Opening one eye a hesitant crack, he faced himself.

The very *image* of a steady, confident father stared back at him. Hair standing on end, whisker stubble on his face, the black jeans he'd slept in unbuttoned, no shirt, and one boot missing.

He couldn't go on like this much longer. Neither could Amanda. As much as it pained him to admit it, he was *not* getting through to his child on his own. Frowning at his reflection, he mentally chided himself. Was he going to let his own reluctance to get close to people, his own *pride* keep him from getting the assistance he knew Amanda needed?

No.

"Kincaid," he said, wincing at the noise, "it's past time to admit it. You need help."

Faith stepped out onto the boardwalk smiling. Glancing up at the cloudless blue sky, she breathed deeply of the fresh morning air. Clasping her books and papers to her chest, she started off for the schoolhouse. It didn't matter if she was early. She could always use the extra time in getting prepared for the children.

Children. Amanda. Her steps faltered slightly, and she pursed her lips thoughtfully. The poor little thing must've been so embarrassed last night, she told herself. With everyone staring at her.

Faith shook her head. She'd known all along that forbidding a child to pretend would never work. But somehow it was small consolation to know she'd been proven right.

She remembered vividly the beaten look on Kincaid's face. The stunned surprise in the room.

Sighing, she walked on. There had to be something she could do to help. Oh, not for Kincaid Hutton's sake, she told herself firmly, but for Amanda's. Maybe now the stubborn man would be willing to accept her offer of assistance.

A gust of wind danced past her, and Faith reached up instinctively to check the coil of hair at her nape. Then, clutching the hem of her black skirt, she climbed the steps to the schoolhouse.

Her footsteps echoed solemnly in the empty building. As she came around the edge of the cloakroom wall into the main room, she gasped and stopped in her tracks.

"What are *you* doing here?" she said, surprise etched in her voice.

Kincaid winced and rubbed his temples with his fingertips. "Shh. Please," he added hastily. "I, uh ... needed to talk to you, and I didn't want to do it where anyone else could hear."

"For heaven's sake, Mr. Hutton," Faith went on and walked past him to her desk, "you gave me quite a start."

"Don't call me Mr. Hutton anymore, Faith. Please?"

She set her things down on her desktop and turned to face him. He looked dreadful. His usually sharp green eyes were bleary, and his clothes looked as though he'd slept in them. Her eyes widened slightly as she noticed for the first time that even his boots didn't match.

"What's wrong, Kincaid?" she asked and fought down the urge to go to him.

He grimaced slightly, walked to the front row of chairs, and perched unsteadily on the edge of a desk. "Thank you," he said quietly and glanced at her from the corner of one eye. "For calling me Kincaid, I mean."

Faith smiled even though he didn't see it. Whatever it was that was bothering him, she felt sure that it was more than just Amanda's behavior the night before. Patiently she waited for him to speak again. To explain his presence. She didn't want to jump to any conclusions and be shouted down. *Or* told to mind her own business again.

"I, uh . . ." He exhaled heavily and raised his gaze to hers. "Well, I suppose you can see that I'm not feeling any too good this morning."

"Yes," she agreed and wondered if she should say more.

"It's my own fault." He shook his head wearily. "After getting Amanda to bed last night, I went to Cord's place and . . ."

Faith leaned against her desk. She'd thought his "symptoms" looked surprisingly familiar. Her father wasn't a drinking man by any means—but every time Faith's mother had delivered a child safely, her father had celebrated. And with seven Lind children, Faith had seen the resulting effects too often not to recognize them.

Though she doubted Kincaid had been "celebrating."

"I see," she said quietly.

He snorted a laugh, then moaned gently. "I'm glad you do, because for the life of me, I don't. It was stupid, I know. But I was—"

"It's all right, Kincaid. I understand." She stepped off the platform and stood beside him. Immediately she wished she hadn't. Being this close to him brought so many feelings to the surface. Her breath quickened and some indescribable flutter of excitement flowered in the pit of her stomach. Faith swallowed nervously, but didn't move away.

Kincaid Hutton had fascinated her since the day he and Amanda had moved into the boardinghouse. And now, seeing him this . . . bereft stirred the embers of that fascination until it was a raging fire inside her.

He looked at her, and Faith noticed that his breathing, too, was ragged. The stamp of self-assurance she'd come to associate with him was gone.

After a long pause the corners of his lips curved into a sad smile. "I believe you *do* understand," he whispered. Then added under his breath, "Though I don't know why you do."

"What did you want to talk to me about?" she asked and laid one hand on his arm.

His gaze locked on her small hand, he said quietly, "I wanted to apologize."

"For what?"

He grinned suddenly and glanced up at her. "For which specific offense, you mean?"

"No. I didn't mean that. . . ."

"I know you didn't." Kincaid snorted derisively and shook his head. "Though God knows you should."

He covered her hand with his own, and tingles of pleasure shot through Faith in response.

"I'm apologizing for telling you to mind your own business. That I could handle Amanda on my own. That you were"—he paused and let his gaze roam over her—"too 'young' to know anything." He snorted a chuckle. "If age held the answer, I *could* fix it. Lord knows I feel about a hundred years old today."

"You don't look a day over eighty!" Faith quipped, her lips quirking.

He looked up at her in surprise, then smiled himself. "Thanks, I'm sure." Squeezing her hand, he rushed out, "Faith, I need your help with Amanda. I just don't know what to do anymore." He shook his head again, sighed, and looked past Faith at the window on the opposite wall. "She . . . *likes* you, and I thought . . ."

"I'd be glad to help," she said quickly, knowing what this apology and appeal had cost his pride. Granted, he *had* hurt her feelings before, when he'd refused her help. But making him grovel for forgiveness wasn't as important to Faith as helping Amanda.

From outside came the unmistakable shrieks of the approaching children. Kincaid released her, and Faith stepped back.

"Why don't I stop by the workshop after school and we can talk more about this?" she offered.

"All right."

He stood only an arm's reach away, staring down at her with an unreadable expression in his eyes.

Slowly, hesitantly, he stretched out one hand and tugged gently at a lock of her hair. Smiling, he said, "Your hair's slipping out of that knot."

The small but somehow *intimate* gesture flustered Faith as she reached up and tucked the errant lock of hair back into place. Desperately she fought to control the trembling sensation coursing through her. Finally she looked up to find his eyes still fixed on her.

"You ought to wear it down sometimes," he said, his voice low, hesitant.

Faith felt herself leaning toward him. Something in his eyes drew her to him. She tilted her head back and closed her eyes. Breathless, every nerve in her body suddenly more sensitive, she waited for the kiss she felt sure was coming.

After what seemed an eternity, though, he cleared his throat nervously, and she heard him take a step back.

Her eyes flew open in time to see a sad smile fade from his lips. Regret shone in his eyes, and Faith fought to keep her disappointment from showing on her face. Time crawled by as they stood in the silent room, their gazes locked.

And then the spell was broken abruptly. Harry Taylor raced into the room, shouted, "Morning, Faith!" and took his seat.

They both heard the other children approaching. Kincaid took a deep breath, turned to go, then stopped dead. Looking over his shoulder, he asked quietly, "Who was that cowboy you were with last night?"

Her brow furrowed. "I wasn't *with* anyone last—" She gasped and added, "Oh! You mean Danny Vega. He sometimes rides shotgun for the stage on this route. Why?"

Kincaid frowned slightly, then shrugged. "No reason. Just wondered who he was. I'll, uh . . ." He stepped out of the way as Gary Lind raced past him. "See you later, Faith."

She nodded and watched him thoughtfully. She saw him bend down and tenderly stroke Amanda's hair as she entered the schoolhouse. When the little girl stiffened and brushed past her father, he straightened up and left the building.

Sarah tugged at Faith's skirt, and Sissy Taylor was clamoring for her attention. But Faith couldn't seem to tear her gaze away from the door where Kincaid had disappeared.

"What you got there, Kincaid?" Maisie asked.

"Huh? Oh." He tapped the long yellow envelope against his fingertips and sat down at the scrubbed kitchen table. "It's a letter from Jonas Smithfield." He looked up at the older woman, but her back was turned as she pulled a batch of corn muffins out of the oven. "My lawyer back home?"

"Oh, yes," Maisie said and plopped the muffin pan onto the table. "I remember him. Little fella. Big Adam's apple. What's he got to say for himself?"

Kincaid reached for one of the hot muffins, avoided Maisie's slapping hand, then took a bite. After he swallowed, he said softly, "He says the buyer he had for the store backed out of the deal."

"Aw, no." Maisie dropped her dishtowel and put her hands on her hips. "I *am* sorry to hear that, Kincaid. I know how you were countin' on it."

He nodded. "Jonas also says that Cassidy has been asking for me." Kincaid took another bite and glanced up at his aunt.

Her mouth puckered up, Maisie snorted indelicately. "Well, why in heaven's name is he botherin' to tell ya that? Don't the fool know you're not sellin' whiskey anymore?"

"Yeah, Maisie," he said quietly, breaking the steaming corn muffin up in his fingers. "He knows. It's just that, well, I guess Cassidy wants me back."

"Back?" Maisie pulled out a chair and dropped onto it. Staring across the table at her nephew, she asked, "You're not actually thinkin' about goin' to work for that man again, are you?"

Kincaid sighed and leaned back in his chair. "I don't want to," he conceded. "But, Maisie, pretty soon I may not have much choice."

"What do you mean?"

"I can't very well go on being your handyman for the rest of my life." He smiled tenderly at the older woman. "Though I'm thankful you gave me the job and a place to come with Amanda."

"Hush!" Maisie waved one hand at him. "Where else would you go, I ask you? Family is family, boy. You remember that."

"I will," he assured her. "But, Maisie, I can't stay with you forever." He leaned one elbow on the table. "I've got to be able to make my own way. And if I can't sell the store, then I'll have to go back to work for Cassidy. Whether I like it or not."

"And what about Amanda?"

"Don't you think I've already thought of that?" He shoved away from the table and walked across the room. Staring out the window at the schoolhouse, he went on. "I know my traveling is what caused all this trouble in the first place. But what else can I do? It's either work for Cassidy or pack up and go back to South Dakota."

"No!"

He heard the disappointment in her voice and turned to face her. Shaking his head, Kincaid said, "I don't want to go back, Maisie. It's better here. For Amanda. *And* for me. But—"

"Now, don't you—"

A knock at the front door interrupted Maisie, and she shoved herself to her feet. Wagging one finger at her nephew, she said, "I'll be right back. We ain't through discussin' this by a long shot, Nephew!"

When she was gone, Kincaid smiled and turned back to the window. The bright yellow schoolhouse captured his attention, and he let his mind wander to the woman inside it. As it did more and more often lately.

If he left Harmony, he'd never see Faith Lind again. A sharp stab of . . . something hit him, and he was staggered by it. Regret? Loneliness? Longing?

He shook his head wearily. Hell, he didn't even know what he was feeling anymore. The only thing he was sure of was that he didn't want to leave Faith.

And that knowledge scared him to death.

CHAPTER

SEVEN

FAITH STOOD in the open doorway of the workshop and looked at Kincaid. His back to her, he held a dipper full of water over his head and poured the cool liquid over himself. Her gaze followed the path blazed by the drops of water from his shining black hair across his wide shoulders, down to his narrow waist until they slid beneath the waistband of his black jeans.

Her mouth suddenly dry, Faith licked her lips self-consciously and tried to look away. But she couldn't. And when he turned suddenly to face her, Faith's heart hammered wildly. He looked so . . . strong. So invincible. And yet, he'd come to her for help.

That thought brought her imaginings to a halt. He'd asked for her help. A parent's request of a teacher.

Nothing more.

She'd do well to remember that.

Dragging a breath into her lungs, she stepped into the relatively cool shade of the building. Desperate for something to say, she found herself blurting out, "If it's this hot in April, summer will be unbearable."

His eyes moved over her slowly, thoroughly. "I keep hoping it'll rain. Cool things off a bit."

She nodded jerkily, like a broken doll, and finally let her gaze slide away from his. Grasping blindly for *something* intelligent to say, her eyes fell to the work-table, and she asked, "What are you making?"

As if she'd cut strings tying him in place, Kincaid walked to the table and stopped only inches from her side. His lean, tanned fingers smoothed over the polished piece of wood. "It's a rack for Maisie's pans and things." He glanced at her. "She's always complaining about having to reach down to the cupboard to find anything. Claims it hurts her back." He smiled, shrugged, then added, "Anyway, once I get the hooks on, she'll be able to just hang the pans she uses most often on this."

"That's a wonderful idea," Faith said softly.

He snorted a laugh. "Oh, yeah, I have *lots* of wonderful ideas. Just ask my daughter."

Instinctively Faith reached out and laid her hand on his arm. Just as before, Kincaid's eyes slid to her hand. But this time he stepped back slowly, away from her touch.

Faith sighed, then told herself she was being foolish. For heaven's sake. She was supposed to be there discussing Amanda. Why on earth did she continue to have the *need* to touch him?

No wonder he was keeping his distance.

"I, uh . . ." she said quickly.

"Do you . . ." Kincaid started at the same time.

Faith laughed uncertainly. This was getting them nowhere. "Please. Go on."

He took a deep breath, turned, and reached for his shirt, draped over a nearby stool. As he pushed his arms through the sleeves, he said, "I appreciate your helping me with Amanda. She seems to like you, as I said before. And I thought, if you wouldn't mind spending some extra time with her . . ."

Faith met his gaze evenly. If this was going to work at all, she knew that it would take both of them

to help Amanda. Right now she had no doubt that
Kincaid was feeling sorry for himself for having
failed so miserably. But he would just have to get
over that.

A low rumble of noise sounded in the distance.
The Friday train was coming.

"I'd be delighted to spend more time with
Amanda, Kincaid." He grinned in relief. "But"—his
eyes narrowed as she continued—"even though
Amanda likes me . . . I'm just her teacher. *You're* the
important one in her life. You're her father. If you
want my help, you have to be involved, too."

"Of course, but—" He shrugged helplessly.

The rumbling grew louder, and the workshop itself
seemed to echo the thunder.

"Spend time with her yourself, Kincaid. You have
to show her that she's loved. That you care. If you
think that will be easier if I'm with you both, then
that's what we'll do."

"Good." He smiled again.

"But remember, Kincaid. *You're* the one she needs."
She watched him and saw the worry flash in his
eyes. For some reason, Kincaid Hutton was as alone
in his own way as his daughter was. Maybe, Faith
told herself, while they tried to reach the child,
maybe *she* could reach the father.

Across the wide street, behind the mercantile, the
Kansas-Pacific train roared through Harmony, leaving only a lonely whistle to mark its passage.

"Where you three off to?" Minnie cocked her head
and looked at them.

"We're takin' a walk, Minnie!" Amanda smiled and
glanced from her father to Faith.

"Well, good!" The older woman nodded, appar-
ently delighted to see a smile on the child's face. "We

all ought to. Maisie means well, y'know. But those corn dodgers of hers sit like stones in your belly after a while."

"I heard that, Sister!" Maisie's raised voice floated out to them from the kitchen.

"Meant that you should, Sister!" Minnie called back, "Don't believe in keepin' secrets!"

"You don't seem to mind keepin' your age a secret, you ol' . . ."

"We'd better go." Kincaid laughed and ushered his daughter, then Faith out the front door and closed it firmly behind him.

Amanda grabbed Faith's hand and tugged her down into the street. Looking back over her shoulder, she called, "C'mon, Papa," and held out her free hand to Kincaid. Clearly surprised, but pleased, Kincaid clasped his daughter's hand in his, and the three of them began their walk down Main Street.

In the companionable silence Faith let her gaze move lovingly over Harmony. Zeke's barbershop was dark and deserted, but across the street at You Sew and Sew, she could see Jane Carson in the lamplight, head bent and hard at work. Shaking her head slightly, Faith looked past Jane's shop and wasn't the least bit surprised to see the wavering light of the blacksmith's forge. Almost every night after dinner, Jake would head back to his livery stable to work.

From farther down the street came the unmistakable sounds of revelry from the two saloons. Though Cord Spencer's place was noisy, things stayed pretty much in hand.

However, at the First Resort, you never could tell what might happen. Oh, not that Faith had ever been inside herself. But in a town the size of Harmony, people talked. And folks talked most about Lottie McGee, the owner and madam of the place. According to gossip, Lottie was such a character, no one was ever sure what she'd be up to next. Faith had even heard that Lottie'd taught her parrot to say "Take your boots off!" and "Ride 'em, cowboy!"

She chuckled just thinking about it.

"What's so funny?" Kincaid's deep voice interrupted her thoughts, and Faith was glad it was so dark. She could feel a blush staining her cheeks. She could hardly admit to him that she'd been thinking about the local madam, so she said the first thing she could think of.

"Nothing, really. Just Maisie and Minnie."

"Oh." He nodded, then asked, "Have they always been like that?"

"Of course. But you should know that, Kincaid." She cocked her head at him. "Maisie's your aunt, isn't she?"

"Only by marriage."

His brief, gruff answer only served to make her more curious, but her next question was cut off unexpectedly.

"Maisie's my aunt, too," Amanda said proudly, then added, "and Minnie says she can be my aunt if I want her to."

Faith smiled at Kincaid, then looked down at the little girl. "That's very nice, Amanda. Do you like living here with your aunts?"

"Oh, yes." The girl sighed and kicked at a pebble. "It's much nicer than that old preacher's house, y'know."

Kincaid frowned slightly but didn't interrupt.

Carefully Faith asked, "What was wrong with the preacher's house?"

Amanda tugged at the adults' arms, jumping into the air occasionally as she walked. "It smelled funny."

"What?" Kincaid's voice sounded harsh, but Amanda didn't seem to notice.

"Yeah." The girl nodded and leapt forward. "It smelled like old books and peppermint. So did the preacher."

"You didn't like him?" Faith prodded.

Amanda shook her head, then leaned far back to stare up at the night sky. "He was all the time reading to me from the Bible. Boom didn't like him, either. But his wife was nice. She made me cookies."

Kincaid stopped suddenly and dropped to one knee. Pulling Amanda around to face him, he stared into her eyes and cupped her cheek with one hand.

Faith watched father and daughter together for a moment, then decided to slip away quietly. It would be easier, she told herself, for Kincaid to talk to his child without an audience.

"Faith," he said huskily, "don't go. Please."

Amanda turned and smiled at her teacher before looking back at her father.

"Amanda . . ." Kincaid shook his head and swallowed nervously. "I didn't know you were unhappy with the preacher and his wife."

The little girl nodded, laid one hand on his knee, and watched her own fingers pick at the fabric of his pants.

"If I had," he went on in a strangled voice, "I would have come for you sooner."

She nodded again but didn't look up until Kincaid's fingers beneath her chin forced her to meet his gaze. Quietly, firmly, he said again, "I would have come for you sooner, Amanda. I didn't know. I'm sorry, sweetheart. I'm so sorry."

Faith's eyes burned with unshed tears, and she blinked frantically while watching Amanda for a reaction. It seemed to take forever, but finally the child's bottom lip began to quiver. She sniffed, rubbed her nose viciously, and jerked a short nod. But this time Kincaid must have seen something different in her eyes, because he leaned over slowly and kissed Amanda's forehead.

This time the girl didn't pull away.

Faith's lips curved in a gentle smile. Silence stretched out until it became almost unbearable. Then she heard herself say softly, "All right, you two. Are you tired of walking already?"

Kincaid looked up at her and smiled. With one last quick glance at Amanda, he pushed himself to his feet. "No, ma'am. I believe we're ready to go again now, aren't we, Amanda?"

Wariness still shone in the child's eyes, but it had been softened just a bit by the tiniest glimmer of happiness.

"Can we go to the river?" she finally asked.

"That's a good idea." Faith held out her hand, and Amanda took it, then reached for Kincaid's.

Slowly they began to move down the street again. A companionable quiet accompanied them as they passed the sheriff's office. Inside, they saw Travis in the lamplight, head bent, busily tackling his paperwork. As they came even with the First Resort, a sudden movement on her left caught Faith's eye. She glanced quickly at the second-story balcony and was in time to see the new girl at Lottie's, Abby Newsome, dart inside.

Faith stopped and stared up at the closed door. She'd only seen Abby once or twice at the mercantile, but she seemed such a sweet, shy girl. It was hard to imagine her working for Lottie.

"Something wrong?"

She turned to Kincaid. Smiling, she answered,

"No. I'm sorry. I guess my mind tends to wander sometimes."

"That's all right," he conceded. "Sometimes I think I've *lost* mine. Like right now." Kincaid pointed at the Last Resort. "See over there?"

Faith squinted into the darkness and saw a huddled shape sneaking under the double doors leading into the saloon.

"Isn't that Billy Taylor?" Kincaid asked.

For a brief moment the lamplight from the saloon fell on the creeping boy, and Faith nodded. "That's him."

"He's only fourteen, isn't he?"

"Uh-huh."

"Well, what in he—heck is he doing sneaking into a saloon?"

"I'm gonna tell," Amanda began to chant.

Faith shook her head and spoke up over the child's voice. "My guess is he's looking for grist for his gossip column in the paper."

"Could be." He nodded. "The doings at the Last Resort seem to be a favorite topic of 'Under the Shell.' "

Amanda tugged at their hands impatiently, and the two adults let themselves be dragged along. Once they'd passed the twin saloons, the silence of the prairie opened up to them. Without speaking, they headed in the direction of the river.

Closer to the water, Amanda dropped the adults' hands and sprinted for the bank.

"Be careful," Faith called.

"Stay back from the edge," Kincaid warned.

As they walked by the mill, shut down for the night, Faith tripped on a stone, and Kincaid's hand shot out to steady her. She felt the jolt of his touch down to her bones and was more pleased than she could have said when he tucked her hand through the crook of his arm before they continued on.

The dry grass crunched beneath their feet, and the sound of the river reached them long before they could see it. When they stopped on the riverbank, within sight of Amanda, Kincaid said softly, "Like to sit for a while?"

She nodded and sat beside him on the wide flat rock the younger boys in town sat on to fish. Moonlight fell across the water and shimmered uneasily on the racing surface. Faith's gaze followed the energetic little girl as she raced up and down the grassy bank, tossing pebbles into the water. Hesitantly Faith asked, "How long has Amanda been playing with Boom?"

He shouldn't have been surprised by her question, but he was. Kincaid glanced at her, then looked back at the river and his daughter. Drawing his knees up, he locked his forearms around them and tried to sort through the emotions tumbling through his brain.

Since stepping out into the night with Faith, he'd been experiencing such strong and *varied* feelings, he hardly knew what to make of them. The desire she evoked in him was more powerful than ever, yet she also gave him a sense of peace that he hadn't felt in years.

Something deep within him stirred to life, and he knew he couldn't afford to encourage it. Then Amanda giggled. The soft, delightful sound drifted to him, and he smiled. It had been too long since he'd heard it. And this, too, he owed to Faith.

"Kincaid?" she whispered, and he felt the warmth of her breath on his cheek.

The ever present ache in his groin intensified, and he shifted position uneasily. Finally, reluctantly, he answered her. "Since not long after her mother died."

He heard her sharp intake of breath and steeled himself for the next question.

"How did her mother die?"

He sighed heavily. There it was at last. Mary Alice had joined them there on the riverbank.

"If you'd rather not talk about it—" she said quickly.

"No, it's all right." He shook his head firmly and kept his gaze locked on Amanda. Maybe talking about his late wife would help. Maybe, he told himself hopefully, if he talked enough, the painful memories would start to fade.

But, he thought with a quick glance at the woman beside him, the old images of Mary Alice blurred in his mind. In the moonlight Faith's skin glowed like old porcelain, and her hair looked like old silver. He was in trouble and he knew it.

"It's just . . ." he started and watched as Amanda heaved a fist-size rock into the water, then darted back to avoid the splash. "I haven't talked about Mary Alice in such a long time."

"Pretty name."

"She was a pretty woman," he said thoughtfully. Strange, he'd almost forgotten that Mary Alice was pretty. So much had been lost in their unhappiness together. Just the thought of that time should be enough to strengthen his resolve to keep his distance from Faith Lind. But even as he told himself that, he silently admitted that staying away from her was the furthest thing from his mind at that moment.

He took a deep, shuddering breath. "She, uh, died of diphtheria."

"I'm so sorry," Faith breathed.

He nodded and forced himself to ignore the compassion in her voice. "It picked up and set down all through the town like a tornado. There was no telling whose house it would enter and whose it would pass by."

"Did you and Amanda get it, too?"

"No." He shook his head and shrugged. "No. We were fine. In fact only two people in town died that winter of the illness. Mary Alice and the doctor's wife."

"I'm so sorry, Kincaid."

She laid her hand on his, and his thumb moved over her soft skin gently. His heart pounding, his whole body aching with need for her, Kincaid forced himself to his feet suddenly. Reaching down, he took her hand in his and pulled her up.

"We'd better get back," he said softly, and couldn't stop himself from smoothing his fingers through a long curl that had escaped her hairpins.

"Papa!" Amanda squealed imperiously. "Papa, come look! Oh, Faith, did you see it? A fish jumped, Papa! Right in front of me!"

Kincaid glanced toward the excited little girl, then turned back to meet Faith's gaze. He saw the confusion, the desire spark in Faith's eyes, and he gave silent, fervent thanks for Amanda's presence.

"We're coming, Amanda," he called, then stepped back to let Faith pass.

In a charged silence they walked down the incline to join the little girl.

CHAPTER

EIGHT

DURING THE last four days Faith had seen a real change in Amanda. True, the child still spoke to Boom more often than Faith *or* Kincaid would like— but at least it wasn't a constant thing like before.

Faith pushed away from her desk and walked to the window. Through the shining glass pane, she watched the children playing and smiled to see Amanda jumping rope with Sarah and Sissy. It was so good to see the little girl joining the other kids instead of sitting apart, sulking.

Fingers tapping on the windowsill, Faith let her gaze slide to the pink workshop behind the boardinghouse. Kincaid would be there, she knew. Nervous flutters of excitement stirred in her stomach, and Faith breathed deeply, trying to calm herself.

It wouldn't work, though, and she knew it. Heaven knew, she'd hardly been able to think of anything except Kincaid Hutton for days.

Deliberately she turned her back on the workshop and walked back to her desk. Plopping down onto her chair, she braced her elbows on the desktop and propped her chin in her hands. Closing her eyes, she saw his face again as he watched Amanda playing at the river's edge. She smiled at the remembered look of tenderness on his face. And it was truly amazing, she thought, how the little girl had responded to her father since his apology that night.

Like a water-starved garden after a spring rain, Amanda blossomed with so many different colors of emotions it was hard to take them all in at once.

Straightening, Faith told herself that it wasn't only the little girl going through so many changes. In the last four days she'd noticed the shadows in Kincaid's eyes fade a little more with each passing day.

And as the Huttons healed, Faith felt herself drawn more and more to the man she'd once thought cold, distant. In fact, she thought firmly, it was time she started remembering that Kincaid Hutton hadn't sought her out because he wanted her company. He'd come to her for help with his child.

Nothing else.

"Lord!" Maisie commanded the Almighty's attention, and everyone at the table jumped. "I understand how you might have thought a tie would be the only fair way to end that damn—er ... *durn* spelling bee the other night."

Faith sighed gently but kept her gaze on her folded hands. She hoped her stomach wouldn't growl. It appeared that tonight's "grace" was going to be a long one.

"But," Maisie continued in a more wheedling tone, "this Sunday after church, we'll be havin' a picnic. Now, Lord, you know we always have a tug-of-war at these to-dos. And since you disappointed both me and my sister last Thursday, I feel it's only fair to expect you to help us ladies win this contest."

"Amen, Sister," Minnie concurred.

"Now, Lord, I know it's only Tuesday, but I wanted you to have plenty of time to set your schedule up. Me and Minnie'd appreciate it if you'd attend the picnic and see to settin' things straight around here." She took a breath and added one last thought. "Oh, yes. If you'd be kind enough to help our boarders here chew this venison roast tonight, I'd appreciate it."

Minnie sucked in air in an angry hiss.

"It ain't Min's fault this beast is tough, Lord. Hell—I mean shoot. Deer prob'ly died of old age. Bound to be a little chewy. Amen."

"Amen," the boarders echoed and reached for the food in the center of the table. No one spoke much over dinner. It would have been hard to be heard over Minnie and Maisie.

"Is there really gonna be a picnic on Sunday?" Amanda asked Maisie as she handed the older woman a ball of red wool yarn.

"Oh, my, yes," Maisie said as she looped the yarn over her knitting needle and began to cast on stitches. Her rocking chair moved rhythmically as she continued, "We'll have a pie-eatin' contest and three-legged races and a tug-of-war like I said. Maybe you youngsters will play some hide-and-seek, too. Would you like that?"

"Yes, ma'am," Amanda sat on the footstool in front of Maisie's rocker. Her gaze locked on the woman's nimble fingers, she asked, "Does everybody go to the picnic?"

"Surely do." Maisie smiled, reached out, and cupped Amanda's cheek. "Folks make a point of it. After a long cold winter it's good to be out in God's fresh air celebratin' with your neighbors!" She gave a quick glance around her, then said " 'Manda honey, would you run upstairs and fetch my new blue yarn for me? It's in the carved rosewood chest in my room."

"Yes'm," Amanda agreed and left the front parlor. As she started up the stairs, she saw Kincaid coming down. "Papa?" she asked. "Are we goin' to the church picnic on Sunday?"

Halfway down the staircase Kincaid stopped dead. He stared into Amanda's expectant gaze and knew that he'd have to agree. He could hardly refuse when most of the people in this part of the county would be attending.

And yet, the thought of spending an entire day with his own child, just the two of them, was a daunting one. She'd been doing so well lately, he was terrified that he'd make some sort of stupid mistake that would send her scuttling back to Boom and silence.

The only real way to keep that from happening was to have Faith join them. And that was worrisome in a completely different way.

"Papa?" Amanda repeated.

"Huh? Oh. Uh, all right, Amanda, we'll go." He forced a smile and was rewarded by an answering grin from his daughter. She charged up the stairs, paused beside him long enough to hug him briefly, then ran past him.

Kincaid descended the stairs slowly, thoughtfully. That too-quick hug was the first time she'd shown him any affection impulsively since right after Mary Alice's funeral.

He felt the unmistakable sting of tears fill his eyes, and he blinked them back quickly. Behind him, he heard the sound of Amanda's charging footsteps. Embarrassed, he hurried across the entryway and slipped out the front door. The last person he wanted to witness his loss of control was Amanda.

Outside, he walked past the newspaper office, barely glancing at Samantha as she worked at her desk. His long legs carried him across Main Street, around the mercantile to the bridge that spanned the Smoky Hill River. He didn't even bother to wonder why it seemed that he always ended up going to the river's edge to think. He only knew that he needed to be alone.

He had to figure out what to do about Faith.

He stopped suddenly, and the ever present wind pushed at him as if encouraging him to move on. Instead, he tilted his head back and stared up at the night sky. The stars were close enough to touch, adding their light to the full moon's.

"It's no good," he mumbled to no one. "I've tried to keep my distance. I've tried to see her as Amanda's teacher, nothing more." He exhaled heavily and continued to whisper into the night. "But I can't. She's . . . *more* than that. Much more. Maybe *too* much more."

From somewhere in the town a dog howled longingly at the moon, and Kincaid, startled, shook his head and laughed shortly. Fine, he told himself. Amanda's not talking to herself anymore. *You* are!

Disgusted with his own indecision, he started walking again. He stepped around the weathered old trunk of the ancient tree that bordered the bridge and stopped dead.

Faith.

Partially hidden by the low-hanging branches, Kincaid took a moment to study her. Her hands on the railing in front of her, she stood in the center of the bridge, her face tilted up to the sky, the wind tossing her hair about her shoulders playfully. The same wind smoothed her simple pale blue dress tight against her until it hugged her body like a lover.

Kincaid breathed deeply, evenly, trying to control his suddenly racing blood.

For the space of a single heartbeat Kincaid let himself forget Mary Alice. He mentally brushed aside his failures with Amanda and the guilt that had become his constant companion. For that one instant he watched the smiling young woman and wished that everything were different.

That *he* were different.

Then a blast of cold wind slapped him, and the fantasy died. Slowly he stepped up onto the bridge and walked to her side.

Faith shook her head gently, letting her hair twist and fly in the night breeze. It felt wonderful being out in the open again. Since she moved to town, she'd hardly had a chance to be outside. She went from the boardinghouse to the school and back again.

The one thing she really missed in town, besides her family, of course, was being in the open with the wind. She smiled when she realized how few people would understand how she felt about the strong, gusty breezes that swept across the prairie. Most people, women especially, hated the wind.

She'd heard all the reasons from her own mother. How it kicked up the dirt, blew hats off your head, tossed clean laundry off the line onto the ground ... Oh, there were so many she couldn't even remember them all. But ever since she was a child, Faith had loved the sound and feel of the Kansas wind.

Tonight especially, she welcomed it. She'd deliberately escaped the confines of the boardinghouse as soon as she was able. Between the schoolchildren she dealt with daily and all of the other boarders, she felt as though she hadn't had a moment to herself in days.

Laughing softly, Faith told herself that was nonsense. Her problems had nothing at all to do with the children or the boarders. It was Kincaid Hutton alone who'd driven her out to the bridge hoping for a respite from thoughts of him.

All at once, she raised her arms high above her head, turned in a slow circle, and let the cool breezes flow around her. And just like when she was a girl, Faith felt ... *powerful*. The sting of the chill air brought goose bumps to her flesh, but it also seemed to welcome her like an old friend.

Still smiling, she dropped her hands to the bridge railing and, with her eyes closed, listened to the sounds around her. The river below, rushing over rocks and fallen branches, the gentle rustle of the cottonwoods, footsteps on the wooden bridge.

Her eyes flew open and she half turned.

"Evening," Kincaid said and stepped up beside her.

"Hello." Faith pushed her windswept hair out of her eyes and stared up at him. Waiting.

"I didn't mean to disturb you," he said softly.

"No, you didn't. I was just leaving anyway, and—"

His hand shot out and grabbed hers. "Don't go, Faith. Not yet."

She looked down at their joined hands and slowly nodded. This is what she'd been hoping for and dreading the last four days. To be alone with him. To hold him tight and listen to the steady beat of his heart.

But now that the moment was here, Faith was ... uneasy.

"I came out here to be alone," he started and dropped her hand.

"So did I." she admitted with a smile.

He nodded as if he understood all too well her

need to get away, and Faith wondered if his thoughts had been mirroring her own.

"We really haven't had a chance to talk since . . ." Kincaid's voice trailed off, and he turned to stare down into the moonlit river water.

"I know," she said nervously, "and I've wanted to talk to you about Amanda." Her fingers curled tightly around the rough wooden railing. "She's been doing so well, Kincaid. Of course, she still talks to Boom now and then, but"—she smiled up at him— "she plays with the other kids now, too. It's almost as if she doesn't have too much time for Boom anymore."

"You were right," he admitted quietly. "The last few days have been good for Amanda *and* me. Spending quiet time with her over her homework or having her out in the workshop with me has been"—he took a deep breath—"*good*. A simple word, I know. But it's true."

Faith glanced down at his hands and saw that he was squeezing the railing with all his might.

"And I'd almost forgotten what that was like." Abruptly he turned and looked at her. "I owe you that, you know. You're giving me back my daughter."

She shook her head. "You never really lost her, Kincaid."

He snorted. "Oh, yes, I had. Hell, I lost her even before Mary Alice died."

Shaking his head, he shoved both hands through his hair, as if he wanted to reach inside his head and pull out the memories that tortured him.

"I don't understand," Faith whispered, her hand instinctively reaching out for him.

He saw her movement and stepped back regretfully. "I know you don't. But you have to. *Jesus!* I never expected to be having this conversation."

"What is it?"

"No." He shook his head, pulled in a deep breath again, and blew it out in a rush. "Dammit, I'm not going into that now. I can't. At least, not yet." Suddenly he grabbed her forearms and pulled her close. "Faith, whatever it is that's between us . . . it *can't* happen. I won't *let* it happen. Do you understand?"

"No." Confused and more than a little hurt and angry, Faith pulled away and stared at him. "No, I *don't* understand, Kincaid. I thought we . . . is it because you still think I'm just a child?"

He laughed outright. "God, no! If only you were! Then I could be noble, turn my back and tell myself it was for your own good."

"Then what?" Hands on hips, she faced him. "What is it you're not telling me?"

"Never mind." He shook his head again and cleared his throat. "What I need to know is, are you still willing to help me with Amanda, knowing that I can't—won't . . ."

"What kind of woman do you think I am, Kincaid Hutton?" Faith closed the small space separating them and glared up into his eyes. "Do you really think I would turn my back on a little girl just because her father is a jackass?"

"No, but I had to—"

She cut him off. "Fine. You've done the 'noble' thing. Your conscience is clear. You've put the little schoolmarm in her place and—"

"Faith—"

"Don't," she said quickly when he reached out to her. "Just don't say or do anything else, Kincaid. Not now." A gust of wind tossed her hair into her eyes, and she shook it back. Cocking her head at him, she asked, "Disappointed, Kincaid? Expect me to fall on

the ground at your feet and beg you to please kiss
me?"

"Faith, dammit—" His voice was rough, hard.

She saw an anger to match her own cross his features and was glad. She couldn't bear it right now if
he acted as though he were sorry for her.

"Well, don't you concern yourself for me, Kincaid.
I'll help with Amanda. I'll save my affections for that
little girl and not trouble you with them again." She
turned sharply and took a half step before assuring
him, "Believe it or not Kincaid Hutton, there are a
few men in this county who would be pleased as
punch to have me kiss them!"

"Like Danny Vega, maybe?" he shot back.

She looked back at him over her shoulder. The fury
on his face did her heart good. As she started walking, she called back, "*Exactly* like Danny Vega!"

Almost before the words left her mouth, Kincaid
caught up to her and spun her around to face him.

Her heart pounding, Faith looked up into his blazing green eyes. His hair tumbled over his forehead,
and she felt the barely controlled rage in him wash
over her. But she wasn't afraid. Even in the grip of
his fury, Faith knew that she was safe with him. Besides, her own temper made them equal adversaries.

"Danny Vega?" he muttered thickly, and his voice
was almost lost in the rush of the river below.

She nodded and lifted her chin.

The wind suddenly picked up, moaning softly as it
raced by them. Cottonwood trees rattled and danced
to the wind's music, and Faith had to strain to hear
Kincaid even though his mouth was just a breath
away from her own.

"No, Faith," he said. "God help me, no one but
me."

His eyes moved over her face like a pauper staring

at a king's banquet. His strong, warm hands moved
to cup her face, and she felt his thumbs trace gently
over her cheekbones. Faith held completely still,
afraid to move lest she break the spell that held
them.

She caught her breath, and his mouth came down
over hers. Hungrily, fiercely, he wrapped his arms
around her, clasping her to him, and Faith welcomed
the embrace. Wrapping her arms around his neck,
she kissed him back with all the passion that had
been building in her the last four days.

When his tongue touched hers, she moaned softly
and leaned into his strength. Deliberately Faith
rubbed her breasts against his chest, delighting in the
powerful sensations that racked her body. His hands
moved over her back and hips, and when he cupped
her behind and pulled her tight against him, she felt
the rigid proof of his need.

He broke the kiss then, leaving her gasping for
breath as he once again tasted the length of her
throat. His teeth teased her flesh, and she let her
head fall back on her neck to make his task easier.

Slowly he snaked one hand up to caress her breast
and Faith covered his hand with her own.

"Kincaid . . ." She sighed and felt the wind snatch
her breath from her. "I need . . ."

He pulled back from her then. With his thumb still
stroking the bud of her breast, he smiled regretfully.
She watched the passion fade from his features to be
replaced by a grim determination. "I know, Faith."
His other hand came up to cup her cheek, and she
leaned into it, struggling for breath.

Desperately she wanted to recapture the emotions
of only a moment ago. But when he spoke softly, she
knew it was no use to try.

"This is what I'd hoped to avoid," Kincaid went

on. "But I . . ." He sighed, drew her into his embrace, and held her tight.

Her head on his chest, Faith listened to the pounding of his heart and knew that he shared the incredible feelings still coursing through her. There would be time later to convince him that what they felt was right.

She closed her eyes. For now it was enough to be held.

CHAPTER

NINE

"HARRY TAYLOR!" Maisie yelled, waving a wooden spoon in the air. She hopped from foot to foot, watching as the short, redheaded little thief weaved in and out of the crowd, carrying at least a half dozen of Maisie's cookies.

"Durn that boy anyway!" she muttered and turned back to the food table in time to see Billy Taylor reaching for a piece of fried chicken. Quickly she slapped his hand with the back of her spoon. Yelping, Billy jumped back, glaring at Maisie. The older woman didn't bat an eye. "Don't your ma never feed you young'uns?"

"We're s'posed to eat here, Maisie," Billy complained. "It's a *picnic!*"

"Hell, I know that, but you all will eat when *we* say so and not before! Now, git!" She raised her spoon again warningly, and Billy backed off, grumbling something about writing about this in his column.

With a snort of delight Maisie called out, "Just spell it right, Billy. Maisie Hastings and Minnie Parker. And whatever you do, don't ask your pa to help you spell it!"

Several of the nearby women laughed, Billy's face flushed a beet red, and Maisie smiled triumphantly.

Faith stepped up behind her, took a hard-boiled

egg from a platter, and asked, "Have you seen Kincaid or Amanda?"

"Nope," Maisie answered and frowned at the egg Faith held. "Don't you let anybody see you eatin' that, mind. It ain't time for supper yet."

Grinning, Faith hid the egg in the skirt pocket of her lemon-yellow dress. Still smiling, she watched Maisie turn her hawk eye back on the mounds of food and told herself the older woman would have made a great general. Her smile dropped away when Maisie spoke again, though.

"So, why you so interested in Kincaid?"

"Oh, no reason. I, uh, promised Amanda I'd spend the day with her and . . ."

Maisie shot her a sardonic glance. "Uh-huh."

"What?"

"Nothin', nothin'." Maisie waved her hand over the three-layer chocolate cake, brushing away flies. "It just seems strange to me that you should be so interested in seein' Kincaid, is all. The two of you've been avoidin' each other all week long. Whenever one of ya's in the room, the other leaves." She shook her gray head. "Perplexin', is all."

Faith inhaled sharply. She should have known that Maisie would notice the uneasy truce between her and Kincaid. Maisie didn't miss anything. And if for some reason she did, well—Minnie was right there to keep her informed.

It was all so ridiculous, she told herself with a frown. Instead of bringing them closer, the kiss they'd shared only seemed to pull them further apart. She shook her head slowly. And Kincaid's reaction was really puzzling.

She wasn't such a fool that she didn't know when a man was interested in her. But Kincaid's actions were so confusing she wasn't sure what to do anymore. The way he kissed her, the way he held her so tenderly, she *knew* he cared for her. *Knew* that he felt the strength of the . . . "attraction" that lay between them. But while she wanted to enjoy these new feelings and revel in them—they only seemed to make Kincaid angry.

And his unspoken rejection fed the flames of her own well-known temper. With them both concentrating on their own feelings, nothing was being settled. Faith bit at her lip and nodded slowly. Enough is enough, she thought with a new determination. It was time to get to the bottom of all this, whether Kincaid liked it or not.

She wasn't about to spend another week like this past one. If Kincaid wasn't interested in pursuing this . . . *feeling* they shared, then she'd rather know it right now. She was tired of being ignored.

Telling herself that learning a little more about him might help her to understand what he was thinking, Faith decided to start with his "aunt by marriage."

"Maisie," she began in a soft tone, "how much do you know about Kincaid?" When Maisie threw her a sharp glance, she said quickly, "I mean, did you know him well before he came to Harmony?"

"Well enough, I suppose," the woman said and cocked her head at Faith. "He *was* married to my niece Mary Alice."

"Uh-huh." Faith let her fingers trail lightly across the plain white bedsheet that covered the food table. "And what was she like? Mary Alice, I mean."

"Don't you think you should be askin' Kincaid this?"

"Why?" she asked innocently. "Mary Alice was *your* niece, wasn't she?"

After a long, thoughtful moment Maisie nodded and sighed. "Yeah. That she was."

"What was she like, Maisie? I need to know."

The older woman studied her carefully and slowly smiled. "I guess you do at that." She pulled in a deep breath and began to speak in a low undertone. "Mary Alice was my husband's brother's girl. Now, Lord knows, I don't like to speak ill of the dead, but that Mary Alice would have tried the patience of Job." Shaking her head, she added, "Such a pretty little thing. Tiny, like you, Faith, but the girl had none of your backbone. Since she was an only child, her daddy spoiled her somethin' awful. Used to gettin' her own way she was, and when things didn't work out just right, that girl could whine and sulk with the best of 'em."

Faith stared out over the crowded churchyard. But she wasn't looking at any of her friends and neighbors. Instead, she watched a hazy image in her mind. Kincaid, bending solicitously over a small, dark-haired woman with pouting lips. As if from a distance she heard Maisie continue.

"When she saw Kincaid Hutton at a dance, Mary Alice decided she wanted him. Hmmph! Couldn't have been too hard for her to get him, either. Pretty as she was, she'd learned early how to play a man like a fish in a river. Before he knew what hit him, Kincaid was married and tryin' to make her happy." She paused and Faith turned to look at her. Maisie confided, "Not an easy task, by any means." She inhaled, cleared her throat, and finished brusquely, "Still, Kincaid did all he could. I always liked that boy, y'know. And after Amanda came—" The older woman laid one work-worn hand on Faith's arm. "You wouldn't know it now, to look at the two of them together . . . but when that child was born until a couple of years before Mary Alice died, Kincaid and Amanda were thicker than molasses in winter.

Always together." She straightened up abruptly. "I visited them a time or two some years back, and them two were a pure delight to watch together. Yeah, it was a shame to see them so separate when they come here. But it's gettin' better now. Gettin' better."

"Maisie!" Minnie's voice called out. "They're fixin' to start the pie-eatin' contest! C'mon over here, Sister!"

"Better get movin' or that ol' woman's likely to have a stroke." Maisie started walking, and Faith said, "Thanks, Maisie."

The woman nodded but added, "You want to know any more, you best ask Kincaid, y'hear? And Faith, don't you go givin' up too soon, now."

Faith nodded absently. Her mind was on Mary Alice. The sulky, spoiled wife Kincaid couldn't make happy. But after all she'd just learned, Faith had her own ideas about what had gone wrong in the Hutton marriage.

Kincaid had stalled as long as he dared. Amanda wasn't going to be put off another minute. She'd waited while he changed out of his church clothes, she'd stood still for him to rebrush her hair, she'd even waited for him to straighten up the wookroom just a bit. But now his little girl stood looking up at him, silently demanding that they leave for the picnic.

There was no way to avoid it, he knew. Maybe it would be better to just go and get it over with. He only wished that he'd never asked Faith to spend the day with them. But, he argued with himself, how was he to know that by the end of the week he'd be desperate to avoid her?

"All right, Amanda" he said softly. "You run ahead. I'll be right along."

She opened the door, stepped out onto the boardwalk, and stopped. Glancing over her shoulder at him as if waiting to make sure he was coming, she didn't move again until he was standing right beside her.

Kincaid smiled reluctantly. "Go ahead. I'm coming. I promise."

She cocked her head at him, grinned suddenly, then jumped off the boardwalk steps and raced toward the churchyard. Kincaid stared after her for a long moment and felt a smile tug at the corners of his mouth.

It was good to see her like this, he told himself. Happy, excited, she was almost the girl she used to be. And he knew that he owed a great deal of Amanda's progress to Faith Lind.

Faith. Even her name carried a rush of emotion he'd thought long dead. He'd avoided her for the last five days, and still his hands itched to touch her. He hardly slept at night anymore. Every time he closed his eyes, Faith's image rose up to taunt him. And on those rare occasions when he *did* manage to drift off to sleep, dreams of her would have him waking abruptly, his body aching with the need only she could ease. He shook his head wearily and stepped off the boardwalk into the street. As he slowly walked toward the gathering of people in the distance, he told himself that Faith's attitude hadn't helped much, either.

Oh, he couldn't really blame her for doing her best to avoid him, too. But when she *did* look at him, all he saw in her hazel eyes was the reflection of her utter confusion. He'd expected many different reactions from her, of course. After living with Mary Alice for

several years, he'd become accustomed to the sulking, the pouting, the whining list of complaints rang-
ing from his insensitivity to his "disgusting appetite
for carnal pleasures."

Kincaid snorted and frowned. He'd been ready for
just about anything. Except being ignored.

Even when they inevitably passed each other on
the stairs and it was just the two of them, Faith kept
her composure while still managing to let him know
of her disappointment, bewilderment.

Sighing in exasperation, Kincaid forced himself to
hurry when he noticed Amanda waving at him excitedly. He didn't even remember a time when he
wasn't confused anymore.

Two long lines stretched out across the open yard.
Facing each other across a distance of five feet, the
entrants in the egg toss waited as Lillie Taylor
walked the length of one line, handing a raw egg to
each person.

Her husband, James, stood in the center of the
yard, shouting out the rules.

"All right, now," he called. "When I give the sig-
nal, you bunch with the eggs, toss it over to your
partner. And every time you catch the egg, both of
you have to take one step back!" He let his gaze
sweep over the murmuring crowd. "No cheatin',
mind! We'll be watching!"

Kincaid looked at Amanda and couldn't hide his
smile. Dancing excitedly in place, she'd be lucky not
to break the egg she held before she got a chance to
throw it to him!

Suddenly his daughter looked into the crowd of
bystanders and crowed, "Faith! Watch us! We're
gonna win!"

Reluctantly he followed Amanda's gaze and saw

Faith standing alone at the edge of the group of people. She smiled at the little girl, then turned to look at him. Her expression was clear. Mixed with the confusion he'd come to recognize lately was a desire to match his own.

"All right, folks!" James shouted and ran for cover. "Let 'er go!"

At once ten raw eggs sailed high into the air. Kincaid watched his and concentrated. Cupping his hands, he caught it carefully, then he and Amanda each stepped back.

He hardly noticed the people on either side of him. He was much too busy willing Amanda to catch the egg flying toward her. When she did, he sighed in relief and dutifully stepped back again.

She tossed the egg back to him, higher this time. His eyes locked on the fragile bullet, he prepared to catch it. Then he heard someone shout out "Faith!" Instinctively Kincaid turned to see who was calling her. The egg crashed onto his forehead at the same time Amanda yelled out a warning.

Laughter erupted from the watching crowd, but Kincaid didn't notice. All he saw was Faith's pleased grin. Then, as the slimy egg white slid down his cheek and under the collar of his shirt, he reached up and brushed the broken shells off his face. Served him right.

"Papa!" Amanda laughed delightedly and rushed up to him, "*You* broke it! I thought *I* would, Papa!"

Kincaid stared down at his little girl. Her eyes bright, cheeks flushed with happiness, he knew he wouldn't mind a *dozen* eggs smashed on his head. The good-natured laughter faded away, and Kincaid saw only Amanda's smile.

"Bend down, Papa," she said and held up a handkerchief. "Bend down so I can clean you all up!"

With a quick glance at Faith, Kincaid went down on one knee and let his little girl mop his face.

"Faith?"

She turned her back on Amanda and Kincaid at the sound of her sister's voice. A smile still on her face, she watched as Suzanna "Zan" Lind walked up with a long, easy stride. Faith shook her head gently. She'd always envied Zan's height and willowy figure. Even dressed as she was now—an old checked skirt and a striped blouse, her long, sun-bleached hair hanging down her back in a single braid—Zan managed to look pretty.

Why, compared to her one-year-younger sister, Faith felt like a too plump puppy!

Zan's honey-brown skin, darkened from too much farm work and too little protection from the sun, emphasized her sparkling hazel eyes. When she grinned, Faith couldn't resist smiling back.

"Why're you standing off here by yourself, Faith?"

"Just . . . thinking, I guess."

Zan laughed and grabbed her sister's arm. "This is no day to be thinking. C'mon, they're starting up a round of hide-and-seek. Let's see if you can still beat me!"

Hitching up her skirt, Faith pushed thoughts of Kincaid to the back of her mind and crowed, "You never could beat me, Zan Lind. And you're not about to start now!"

Zan turned too quickly and bumped smack into Edward Winchester. "Will you kindly watch where you're going?" he snapped.

Leaning back, a smirk on her face, Zan retorted, "I'm *so* sorry, Your Worthiness!"

Edward frowned, but Zan just laughed at him,

grabbed Faith, and took off like a shot for the gathering crowd.

Glancing over her shoulder, Faith saw the Englishman still standing where they'd left him, staring after them.

"Honestly, Suzanna! You didn't have to be rude!"

"What? To *him*?" She waved away her sister's concern. "Ed Winchester could *use* a little rudeness now and again. Just to keep him human!" Then Zan shouted, "Mr. Evans! When did you get back?"

Faith spun about to see Alexander Evans, Samantha's father, striding up to them.

"Last night," he offered. "Why do so many things happen around here whenever I take off for Salinas for a while?" He grinned at Faith. "I hear a spelling bee almost touched off another civil war!"

"It came much too close," Faith agreed, smiling up into Alex's warm blue eyes. It was sometimes hard to believe that any man as handsome and youthful-looking as *he* could be Samantha's father.

"Are you ready to play hide-and-seek, Mr. Evans?" Zan challenged with a laugh.

"No," he said thoughtfully, looking past them. "I think I'll sit this one out."

Faith followed his gaze and saw Jane Carson sitting by herself on a blanket under a tree.

When Alex noted Faith's glance, he cleared his throat uneasily and added, "I'm *much* too old and tired to be running around in the afternoon sun!" Tipping his hat, he excused himself and started walking.

Turning slightly, Faith saw him head directly toward Jane. "Hmmm," she mused aloud, "now I wonder if there's something happening there. . . ."

Zan turned, saw Alex sit down beside Jane, and snorted. "Your head's in the clouds, big sister. More than likely, he's gone to talk about Sam's clothing bill! I swear, someday Jane Carson's going to be a rich woman if Samantha keeps this up!"

Her eyebrows quirking slightly, Faith looked her sister up and down pointedly. "It wouldn't do *you* any harm to wear a fashionable dress once in a while, Suzanna."

Cocking her head, Zan shot back, "Now, where did *that* come from? Besides, can't you see me walking behind a plow with my train over one arm?"

She struck a comical pose, and Faith chuckled delightedly. The image she'd just described was so ridiculous, even *Zan* laughed! Fashionable or not, Faith thought with a sigh, she wouldn't change one hair on her sister's head.

Zeke Gallagher and Charlie Thompson were still complaining loudly, but none of the women paid the slightest bit of attention.

"It wasn't fair, Maisie," Zeke proclaimed for the tenth time.

"Oh, hush, all's fair, y'know!"

"That's 'in love and war,' " Charlie reminded her.

"Or," Charlie's wife, Cora, tossed in with a laugh, "love and tug-of-war!"

"Ticklin' the men so's the women could win wasn't fair no matter how you slice it, Cora!"

"Maybe you men'll have better luck at hide-and-seek," she teased her husband and was rewarded by a reluctant smile.

"I'm too durn old for hide-and-seek," Zeke grumbled.

"Then you come with me, and I'll feed you some cake," Maisie offered and bent down to the little girl beside her. At five years old, Charlie and Cora's oldest child had been a favorite of the older woman's ever since the night she'd delivered little Maisie.

The child's curly black hair was tied back with a bright yellow bow almost as big as she was. Her starched, ruffled white pinafore looked as fresh as if she'd just put it on. Maisie shook her head smiling. Obviously, the girl was going to grow up as persnickety about cleanliness as her mother. "How 'bout you, little Mae?" she asked the child. "You want some cake too?"

Cora Thompson's hand rested on her daughter's head gently for a moment. "You know her, Maisie. She's always ready for chocolate."

"Course she is. She's my goddaughter, ain't she?" Maisie tweaked the laughing little girl's nose gently. "And I got some cake over there just the color of your eyes, sweet thing." She glanced over her shoulder at Cora and Charlie. "You two go on and join in the hide-and-seek. Me and Zeke'll keep an eye on Mae and Lincoln."

Cora grinned up at her husband, eager to take her friends up on their offer. With a sigh Charlie handed his two-year-old son into Zeke's care. "You watch out for him, now, Zeke. He's a terror!"

"Hmmph! So'm I!" The older man grinned when Lincoln tugged on his beard. "Go on, you two, leave us be!"

Charlie and Cora ran hand in hand up to the small group of adults and children waiting for the next game to begin. Faith smiled hello when they stepped up beside her, then reached down to smooth Amanda's hair back from her forehead.

"So," Travis Miller announced, looking at the little group. "It's decided. Kincaid here is 'it.' "

Faith risked a glance at Kincaid and was pleased to

see a resigned expression cross his face. There were traces of dried egg white still clinging to his jaw.

"You all have to the count of thirty to go hide," Travis continued. "So, Kincaid, you close your eyes, and the rest of you, get goin'!" As they all darted off, Travis yelled out, "The winner gets the first bowl of Lillie's fresh peach-preserve ice cream!"

In the first rush of people, Faith lost track of Amanda. No doubt the girl was too busy hunting her own hiding place to worry about sticking close to Faith.

Laughing, Faith glanced around at the people she'd known all her life and was glad she'd set aside her confusion with Kincaid long enough to enjoy the day's fun. She hiked her skirt up to her knees and ran into the stand of cottonwoods. Vaguely she could still hear Kincaid counting. He was nearing twenty already.

Faith grinned and told herself that *she* was going to win that ice cream! After all, growing up with six brothers and sisters, the *one* thing she knew how to do better than anybody else was hide. She slipped around a knee-high bush and passed two young trees, their trunks much too small for what she had in mind.

Deeper and deeper into the stand of trees she ran. If Kincaid was going to find *her*, she told herself . . . he'd really have to work at it! She'd left everyone else far behind her. The sounds of the picnic were distant, muted.

Finally, as she heard Kincaid yell "twenty-five," she found the tree she'd been watching for. Tall and sturdy, its trunk was as big around as a horse's middle. Grasping the lowest branch, she swung herself up off the ground and began to "walk" her feet up the trunk, swinging her body around as she went.

When she was standing on a limb about five feet off the ground, she decided she wasn't high enough and climbed another two or three feet up. Then, as Kincaid shouted out "Thirty!", she pulled the edges of her skirt together into her lap, straddled the branch, and hung on.

From her vantage point she could watch as Kincaid stepped into the copse of trees. A couple of the younger children were "hiding" almost in the open. She knew he *had* to have seen them. But he walked by them without even a flicker of a glance. Faith smiled to see the delighted expressions on the kids' faces as they skipped out of hiding and raced to tag themselves home free.

Her foot slipped a little, and she tightened her grip on the gnarled limb.

When Kincaid came face to face with Charlie suddenly, startling both men into gasping, it was all she could do to muffle her laughter.

Between the shouts of people tagging in safe and Kincaid's crowing whenever he found someone, Faith knew that if she wasn't the last one out, she was close to it. One by one, almost everyone had been eliminated. It was time to make her move, she told herself and took a look around at the ground below her.

No one in sight. Slowly, carefully, she edged her way down to the lowest branch. Then she sat down, swung her legs over and hung by her hands from the limb for a moment. Dropping almost soundlessly onto the leaf-strewn ground, Faith started creeping toward the home-free area.

The only problem with hiding as deeply into the stand of trees as she had was having to run that great a distance to tag free.

She stopped suddenly at a sharp snap from behind

her. Tossing a glance over her shoulder, Faith saw Kincaid approaching. He must have stepped on a twig, she thought, grateful for the warning. It was quite a ways still to the edge of the trees, then a shorter run and she would be safe. She'd win.

Gathering up her skirt, Faith looked back once more and saw that he'd spotted her! She darted off suddenly, sprinting for victory and the edge of the trees still so far away. Behind her, she heard him running and risked another glance at him to check on his progress.

Almost upon her, she saw his proud grin and heard him yell triumphantly, "Got you, Faith!"

She turned back around quickly but not quick enough to see the tree root that snaked up in her path. The top of her foot slid under the root, and she fell facedown into the dirt, knocking the breath right out of herself.

Too stunned by the impact to move at first, she couldn't get out of Kincaid's way as he fell directly on top of her. She grunted her surprise when he landed on her back, and from a distance, she heard Cora shout delightedly. "I heard that! I heard Kincaid shout that he caught Faith!" She let out an excited squeal. "That means *I* win!"

"All right, everyone," someone else called out. "Time for the three-legged races!"

Disgusted with her own clumsiness, Faith spat the dirt and leaves out of her mouth and poked Kincaid with her elbow. "Get *up*!" she ordered in a whispered shout. "I can hardly breathe!"

He chuckled softly, and she felt an answering smile tug at her lips. As he shifted position slightly, Faith turned onto her side and tried to push her hiked-up skirt back down over her thighs and legs. Still grinning, she looked up into Kincaid's suddenly sober expression, and her breath caught.

Slowly, hesitantly, he covered her reaching hand with his own and stilled her movements. Instead of straightening her skirts, she felt him slide the material up even higher on her thighs, his hand caressing the length of her leg as he went.

Lips parted, her breathing no more than ragged gasps, she stared up into his passion-glazed green eyes and knew that she wouldn't stop him. That she wanted him to touch her. She'd dreamed of loving a man and being loved for most of her life, and now that she'd found him, she would deny him nothing.

Her anger forgotten, Faith concentrated solely on his face. Tenderness was etched into his features along with a hunger that gripped her as well. From somewhere deep inside her, she accepted the certain knowledge that she loved Kincaid Hutton. Maybe she had from the first.

Despite everything, even knowing that he fought madly against any closeness between them, she loved him. She'd had no promises from him. No declarations of undying affection. And there was no guarantee that she would *ever* get them.

All she knew for certain was that when he touched her, she felt alive.

The laughter and snatches of conversation from the crowd so very far away faded into the background. As if they were the only two people for miles around, Faith heard only Kincaid's breathing and the beating of her own heart.

A canopy of low-hanging branches and wide bushes hid them and sheltered them in a dark, lush cavern of green.

She lay back on the grassy ground, staring up at him. Her hands moved up his arms to cup the back of his head, and slowly she drew him down to her. As she pressed her lips to his, he slid his hand up to the juncture of her thighs.

Through the soft white fabric of her drawers, Faith felt the warmth of his flesh cupped against her center, and she arched against him. As he began to rub and stroke that most sensitive part of her body, Faith groaned softly and pulled her mouth away from his, trying to breathe.

Eyes wide, she stared up at him and lost herself in the gentleness she saw in his gaze.

"Let me touch you, Faith," he whispered and planted a gentle kiss at the corner of her mouth.

Wildly Faith told herself that she thought he already *was* touching her, but she nodded anyway, unable to speak. As if from a great distance, she heard again the shouted conversations and snatches of laughter from the townspeople, and she knew that she should be concerned that someone would enter the copse of trees. That someone would see the two of them.

But at that moment she didn't care. All she cared about was Kincaid's hand moving over her body gently, bringing with him a fire she'd never dreamed existed.

Then she jumped, startled, as his fingers moved over her naked flesh. He'd untied the strings at her waist and slipped his hand beneath the fabric of her underthings. She'd never known the intimate feel of flesh against flesh. The gentle chaos of emotion that charged through her brain, leaving her whimpering softly.

His long fingers dipped lower still, and she held her breath, not sure what to expect. Then her breath left her on a sigh as Kincaid slipped his fingers into her body's warmth. Instinctively she spread her legs farther apart, welcoming him. His thumb stroked a hardened bud of desire while his fingers dipped in and out of her slick warmth, and Faith's head tossed from side to side breathlessly.

"Dear God, Faith," he whispered and kissed her eyes, her cheeks.

"Kincaid," she breathed heavily, arching her hips into his touch, "Kincaid, help me."

"I will, my love, I will" he promised and lowered his mouth to hers.

His tongue darted inside her mouth and kept rhythm with his questing fingers. Faith held on to him tightly, sure that if she released him, she would spin off the edge of the world. Eagerly she matched his tongue's movements, and groaned as the sensations growing in the center of her body threatened to explode.

And finally, when her entire body ached with need, Kincaid gave her the release she'd been striving toward. As her flesh convulsed around his hand, he swallowed her groan of pleasure.

"Anybody seen Faith?" Mrs. Lind stepped up to the food table and picked up a corn muffin. Her quick, happy gaze moved from one familiar face to the other.

"Haven't seen her since the game started," Cora answered and took another bite of her ice cream.

"Well," Minnie announced suddenly, smacking Gary Lind's reaching hand away from the chocolate cake, "I don't know where Faith is, but I've been lookin' all over for Kincaid."

"He's gone, too?" Cora asked thoughtfully.

Minnie nodded. "Ain't seen hide nor hair of him, and Amanda's been askin' after him."

"Hmmm . . ." Maisie smiled slowly. Kincaid and

Faith both missing. She glanced at Inga Lind and saw the same curious interest on Faith's mother's face.

Maybe, Maisie told herself with a silent chuckle, maybe that boy's got some sense after all. Deliberately she tamped down the smile hovering around her lips and changed the subject.

No sense workin' everybody up into startin' a search party that *could* prove embarrassing! "So, Inga," she said firmly, "you and Tom gonna be comin' into town for the next spelling bee? We missed you last time."

CHAPTER

TEN

HER HEAD on his chest, Faith's body still trembled. She cuddled in close to him as Kincaid smoothed her skirt gently down over her legs. One arm wrapped around her, he laid back on the grassy earth and tried to calm his racing heart.

"Kincaid," she whispered, "I've never felt anything like that before."

"I know, Faith." His hand moved up and down her back soothingly. He smiled, kissed the top of her head, and held her tighter. Her breathing ragged, she curled snuggly against him, and an incredible feeling of peace rushed over him. As long as he lived, Kincaid knew he would never forget these last few moments alone with her under the canopy of trees, sheltered in the shadows.

She ran the flat of her hand across his chest, and he snatched it, holding it still. Her slightest touch was almost painful. His entire body aching with unfulfilled need, all he could think of was how he wanted to bury himself in her. He wanted to watch her eyes as he entered her body. He wanted to feel her warmth surround him, welcome him.

God, he groaned silently, and desperately fought to clear his mind of the images taunting him.

She rubbed her cheek against his chest and spoke

on a sigh. Kincaid tensed, breath held. "What did you say?" he asked hesitantly.

Tilting her head back, she looked at him and smiled shyly. "I said I love you."

Sweet Jesus! his brain screamed. Somehow he managed to move carefully. Gently disentangling himself from her, he sat, drew one knee up, and rested his forearm on top.

He should have known what would happen. What had been happening all along. Hell, maybe he *had* known. Maybe he'd just been hoping that . . . *what*? he asked himself. That you could use her warmth, her heart for a while, then toss her aside?

No. Faith Lind wasn't the kind of woman you trifled with, he knew that. Wasn't that exactly why he'd been so damn scared? She's the kind you marry. Have children with. Hell, what he'd done to her already was enough to warrant her father coming after him with a shotgun!

"Kincaid?" Faith said softly.

As if from a great distance, he heard snatches of conversations and short bursts of laughter from the picnic yard. He should have stayed in the crowd. He should never have trusted himself alone with her. His eyes squeezed shut. But God help him, he'd needed to touch her so badly that even now he couldn't regret it. The only thing he regretted was the fact that he had to hurt her now.

"Faith, don't," he whispered, shaking his head.

"Don't what?"

"Don't love me." He snorted a half laugh and stared blankly into the surrounding trees. "I'm a bad risk."

"What do you mean?" she asked and sat up. Keeping a small space between them, Faith brushed at the leaves and dry grass on her skirt.

"I mean, I've *been* married, Faith. And I did a right poor job of it." He rubbed one hand across his jaw and tried to think of the right words. No matter what he said, he knew she'd be hurt, but maybe she could understand that what he was doing was best for her in the long run of things. "You're the kind of girl— woman—" he corrected quickly, "who *should* be married. God knows, if things were different, I'd—but anyway. You want a husband. Children. And rightly so."

He glanced at her regretfully. "And I can't give those to you."

She stared at him, and Kincaid wasn't sure if it was anger or confusion in her soft hazel eyes. When she spoke, he still wasn't sure.

"I don't understand what you're trying to tell me, Kincaid. Nobody said anything about marriage."

"You said you loved me." He turned away. "Another woman said that to me once. And I managed to make her life miserable." His voice turned harsh when he added, "I won't do that to you. And *children*?" A bitter laugh shook him. "Hell, Faith, you've seen my child. Look what I did to Amanda! You think I want to mess up more children's lives?"

She stared at him for a long moment, and Kincaid would've given anything to know what she was thinking. But her expression was unreadable. He could only hope that what he'd said had taken root.

No matter how badly he wanted her, he wasn't about to let another woman into his life. Not again.

Faith stood up suddenly and began to straighten the fall of her skirt. Slowly, deliberately, her hands moved over the fabric, and as he watched her, Kincaid felt as though she was brushing him aside as effectively as she was the grass and leaves.

"Why don't you go on back to the picnic,

Kincaid?" she said softly. "If we don't get back soon, folks will start talking."

He stood up, keeping a safe distance from her. If he got too close, he might just forget all of his fine, noble words and clutch her to him. "What about you?" he asked.

She flashed him a glance, then moved to pull leaves from her hair. "I'll walk through the trees a bit and come around from the other side. No sense feeding the gossips any more than we have already."

"Faith—"

"Just go, Kincaid." She took a deep breath. "Now." She turned and began to walk through the copse of trees.

Helpless to undo what he'd done and unwilling to call her back and disregard what he knew to be right, Kincaid watched her until she disappeared into the shadows of the trees.

"Well, Faith dear," her mother called out, "there you are!"

Faith stopped dead, took a shuddering breath, and turned to face Inga Lind. Of all the people she could have run into at that moment, why on earth did it have to be her mother?

The short, plump blond woman was hurrying up to her, and Faith knew she wouldn't even have an extra moment to compose herself. She groaned inwardly, wishing her mother didn't have such sharp eyes. But Inga Lind never missed a thing. When it came to her family, she almost had a sixth sense. She always seemed to know when her children were happy or when something was wrong.

For one brief instant Faith found herself wishing that she could turn and run, but it wouldn't do the slightest bit of good. Inga would hunt her down if it took all day. Better to get it over with right away.

"Where in heaven have you been, girl?" Inga asked breathlessly as she came to a sudden stop just inches from her daughter. Right hand splayed against her heaving bosom, she added, "You disappeared during hide-and-seek, and your papa and I wanted to say goodbye before we went home."

"You're leaving already?"

"Yes." Inga frowned and tugged at the ribbons on her straw bonnet. "Your brother Ben ate so much of Lillie Taylor's ice cream, he has a bellyache."

Though Faith was sorry to hear Ben wasn't feeling well, he was only eight. He'd recover. Right at that moment she was only grateful that Ben's stomach would keep Inga's mind too busy to notice anything amiss with her oldest child. But even as that thought flew through her mind, her mother said, "Maisie tells me that you and her nephew have been seeing quite a bit of each other—"

"What?" A flush crept up Faith's neck and colored her cheeks. She felt the heat of it and knew she couldn't stop it. "Maisie said *that*?"

"Don't take on so, dear." Inga cocked her head and stared at her daughter curiously. "I'm sure she didn't mean anything special by it ... *did* she?"

"Of course not, Mama." Faith shook her head firmly, hoping she looked more convincing than she sounded. "Kincaid and I have only been trying to ... help his little girl."

"Ah, yes." Inga nodded, one blond curl slipping from her bonnet and bouncing with the woman's sharp movements. "Amanda. I met her. Lovely child." Tapping her finger against her chin, she asked, "Is there something wrong, honey? Something you'd like to tell me about? Perhaps ... something your papa should talk to Kincaid about?"

"No!" Good God. That's all she needed, Faith told herself. Her father descending on the boardinghouse armed with a shotgun and righteous indignation! "There's nothing wrong, Mama. Really."

"Inga!"

Thankfully, Faith recognized her father's deep voice. Immediately he shouted again. "Inga, Ben's not gettin' any better waitin' on you!"

"All right, Tom!" the little woman yelled back, waving one hand impatiently. Looking back at Faith, she added, "I have to go or your papa's gonna shout till the trees fall down. You take good care of yourself, honey." She hugged Faith hard, then cupped her daughter's cheek. "If there's ever anything you need to talk over, you just come on home." A sad smile touched her face. "It's lonesome without you."

Despite herself, Faith laughed. "With *six* other children there? You probably don't even know I'm gone!"

"Don't you believe it, girl. Each one of my children is special to me. And when one of them isn't around, it leaves an aching big hole in my heart."

"Oh, Mama," Faith murmured and wrapped her arms around her mother. Briefly she wished she *could* tell Inga about the confusing feelings she was experiencing. She wished she could ask her mother's advice about Kincaid and what she should do about him. She wanted to know if *all* women felt so glorious in the arms of the men they loved.

Then she remembered just how many times she'd seen her parents exchange quiet, secret smiles. And how many times over the years they'd gone to collect the eggs together in the hushed hours before dawn.

Smiling, Faith let her mother go and watched until

Tom Lind greeted his wife with a hearty kiss. With a sigh she realized she'd just received an answer to her question. Her mother would know very well what Faith was talking about.

The rest of the afternoon passed in a haze. Kincaid kept to himself, only joining in the festivities when Amanda insisted.

As he packed up the last of Maisie's and Minnie's things to take back to the boardinghouse, he found himself smiling despite what had happened earlier.

Amanda was very nearly back to her old self. Laughing and playing with the other children, she hadn't talked to Boom once all afternoon. At least, he hadn't seen her.

He raised his gaze and looked over the dwindling crowd, searching for her. Most of the people had already gone home. The farm families had long drives ahead of them, and most of them had set out with their children sound asleep in the backs of the wagons.

His gaze strayed to the cloud-streaked sky and saw the coming sunset had begun to tint the heavens in soft shades of pink and orange. The prairie wind raced across the open ground, kicking up the discarded remnants of the picnic. Standing up and squinting, he once again scanned the field for signs of Amanda.

She'd been so happy today, he thought grimly. He prayed that feeling would stay with her even after Faith began to treat her differently. Having had long experience in dealing with Mary Alice's pouting tantrums, Kincaid was dreading having to put up with Faith's inevitable sulking. He only hoped his tenuous new relationship with his daughter was strong enough to withstand the snubbing he was expecting.

In the distance his eyes caught a flicker of movement, and he squinted, studying the two figures so far away. Even when he'd indentified them, though, he could hardly believe it.

He shaded his eyes with one hand and cocked his head. He wasn't mistaken. It *was* Faith and Amanda. Playing. Frowning slightly, he continued to watch the far-off pair. The little girl ran, her hair streaking out behind her, and Faith was chasing her. On a blast of wind he caught a hint of laughter and recognized the brief snippet of sound as Amanda's voice.

Thoroughly confused, hands on hips, he stared off at the pair of them, shaking his head. Faith had ignored him completely for the last few hours, only speaking politely when absolutely forced to in the presence of others. He'd *assumed* that attitude would continue . . . and include Amanda.

"Kincaid!"

He spun around to face Maisie.

"Boy, you gonna stand there all day gapin' with your mouth hangin' open . . . or are you gonna help us?"

"Yeah. Be right there, Maisie." Dutifully he lifted the box of dishes. With one last glance over his shoulder he started for the boardinghouse. When he passed his aunt, he didn't even notice the telling smile on her lips.

After supper, despite her fatigue, Faith escaped to the front porch. Her face hurt from smiling, and if she had to take part in one more conversation, she was sure she would scream. She breathed deeply of the soft spring night air. A faint perfume from the wildflowers on the prairie drifted to her, bringing a reluctant smile to her lips.

A beautiful evening after what should have been a

glorious day. She closed her eyes and leaned her head against the newel post. For the first time she let herself remember what had happened only a few short hours ago. In her mind's eye she saw Kincaid's face just inches above hers. She recalled vividly the tenderness of his expression and the passion in his eyes.

Her own eyes flew open. She *couldn't* have been mistaken. Surely *no* man could touch a woman so intimately with such gentleness unless he felt *something* for her! Or was she really such an innocent? Was it possible that a man could experience such a thing and feel nothing more than the pleasure of the moment?

No. She shook her head firmly. She wasn't wrong. She *knew* it! He *had* felt something. Something beyond desire. But even if he had, she reminded herself, he'd successfully cut it off.

Faith swallowed heavily, took another deep breath, and pushed away from the porch post. Smoothing her skirt, she sat down on the top step, rested her elbows on her knees, and propped her chin in her hands.

From next door she heard the steady thump of the printing press and knew that Samantha and Alex were busily working. Across the street Jane Carson's lamp was lit as usual. Faith glanced to the left and saw that lamplight shone from behind the windows of the church. It seemed that even Reverend Johnson and his wife, Rachel, were working late.

She twisted the fingers of her hands together in her lap suddenly, wishing she, too, had something to keep her busy. Something to keep her mind off Kincaid Hutton.

Good Lord, she'd been an idiot! Sharing the intimate secrets of her body with a man who afterward calmly said "I'm sorry" and walked away. How could she have been so stupid?

Maybe he was right. Maybe she *was* too young. Maybe if she'd been older, she'd have seen from the first that Kincaid Hutton wanted nothing more from her than her help with Amanda. And yet . . . there was so much more in his eyes than gratitude.

Oh, for heaven's sake! she thought and straightened her spine. Why couldn't she have just fallen in love with a nice, reliable farmer? Someone she'd known forever? Even Danny Vega, for that matter. At least with them, she would know what to expect. She wouldn't go from hot to cold, desire to misery in seconds.

Hmmph! Kincaid had hardly *looked* at her since that breathtaking episode in the trees. Truth to tell, she should be grateful. How would she manage to look him in the eye, knowing that he'd touched parts of her body that even *she* had hardly looked at. She cringed for a moment, remembering the way she'd moaned and twisted under his hand. Remembering how wet her body'd become and how she'd clamped her thighs around his hand, holding him in place.

Good God. How could she face him after all that?

Do you regret it? her mind asked. Do you wish it had never happened?

She thought about it for a long moment and finally found her answer. No. She didn't regret it one bit. And even if nothing like that ever happened to her again in her life, she wouldn't wish it away.

Faith tilted her head back and stared up at the black sky. Deliberately she chose one star from the multitude and focused on it. She'd done nothing wrong, she told herself firmly. Nothing. She'd offered herself to the man she loved, and for one brief moment she'd experienced something that would live in her memory forever.

If Kincaid chose to ignore that, so be it. It changed nothing. Not her feelings. Certainly not his. She still flushed when she remembered how he'd lectured her afterward.

Telling her that he had no intention of marrying again because he'd done such a poor job of it the first time. And imagine, she told herself, he'd used *Amanda* as an example of why he shouldn't have children. That lovely girl. Faith shook her head and lowered her gaze back to Harmony's Main Street.

The man's a fool, she thought fiercely. He couldn't see the truth standing right in front of him. There was nothing wrong with Amanda that his attentions weren't curing. And because one attempt at love had failed . . . well, that didn't mean that you should never love again!

Behind her the front door opened, and Faith tensed, somehow *knowing* that Kincaid was about to join her. She stood up, preferring to meet him standing on her own two feet.

He closed the door firmly after him and crossed the boardwalk to stand beside her. But not too close.

"Faith," he said, looking out over the empty street, "I, uh, wanted to apologize again for what happened today. It never should have. It was entirely my fault." He exhaled on a rush. "And it won't happen again."

"I see." She watched him in the half-light and struggled to keep a tight rein on her temper.

"Also," he added, "I wanted to thank you for not being angry. I'm afraid of what it might have done to Amanda."

"Oh," Faith countered quickly and took two steps back from him, "I'm angry, Kincaid. So save your thanks."

His brow furrowed. "But ... I *watched* you. You were laughing. *Playing*."

She snorted a laugh and shook her head. "What did you expect me to do? Punish Amanda for *your* 'mistake'?"

"That's what—" He broke off abruptly.

"Mary Alice would have done?" Faith finished for him. "I'm not Mary Alice, Kincaid. I'm Faith Lind." She took one step closer to him and had to tilt her head back to look into his eyes. "And even though I'm mad at you ... I'm not about to show it in front of an already troubled child!"

"I'm—"

"How little you must think of me," she fumed, effectively cutting him off again. "Oh, granted, perhaps I asked for it, allowing you such ... *liberties*." She was glad for the darkness. The hot flush of embarrassment stained her cheeks. "Yet somehow, I'd hoped that you would have known me better than that."

"Faith, I—"

"No, Kincaid." She shook her head and closed the remaining space between them. "You had your say this afternoon. It's *my* turn now." Poking her index finger against his chest, she went on, "Entirely your fault, was it? It won't happen again, right?"

He nodded.

"Well, let me tell you something, *Mr.* Hutton. If I hadn't wanted it to happen today, it *wouldn't* have. Don't take so much on yourself. Whether you think so or not, I am *not* a child. I make my own decisions. Some of them good. Some bad." Pausing for breath, she jammed her fists on her hips and finished up, "And I *promise* you, nothing is going to happen between us that you need worry about. If my kisses, my ... *body* ... are so distasteful to you, you may rest assured you won't be bothered with them again."

She half turned for the door but stopped for one more word. "We'll go on working together for Amanda's sake. Lord knows, I would never sacrifice a child, even *yours*, to a fit of temper. But as far as you and I are concerned, Kincaid"—she twisted the doorknob—"consider yourself relieved of *any* responsibility toward me. And I will do the same. Good night."

The door closed quietly after her, leaving Kincaid alone with his thoughts. Stunned by her determination as much as by her words, he felt a familiar swell of confusion rush through him.

Dropping to the top step, Kincaid leaned back against the porch post. He couldn't even remember the last time someone had put him in his place so thoroughly. He'd been prepared for pouting, tears, recriminations. Hell, he was *used* to dealing with that sort of thing. Heaven knew, he'd had enough experience with Mary Alice.

But Faith's calm, controlled anger was something completely new to him. He closed his eyes and let his head drop back against the post with a satisfying thump.

Distasteful? God, if that's what she thought he did with a woman he found *distasteful* . . . Dammit!

He'd made a complete ass of himself. Lecturing her, nobly accepting the blame for letting a situation get out of control. Treating her as though she'd had no say in what had happened. As though because he'd wanted it, it had been so.

Jesus! And he'd considered her too young. Disgusted with himself, he wondered wryly just *who* was the real child. He turned and went inside. It was time to tuck Amanda in for the night.

Taking the stairs quietly, Kincaid reached the landing and paused. Voices. Coming from Amanda's room. He listened carefully for a moment, then groaned inwardly. Faith.

A few short steps brought him to his daughter's open doorway, and he stood, just out of sight, listening.

"I'm not"—Amanda yawned—"ready to sleep yet, Faith."

Faith's chuckle drifted out to him. "Well, everyone else in the house is," she said softly. "We all had quite a day, you know."

"It was fun," Amanda agreed on a sigh. "The best day ever!"

"I'm glad, honey."

Kincaid poked his head around and watched as Faith pulled the quilt up to his daughter's chin and sat down on the bed beside her.

"Wasn't Papa funny with the egg on his head?"

"Yes, he was."

"And he didn't find me when we played hide-and-seek, Faith. I hid real good and he didn't even *see* me!"

"I know." Faith swept Amanda's bangs off her forehead gently. "You played the game very well!"

The little girl nodded and grinned. "Papa caught you, didn't he, Faith?"

Kincaid held his breath and watched the woman's expression. He saw her swallow heavily and recognized what an effort it cost her to smile.

"He surely did, honey."

"I can teach you to hide, Faith. So he can't catch you again!"

Faith's voice came low, thoughtful. "Maybe that's a good idea, Amanda. We'll see."

Sharp green eyes caught his movement in the doorway, and before he could back away, Amanda called, "Papa! Faith is tucking me in 'cause I asked her to!"

His gaze locked with Faith's, Kincaid stepped into the room and walked to his daughter's bedside. "That was nice of her," he said quietly.

Faith jumped up. "I'll be going now, let you two say your good nights. . . ."

"No," both Huttons said at once.

Amanda held out her arms to her teacher. "You didn't kiss me good night."

With a quick glance at Kincaid, Faith leaned down, kissed the little girl's forehead, and stood up again.

"Now you, Papa," Amanda ordered.

Surprised and touched, Kincaid leaned over his daughter and felt her small arms wrap tightly about his neck. She squeezed him hard and planted a kiss on his cheek. Reverently Kincaid's palm cupped her face, and he smiled down at her. For the first time in far too long, his little girl had *kissed* him! Somehow, he managed to swallow past the knot in his throat.

"Papa," Amanda said softly.

"Yes?"

"You won't ever go away again, will you, Papa?" She bit her lip nervously and waited for his answer.

He dragged air into his chest, kissed her forehead, then looked directly into her eyes. In a hushed, nearly strangled voice he vowed, "Never, Amanda. I promise. I won't leave you again."

She studied him for what seemed an eternity before she finally smiled, satisfied. Snuggling down deeper under the quilt, she murmured, "G'night, Papa. G'night, Faith."

Kincaid pushed himself to his feet, looked at the woman beside him, and motioned for her to join him in the hallway.

With Amanda's door closed, the two adults stared at each other, suddenly at a loss for words.

"Faith . . ." he began.

She shook her head. "No, Kincaid. Don't say anything else tonight. Please." Backing up a step, she edged toward her own room. "I'm glad for you. For you and Amanda both. Really. But . . ." Her breath caught, and she suddenly spun around, opened her own door, and slipped into her bedroom.

Kincaid stood alone in the dimly lit hallway. He should be the happiest man on earth, he told himself. His daughter loved him again. He glanced over his shoulder at the little girl's closed door, then turned back to face the door Faith had just shut in his face.

Dear God, he'd finally received the one thing he'd dreamed about for months, and now . . . it wasn't enough.

Kincaid was up and dressed as dawn filled the sky. Irritable, he stared at himself in the mirror as he whipped his shaving soap into foam. Bleary green eyes looked back at him accusingly.

He hadn't gotten a wink of sleep all night. Every time he closed his eyes, visions of Faith sprang up. His body throbbed with the need that was constantly with him. It had been too long since he'd had a woman.

Maybe that's all he needed, he told himself. A woman. *Any* woman. Relief rushed through him. Of course. What a fool he was! He'd been living like a monk and torturing himself with a closeness to Faith. No *wonder* he was so miserable.

He should just stroll down to the First Resort and

take advantage of one of Lottie's girls. If his body found peace, surely his mind would, too.

But even as he thought it, he knew it wouldn't work. He didn't want just *any* woman. He wanted Faith. Even more so since sampling the passion hidden in the little schoolteacher.

Snarling at his own reflection, he began to lather his cheeks viciously. The only answer for him was work. Hard work. And lots of it.

From the room next door came the first sounds of Amanda stirring. He cocked his head slightly and heard his daughter singing in a soft voice. Picking up his razor, Kincaid frowned as he tested the blade gingerly with the pad of his thumb.

He remembered her good-night kiss and the feel of her arms around his neck. Amanda was happy again. A couple of months ago he would have given everything he owned just to hear her singing to herself.

"Jesus," he said aloud to the mirror, "look at yourself. Because you *wanted* Faith, you were willing to sacrifice your child's chance at happiness? What if Faith had refused to help you with her anymore? Then what?" He dragged the sharp blade's edge down one cheek and wiped the lather on a towel. "I'll tell you what," he continued. "Amanda would be talking to Boom right now and blaming you!" As he continued to scrape away the whisker stubble on his jaw, he said softly, "If Faith can put her anger aside for the good of *your* child, then by thunder you can put your own desire aside for the same reason."

Since Faith was willing to help him, he would simply have to swallow what was left of his pride and accept whatever she was willing to give. For Amanda's sake he would find a way to be around Faith without touching her.

It wasn't as if he were a boy, experiencing the first

rush of lust. He was an adult. He could control himself. And he would.

Even if it killed him.

When he was finished, he wiped his face, grabbed his shirt, and stepped into the hall. Bypassing Amanda's room, he hurried downstairs, went through the kitchen, and out the back door. He needed to get into the workshop as early as possible.

He'd start that cabinet Maisie'd been after him for three weeks to make. If he worked himself half to death during the day, he told himself hopefully, maybe he'd be able to sleep at night.

CHAPTER

ELEVEN

THREE DAYS. Three long days, he told himself, and glumly stared through the workshop window at the schoolyard. Kincaid watched as Faith picked up her skirts and jumped rope with the children.

He tried to look away, but his gaze was locked on her legs, shapely even encased in plain black cotton stockings. Graceful even at play, he looked up at her smiling face and realized wistfully how much he'd missed seeing her smile.

Oh, in front of Amanda or anyone else for that matter, Faith was unfailingly polite and even friendly. But as soon as they were left alone, her smile would disappear and she would look through him as if he weren't there.

His grip on the windowsill tightened, and he told himself it shouldn't matter to him. After all, it was Amanda who was important. It was only for *her* sake that Faith had agreed to continue speaking to him at all. If anything, he should be grateful! But he wasn't.

It surprised him to realize just how much her smiles and her conversation had come to mean to him. He missed talking to her. Missed watching the play of emotions on her face. Missed that flash of interest that sparkled in her eyes when he spoke to her.

Dammit, he missed *her*!

"Kincaid?" Minnie called out and stepped into the workroom.

"Yes?" Guiltily he moved away from the window.

The older woman hurried across the room, kicking at the small piles of sawdust as she went, a yellow paper in her hand. "This just come for you. A boy rode in from Ellsworth with it."

He took the telegram and stared at it. From his lawyer in South Dakota. Kincaid's mind raced. He was only vaguely listening as Minnie added, "I keep tellin' folks around here that it's high time we got our *own* telegraph office. But no, nobody wants to listen to an old woman!" She finally paused for breath and asked, "Ain't you gonna open it up, boy?"

"Huh? Oh, of course." Turning it over, his fingers split the envelope and pulled out a single sheet of paper. Quickly his gaze went over the message, and he smiled.

"Good news, then?" Minnie sounded relieved. "Thank heaven! Lord, them things usually bring nothin' but disaster with 'em. What is it, Kincaid?"

He looked up, grabbed Minnie, and kissed her cheek soundly. "Very good news, Min. My lawyer back home finally sold the store. He's sending a bank draft along separately."

"Well, my lands! That *is* good to hear, boy! Won't Maisie be pleased!" She reached up and patted his cheek. "And won't it just ruin her day that *I* was the one that brought it to ya! I'll just run and tell her, shall I?"

"Sure, Min. Sure." As the older woman left, he leaned back against the wall, smiling.

Finally. The past was finished. His last link with South Dakota was severed. Kincaid looked down at the telegram and read the message one more time. It was true. He wasn't seeing things. He inhaled sharply. The end of one life. The beginning of another. Soon he'd have the money he needed to build a future for Amanda and himself. A future right here in Harmony.

There would be no going backward now. No more running away. Here, where Amanda'd already made friends, was the place to build. Here, he thought as his gaze slid out to the schoolyard once more, where Faith lived.

Faith.

Somehow, he *had* to find a way to make her accept him as a friend. Surely, since they were both adults, they could live in the same town without driving each other to distraction.

And this forced politeness of hers was almost as hard to live with as the torture of not touching her. There *had* to be a middle ground *somewhere*. They only had to find it.

He watched, breath held, as Faith dropped to the ground exhausted and the kids sat down around her. The smile on her face captivated him, but he deliberately tamped down the flash of desire she aroused.

If they were to live in such close proximity, he *had* to stop reacting to her like that. And he would, he promised himself. Soon.

Carefully he folded up the telegram and shoved it in his pants pocket. He walked back to the worktable and picked up his paintbrush. As he gave Maisie's cabinet the finishing coat of robin's-egg-blue paint, he let his mind wander, hoping for an answer to his problems.

But he already knew the only answer possible for him. Kincaid set the paint can and brush down on the table and turned back toward the window. Now Faith was playing tag with the children. Somehow,

he was going to have to find a way to deal with her
presence in his life without losing his mind.

He walked to the door and leaned one shoulder
against the jamb. Crossing his feet at the ankles, he
felt a reluctant smile tug at his lips as he watched
Faith run and play. Her delighted laughter floated to
him on the wind, and once again he was reminded of
how much he'd missed hearing it.

But a romance between them wouldn't work, and
all the wishing in the world wouldn't change that
fact. His smile faded slowly. All at once he saw himself in the years to come. He would have to resign
himself to standing back from her. To seeing her be
courted. To someday watching her marry another
man. He swallowed heavily. He forced himself to
imagine her lying smiling beneath another man.
Carrying another man's child.

He groaned aloud, and his fist shot out and
slammed into the doorjamb opposite him. A star-
burst of pain screamed up his arm, and he welcomed
it gratefully. Pulling a deep breath into his lungs, he
clamped his lips shut against the pain and turned
away from the scene in the schoolyard.

"Lord," Minnie began loudly with a quick glance
at the boarders, "thank you again for a fine day. We
all worked hard, 'cept for Kincaid there who durned
near broke his hand doin' only You know what since
he won't tell a soul how he done it."

Faith looked across the table at him and saw the
frown he tossed at the older woman. His hands were
in his lap, though. She couldn't see what he'd done
to himself.

"And, Lord," Minnie went on with another glance
at Kincaid, "make the fool man smart enough to trot

himself over to Jane so's she can have a look at it. Amen."

"Amen," everyone echoed.

"Kincaid," Maisie demanded, "let me see that hand of yours."

"It's fine, Maisie," he retorted. "I already told you. Let it be."

"Nonsense. If you don't want me to see it, then go on over to Jane's. She's the closest we got to a doctor around here."

He only half turned his head to stare at his aunt. "I said it's all right, Maisie."

"Papa," Amanda said and reached for his injured hand, "did you hurt yourself??"

He sucked in a deep breath when his daughter touched him, and Faith jumped to her feet and walked around the table to his side.

"Just a little, Amanda," Kincaid was saying gently, "but I'll be fine."

"Let me see it," Faith said.

He looked up into her eyes and frowned. Her eyebrows quirked. It would take more than an angry glare to make *her* back down.

"Dammit, why is everyone making such a fuss over my hand?" Kincaid shouted, glaring at Faith.

"Kincaid Hutton," Maisie ordered firmly, "you watch your mouth at my dinner table. There'll be no profanity *here*!"

"Sorry, Maisie," he offered.

"What the . . . heck," Travis stumbled over the word, "did you do to yourself, Kincaid?"

"Nothing." He waved his uninjured left hand at the group around the table. "It is *nothing*."

"Then let me see it," Faith repeated, tapping her foot against the braided rug. "*Maybe*, if you'd stop being so secretive about it, people would leave you alone."

"Papa? Is it awful terrible? Is that how come you don't want to show us?"

Faith saw the worry on the little girl's face, and Kincaid must've seen it, too. He leaned toward her and said softly, "No, sweetheart. It's not terrible. And if it'll make you feel better, I'll let Jane have a look at it. All right?"

Amanda smiled and nodded.

"I'll go with you," Faith declared and turned for the front door.

"That's not necessary. I'll go myself after supper," Kincaid protested.

"Oh, I'll keep it warm for ya. Thank you kindly Faith, dear," Maisie called out. "Now I know he'll go."

Faith heard him behind her and only slowed down to snatch her shawl from the hall tree before opening the door for him. As he stepped out onto the porch, she said quietly, her hand extended, "Let me see it, Kincaid."

He heaved a sigh, rolled his eyes skyward, and held his right hand out to her. "Happy?"

"Very." Gently her fingers moved over his bruised and scraped knuckles. Shaking her head, she finally asked, "How on earth did you manage to do this?"

"I, uh, *hit* something," he said and pulled his hand away, wincing.

"I can *see* that," she retorted and started for the steps. "What I asked was how?"

"Jesus, Faith!" He glared at her ferociously. "I'm not your *son*! How I did it is none of your business. Isn't it enough that I'm going over to see Jane Carson?"

Lips tight, she nodded and led the way.

As usual, Jane's lamp was lit, but as they neared her shop, Faith saw through the window that the woman already had a visitor. She pulled the door wide and said, "Hello, Jane, Alex."

Alex Evans left his chair hurriedly and stood smiling. Jane gave them both a timid smile and glanced at Alex when he wasn't looking.

"What are you two up to tonight?" Alex's voice boomed out into the small shop with a false heartiness.

Faith had the distinct feeling that they were intruding on a private moment. One glance at Kincaid's face told her that he was thinking the same thing. While she searched blindly for something to say, Kincaid spoke up.

"Nothing much, Alex," he began, "just saw Jane's light, thought we'd stop and make sure she was all right. . . ."

For heaven's sake, Faith told herself, surely he could have thought of something better than that! Jane worked late nearly every night! Besides, what about his hand?

Before she could say anything, Kincaid grabbed her elbow with his good hand and backed through the door. "Well, good night, now."

It wasn't until they were clear of the shop that Faith pulled out of his grasp and asked, "What was *that* all about?"

He let his head fall back on his neck. "C'mon, Faith, you know we interrupted *something* back there."

"Well, maybe . . ." She looked up at him. "But Jane was supposed to look at your hand."

"It's all right." Sticking his right hand out in front

of him, he flexed his fingers one by one, then made a fist. "Nothing broken. It's just bruised and sore. That'll fade." Silently then, he began to walk, and without thinking, Faith fell in beside him. "Strange, isn't it?" he asked.

"What?"

"We always seem to do most of our talking at night. Did you notice?"

She glanced at him. "Yes. But what with all the people around us during the day, I guess it's only natural."

"Yeah." He nodded. "That's it."

"Kincaid—"

"Faith—"

They spoke at the same time and then stopped suddenly. As their eyes met, Faith found herself almost forgetting the last few days of anger. In fact, she told herself silently, she was lucky she didn't forget her own name when she looked into his green eyes.

"Faith," he said and sucked in a gulp of air. "I'm glad you came out with me ... I wanted to talk to you."

Her heart sank. Surely he wasn't going to tell her yet *again* that he wanted nothing to do with her! But he didn't look hard or cold now, she thought wonderingly. He looked almost ... hesitant. "All right, Kincaid," she agreed warily. "What is it?"

He cupped her elbow and guided her in a slow walk toward the workroom behind the boarding-house.

"Where are we going?" she asked.

"Just out back," he said and kept walking. "I'd rather not be interrupted once I get started."

She stopped and pulled her arm free. Perhaps it

would be better, she told herself firmly, if she spoke *her* mind first.

"Kincaid, I'm willing to listen to what you have to say as long as it isn't the same speech you've already delivered one too many times."

"What?"

She ignored his confused expression and explained herself quickly. "You know which one I mean. It's usually given directly following a kiss?" Cocking her head, she continued. "You remember? When you tell me that I'm too young? That my kisses are distasteful?"

He snorted a choking laugh. "*I* never said that, Faith. *You* did."

Her brow wrinkled in thought, she stumbled after him when he started walking again, quicker this time. By the time they'd reached the workroom, Faith was ready to give him a piece of her mind. After all, she'd agreed to listen! But was it *really* necessary for them to *hide* while they talked? And he had so dismissed her kisses!

Kincaid took one look at her and started talking. "Let me say what I have to say, all right, Faith? Then when I've finished, you can tell me exactly what it is that's about to choke you."

Her lips clamped shut, she waited impatiently.

For what seemed forever, Kincaid paced in a tight circle in the center of the workroom. One hand rubbing the back of his neck, the scowl on his face told her that he wasn't having an easy time straightening out his thoughts.

When her patience was almost exhausted, he stopped in front of her and stared down into her eyes.

"First," he said, shaking his head ruefully, "let me say that your kisses are *far* from distasteful! I . . . enjoyed kissing you very much." Inwardly he groaned at the understatement.

"Then why—"

He held up one hand. "Please. Just let me finish. Today I received a telegram from my lawyer back home."

"Bad news?"

"No. Good news. *Very* good news."

She sighed. "I don't understand, Kincaid."

"I know. I'm doing this badly." He rubbed one hand across his jaw nervously. "Faith, my lawyer finally managed to sell the store I left behind and—"

"That's wonderful," she interrupted. "I didn't know you have a store."

"Had," he corrected quickly and ignored the flash of interest in her gaze. "Now, what I have is the money to build a new life for Amanda and myself here in Harmony."

"Then what's bothering you so and what do my kisses have to do with it?"

A mirthless chuckle escaped him. "Your kisses." He let his gaze slide away from hers. How the hell could he say this without sounding like a pompous fool? Lord knew there was no *polite* way of doing it! Maybe, he thought with a groan, it would be better for both of them if he just spit it out and let the chips fall where they may. Before he could stop himself, he said, "I enjoy kissing you *too* much, Faith. So much so that soon I wouldn't be satisfied with kisses. I'd want more. And the only way to have that is marriage."

She opened her mouth to contradict him, but he cut her off.

"As I've already told you, marriage is out of the question for me. I won't put Amanda through that again. So for *her* sake, I have to put a stop to whatever this is that's building between us."

Faith shook her head and walked a few steps away from him. When at least three feet separated them, she spun around and asked, "Why, Kincaid? What is it you're trying to protect Amanda from? *Me?*"

He inhaled sharply and exhaled again quickly. "No, not you exactly." Jamming his hands into his pants pockets helplessly, he tried to avoid her eyes. Why in the *hell* did this have to happen to him? *Why* did he have to meet Faith in the first place?

He knew without a doubt that if he'd never met her, he could have gone through life happily, just visiting Lottie's whenever the need for a woman became too much to live with. Instead, he had to meet a woman he wanted desperately and couldn't have.

Trying again, he said, "I can't—*won't* let anything happen between us, because if it did . . . when the misery started, it would tear Amanda apart. I won't let that happen again."

"Misery?" she asked, her voice incredibly soft in the shadows.

"Yes," he snapped, fighting against the tenderness he heard in her tone. "Misery." Then sighing, he added, "To understand, you would have to have known Mary Alice."

She took a half step nearer. "Then tell me about her, Kincaid. Help me to understand. Help me to know Mary Alice."

He stared into the darkness but couldn't quite make out her expression. Briefly he considered lighting a lamp, but then again, he told himself, what he had to say would be easier in the dark.

"She was young. Only a year or two younger than you are now when we met."

"You were young, too, Kincaid," she reminded him gently, and he heard her take another step toward him.

A short bark of laughter shot from his throat. "Young?" Shaking his head, he said doubtfully, "Maybe. At first. But not for long."

"What happened?" she breathed. She couldn't take her eyes off him. She'd never seen such a cynical expression on his face before. Not once since she'd met him had his lips twisted into such a mockery of a smile.

Completely lost as to what to do, Faith stood her ground even though she wanted to go to him and wrap her arms around him in comfort.

"Nothing *happened*, really," he was saying and began to pace again. "At least, I can't point my finger at one day in our marriage and say *there*—that's the day everything began to crumble." He stopped his aimless walking and stood stock still. His head dropped back on his neck, and she heard the tired sigh he gave before adding, "It just all went . . . wrong." Kincaid shrugged as if attempting to rid himself of the memories that obviously still tied him to the past. "Mary Alice loved me." He straightened and smiled wearily. "She told me so, often. She fretted over me, pampered me, cosseted me, and in general, did everything she thought would please me and more. Every time I turned around, she was there. With those sad brown eyes of hers staring into me, letting me know what a severe disappointment I was to her."

"What do you mean?" Faith forced herself to ask.

"She couldn't understand why I wasn't happy. She did *everything* a woman could do and more, she'd say. But if I wasn't appreciative enough, she'd com-

plained. Or whined. Or insisted that I was a 'heart-
less beast' of a man."

Faith kept quiet, wanting to hear it all.

"Hell, I *tried*. But I don't think there was a man
alive who could have lived up to what Mary Alice
expected in a husband. And when Amanda came, I
thought she'd be as happy as I was." He shot Faith
a look from the corner of his eye. "But I swear, she
was *jealous* of the baby! Her own *child*! Jesus! If I
even picked Amanda up out of her crib, Mary Alice
was there, harping at me about how I was ignoring
her and how she was fading away from neglect."

Stunned into silence, Faith could only stare at him.
In all her life she'd never heard such a story. It was
beyond her how *any* woman could be jealous of her
own flesh and blood. But it must be true. All of it *had*
to be true. It would explain so much.

Amanda's solitude . . . Kincaid's wariness—no, his
fear of loving anyone. Lord, she thought dismally,
how in the world could she ever overcome the dam-
age Mary Alice Hutton had done to her family?

"Anyway," Kincaid said, shaking his head until
Faith saw his usual rigid control slide back down
over him, "now maybe you'll understand when I say
that as much as I would like things to be different,
it's impossible."

"Kincaid—" she started.

"Faith, it wouldn't work. Mary Alice loved me to
distraction, and I couldn't make her happy." He
looked at her sharply. "Don't you see?"

Walking the few short steps to his side, Faith tentatively laid one hand on his forearm. "It sounds to
me, Kincaid, that *no one* could have made Mary Alice
happy."

"What?"

"To be happy or not." She shook her head and

looked up into his eyes. Even in the gloom of the workroom she saw an interested gleam there. "It's a choice we all have to make for ourselves. If Mary Alice had *wanted* to be happy, she could have been. She had a husband, a child, a home. Don't *you* see, Kincaid? You didn't fail her. She failed herself. And you."

CHAPTER

TWELVE

WAS IT possible? he asked himself wonderingly. Was it really through some fault of her own that Mary Alice had been so damned miserable? Squinting into the darkness, Kincaid thought about everything Faith had just said.

And it made sense. Too much sense to ignore.

But even if it were true—and he wasn't ready to admit that it was—could he take that chance? Could he really risk Amanda's growing confidence and security?

"Kincaid," Faith said, and he was shaken back to the dark workshop.

"Yes?"

"I asked you what your plans are now that you've sold your store."

He'd hardly had time to think of that himself. But then, almost unbidden, came an idea that must have been worming its way into his brain for days. It was the only thing that could explain how swiftly the decision came to him.

"A hotel," he said quickly. "I thought I'd build a hotel."

"Here?" she asked with a smile. "In Harmony?"

"Sure." Smiling himself now, he felt enthusiasm fill him. And with it came a rush of pleasure for the future he'd dreaded only a couple of short weeks ago.

"Harmony's growing. It's right on the railroad line. And Maisie and Minnie's place can only take so many folks. Besides, a boardinghouse is more for long-term guests. Not businessmen or families traveling west."

"True," she whispered and turned her head to follow his progress as he walked the length of the room and back again.

"If I build it near the railroad tracks, it would be convenient. And everyone on the train would be able to see it easily and want to stop. . . ."

She chuckled softly. "Don't forget, the people *in* your hotel would be able to *hear* that same train very easily, too."

He stopped and grinned at her. "Yes, but only on Mondays and Fridays. In the afternoon. At least it wouldn't wake anyone up."

"I think it's a wonderful idea, Kincaid. I really do."

"Faith," he said and walked to her side, "I'd like us to be . . . *friends* if that's all right with you. I can't offer you more than that. Not now anyway. Maybe not ever, I don't know. But I do know that I don't want us to be so cold and distant with each other anymore." He reached one hand out for her, but before he could touch her, he stopped himself and let his hand drop to his side. "Living as closely as we do, our . . . 'battles' are hard on everyone and—" He broke off suddenly. Looking down into her eyes, he waited for what seemed forever before she answered him, a soft smile on her face.

"I'll be your friend, Kincaid. And Amanda's, too, if you still want that."

"Of course I do. You've been wonderful with her, y'know."

Slowly, as if she was afraid of a rebuff, Faith raised one hand and tenderly touched his cheek. Kincaid

summoned every ounce of self-control he possessed
to stand perfectly still under her touch.

"Thank you, Kincaid." she said.

"For what?"

"For telling me about you ... and her."

"Faith, I wish—"

"No." She shook her head. "It's all right. I *do* understand."

Then, as Kincaid held his breath, she raised up on
her toes and kissed his cheek gently. When he found
his voice again, he managed to ask, "What was that
for?"

"Just a *friendly* kiss, Kincaid. That's all." Without
another word she walked to the door and stepped
outside into a patch of starlight. Glancing over her
shoulder, she smiled and whispered, "Good night,
Kincaid."

And then she was gone. He was sure he could still
feel her lips against his cheek. Their warm softness
had all but burned themselves into his flesh.

Alone in the dark, Kincaid stared at the empty
doorway and reminded himself that they were
"friends" now. Merely friends.

This friendship, Faith told herself, was off to a
rocky start.

She tore her gaze away from the sight of Kincaid's
bare back. A mountainous pile of freshly chopped
firewood stood neatly stacked beside the back door
of the boardinghouse. He'd been at it for hours in the
hot afternoon sun, swinging an ax in powerful
strokes, splintering logs into kindling and stove
wood.

For three days they'd abided by the new rules
Kincaid had asked for. The cold politeness was gone
now, replaced by a wary comradeship.

Her gaze slipped back to his broad, bare back. Beads of sweat rolled down his sun-browned flesh and under the waistband of his faded black pants. Faith pulled in a shaky breath and told herself she should move away from the window. There were plenty of chores she could be getting done.

And yet . . . her fingers curled around the window-sill and tightened as the muscles in his back stretched with the movement of the ax again. Friendship! The thoughts that filled her mind had nothing to do with friendship. And she'd felt Kincaid's eyes on her often enough in the last few days to know that he was having no easier a time of this than she was.

He buried the ax blade deep in the chopping block and began to gather up the split wood. Shaking her head, Faith turned her back on the window and walked out of the kitchen. She *had* to abide by their decision to remain friends. She wouldn't do a thing to change their agreement, no matter how she felt inside.

Walking down the narrow hallway to the front parlor, Faith reminded herself of the things she'd told Kincaid not so long ago. That there were plenty of men in the county who would be more than happy to court her. The trouble with that was she didn't want any of them.

Voices from the front parlor reached her, and Faith paused a moment in the hall to compose herself. She was finished behaving like a lovesick child. If Kincaid couldn't see what was right under his nose . . . then bother him! She wasn't about to chase the man down and try to change his mind. They would be friends. And nothing else.

Sooner or later these other feelings she had for him, if ignored long enough, would fade away.

She only hoped it didn't take too long.

* * *

"Afternoon, Faith," Maisie called out as she entered the fussy parlor.

"Maisie, Minnie." Faith nodded at the women who sat opposite each other in matching wing chairs, then wandered over to the drapery-covered window that faced onto Main Street. Grasping the heavy forest-green fabric, Faith pushed the drapes wide, allowing a bright shaft of late sunlight to slice into the room.

"Well, now." Minnie sighed and held up her knitting for a good look. "That's much better. The light, I mean. Thought I was goin' blind there for a spell."

"Faith, honey," Maisie said, "pull them drapes closed again, would ya? That sunlight just fades out my rug something fierce." She waved her hand at the gaudy Oriental carpet lying in the middle of the floor.

Faith moved to shut the drapes again, but Minnie's voice stopped her.

"Hold on, honey." Then, looking at her sister, she went on, "Maisie, I'm commencin' to feel like a bat in a cave in this room. Why the devil should we burn lamps when we got all that good heaven-sent sunshine just waitin' to come in?"

"My rug, Minnie." Maisie lifted her chin and dared her sister to argue with her.

"If you want to know what *I* think—"

"I do not," Maisie countered.

"I think," Minnie went on, "the more faded that rug gets, the better!" She glanced down at the offending carpet and sniffed. "Lord above, that is the *ugliest* durn thing I ever saw!"

Faith watched Maisie uneasily. The woman's lips curled back as if she was snarling and she dropped her knitting into her lap and gripped the arms of her chair.

"You're just jealous, Min, and you know it!"

"Jealous? Of a rug?" Minnie snorted and leaned back.

"Not of the rug, you ninny!"

Minnie's eyes narrowed.

Faith wondered helplessly how this had all started. All she'd wanted to do was sit in a pool of sunshine and read a book—*any* book—in an effort to get her mind off Kincaid Hutton. Now it seemed she'd started a full-scale war.

"You're jealous 'cause my man give me that rug and yours didn't ever give you nothin' but gray hair!"

"If *my* man give me a rug with purple dragons and green flowers plastered all over it, I'd figure he lost his mind!"

"Nothin' wrong with green flowers," Maisie countered hotly.

"Maybe not," Minnie conceded, "but I'd say there's somethin' serious wrong with that orange girl yonder"—she jerked her head at the rug—"*eatin'* one of 'em!"

Carefully, as soundlessly as possible, Faith began to sidle toward the door.

'She ain't *eatin'* it, she's kissin' it!"

"Hah! Kissin' a flower!" Minnie shook one finger at her sister. "*That* makes a whole lot of sense!"

Faith made it through the open doorway and hurried back down the hall and out the kitchen door. Though she and Kincaid were making an effort to get along, it seemed no one else was.

"Faith?"

She groaned silently. Out of the frying pan, she told herself and turned to face Kincaid. Her hungry gaze moved over his still-shirtless chest. Desperately she fought to control her racing heartbeat.

"Faith?" he repeated and took a step toward her. "Is something wrong?"

"No." She sucked in a great gulp of air. "No, it's just Maisie and Minnie, arguing."

He nodded. "The spelling bee again?"

"No, but I think that's what's really behind it. Though neither one of them would admit it. They can hardly wait until next week for the rematch. Right now, though, they're 'discussing' the parlor rug. Minnie says it's ugly, Maisie says she's jealous."

Kincaid wiped his forehead with the back of his hand and grinned. "I have to side with Minnie on this one. That *is* the ugliest rug I've ever seen."

Despite her ragged emotions, Faith answered his smile. "Me, too." Then she added quickly, "But don't say so in there."

"You know," Kincaid said softly and walked toward her, "talking about that rug reminds me of something I wanted to speak to you about."

Faith held her ground. She didn't back away even when he came within inches of her. Staring up into his green eyes, she longed to reach up and smooth his sweat-dampened hair back from his forehead. Instead, her fingers curled around the fabric of her skirt, and somehow she managed to keep a soft smile on her lips.

"What is it?"

He ran one hand through his hair and seemed to choose his words carefully.

"I was down at Cord's place last night, talking to a fellow in from Ellsworth." He reached past her and snatched his shirt off a peg. Shoving his arms through the sleeves, he went on. "He told me about an old hotel just off the main road. Says the owner'd be willing to sell me the furnishings at a reasonable rate."

"That's wonderful, Kincaid. But what does it have to do with me?"

Everything, he wanted to say. He wanted to tell her that his hotel would mean nothing without her, but he couldn't. He'd already made that choice. Now he'd have to live with it. As he buttoned his shirt clumsily, he said instead, "Well, I wanted to know if you'd be willing to come and look at the place with me."

"Why me? I don't know anything about hotels."

"Yeah"—he looked at her and fought down the urge to pull her close—"but I've seen your room here at the boardinghouse."

Her brow wrinkled slightly.

"Oh, just passing glances when you open your door," he said quickly, "but it looks really nice. All the other rooms here seem the same. But you've made that one room look—cozy. Welcoming."

She ducked her head, but not before he saw her smile.

"Anyway," he hurried on, "I don't know about such things. I thought maybe you could help me decide what's good enough to use and what isn't. It would save me a lot of time. And mistakes."

Faith sighed. "I don't know."

"We could take Amanda with us," Kincaid bargained. In fact, he told himself, it would be a lot safer for both of them if Amanda was along.

The last three days had seemed an eternity to him. Everything Faith had said to him the last night they were alone kept repeating itself over and over in his mind. About Mary Alice. Him. Amanda.

He remembered Faith's sweet smile, her gentle touch, and the warmth that seemed to surround her. And though he was glad they'd made that pact to be friends, he had to admit that his frustrations had been easier to bear when they'd been arguing.

At least then he could tell himself that she wouldn't have anything to do with him anyway. But now, with the smiles and comradeship between them, all he could think of was that he wanted more.

And even going to the Last Resort didn't help. He'd found that out right away. There wasn't enough whiskey and beer in the world to cloud his mind enough to forget Faith. And the older he got, the less stomach he had for hard drink anyway.

His gaze moved over her longingly. The Last Resort didn't help, and the First Resort was out of the question. None of Lottie's girls could hold a candle to Faith. And he'd been surprised to realize that he wasn't interested in a quick tumble in the dark with a woman who meant nothing to him.

All of the meaningless nights he'd spent in experienced arms after Mary Alice's death came rushing back to taunt him. And maybe, he admitted grudgingly, it *had* helped at the time. But it wouldn't this time, he knew.

Though it would relieve the ache in his body, the pain in his soul would only go deeper.

She lifted her head to look at him, and he breathed deeply, willing his hunger for her into submission.

"All right, Kincaid," she said finally, almost reluctantly. "I'll go with you and Amanda."

"Good." He grinned and realized just how badly he'd wanted her to say yes. "I thought we could go early Saturday morning if that's all right with you. It will probably take a couple of hours to get there."

She nodded. "I'll pack us a lunch. We could have a picnic."

"I know Amanda would like that." I would, too, he silently added.

"It's settled, then." She smiled up at him, then suddenly squared her shoulders. "Now, I think I'll go over to the schoolhouse and straighten it up a bit. I noticed this morning it could use a good sweeping."

"Do you need any help?" As soon as the words left his mouth, he wanted to drag them back in. The *last* thing he needed was to be alone with her.

"No." She shook her head quickly. "No, thanks. It'll be good to be busy." She walked past him, snatched up the broom leaning against the side of the boardinghouse, and started off.

As he watched her go, his gaze fell unerringly to the smooth sway of her hips. A familiar tightening grabbed his body. Heart pounding, mouth dry, Kincaid walked to the chopping block, pulled the ax free, and set another chunk of wood on the block. He knew just what she meant. Being busy helped. A little.

By Friday morning Faith was more than ready for the weekend. Even when the children were all well behaved, they were a handful . . . and *no* child was well behaved for long.

She looked up from her desk and let her gaze wander over each of the familiar faces. Sissy and Billy Taylor, heads bent, were sharing a copy of *Mitchell's Primary Geography*. Ben and Sarah Lind were studying a worn copy of a *McGuffy's Reader*. Gary Lind sat quietly practicing his alphabet. Amanda was resting her head on her desktop, and Harry Taylor . . . Faith frowned and stood up.

Bent almost double in his desk, Harry was too busy with whatever he was doing to notice Faith approaching. When she was close enough, Faith peeked over the boy's shoulder and saw a scraggly bunch of wildflowers. Harry's dirty fingers smoothed through the blossoms tenderly, laying them all just so and arranging their wilting leaves.

"Harry . . ."

The boy jumped, startled, and straightened up abruptly. Turning a glare on Faith, he wrinkled his freckled nose and said accusingly, "You scared me."

Sighing, she shook her head. "What are you doing, Harry?"

"Nothin'."

"You're supposed to be practicing your penmanship."

"I already done that. See?" He pointed to his slate.

Faith glanced at it and saw that he had indeed filled the slate with wobbly letters.

"You should erase it and start again. School isn't over yet, Harry."

"Durn near."

"Harry"—Faith rolled her eyes—"what are you doing with the wildflowers, anyway?"

"They're a present." He smirked proudly.

"That's nice. For your mother?"

"Shoot, no!"

A titter of laughter from behind her made Faith turn quickly. Her own brother Ben grinned and told her, "Harry's in love, Faith. He's goin' courtin'."

"You hush up, Ben Lind," Harry warned him, "or you'll be talkin' around my fist!"

"Both of you stop it." Faith said evenly and glanced at her pendant watch. Still ten minutes of class time left, but surely it wouldn't hurt to let them all out a little early?

"He started it!" Harry yelled.

Ben leapt to his feet, ready to challenge Harry, but Faith pushed him back into his seat. Then, clapping her hands, she announced firmly, "All right, everyone. Close your books. When you've put your things away properly, you may leave."

"Yahoo!" Harry screeched. Lifting the lid of his desk, he tossed book, slate, and slate pencil inside, grabbed his flowers, and took off like a shot through the open front door.

Faith watched him go and envied him his energy. The boy never walked when he could run. As the other children filed past her, Faith stopped Ben curiously. She couldn't help it, she had to know.

"Who is Harry courting, Ben?"

Ben grinned and shook his head. "Miss Jane, over to the sewin' shop." Chuckling, he sauntered through the doorway. "I think I'll just go watch him for a while. See ya, Faith!"

When Faith turned back to the near empty schoolroom, only Sarah and Amanda were still there.

"My ma said to ask you if you and your pa wanted to come to Sunday supper next week, Amanda. You think you want to? We got us some new puppies and everything."

Faith watched Amanda's eager reaction with a smile. The little girl had come so far in such a short time. Boom was all but gone now, and she'd become good friends with Sarah. Briefly Faith wanted to pick up her little sister and hug her to pieces. Sarah's tender heart had somehow seen beyond Amanda's earlier nastiness to the loneliness inside, and she'd responded to it lovingly.

"Puppies?" Amanda breathed wonderingly. "You really have puppies at your house?" She looked around to Faith for confirmation.

A smile twitched at Faith's lips. Hannah, the Lind family dog, produced a litter of puppies every year, almost without fail. It was getting harder and harder to find a family in this part of the county who *didn't* have a Lind puppy.

"How many did Hannah have this time, Sarah?" Faith asked.

Sarah grinned. "Only four, but they're all cuter'n a button, Faith. Wait'll you see 'em." Turning back to Amanda, she added, "You can have one if you want."

Amanda gasped. Her mouth an open *O* of astonishment, her eyes shone with excitement. "A *puppy*? Of my *own*? Oh, my!" She looked at Faith. "Do you think Papa will say yes?"

Looking down at the little girl's shining face and glittering eyes, Faith said softly, "I think so." In fact, she couldn't imagine Kincaid denying his daughter anything that brought such an expression to her face.

"Sarah," she said softly, "why don't you tell Mama that Kincaid, Amanda, and I will all be out for supper next Sunday."

Amanda looked at her expectantly.

"And," Faith added helplessly, "don't let Papa or the boys give any of the puppies away until Amanda gets to pick hers."

"All right, Faith. I'll tell her." Sarah grinned and told Amanda, "I'll watch 'em real close this week so's I can tell you which one is best."

Amanda nodded happily and watched Sarah as she left. "Oh, my goodness," she breathed. "A puppy. A real, live puppy." Then, turning her gaze up to Faith's, she asked, "And can I name my puppy anything I want?"

Faith smiled gently. It was a sure bet, she told herself, that no puppy on earth would be more loved than Amanda's. Staring down into the little girl's bright eyes, Faith smoothed her dark hair back from her forehead and stopped. Frowning, she trailed her open palm down the side of Amanda's face and cupped her cheek.

It wasn't just excitement glittering in the child's eyes. She had a fever.

CHAPTER

THIRTEEN

SHE LOOKED SO small.

Kincaid pulled in a deep, shuddering breath and laid the cool cloth on his daughter's forehead again. Her fine black hair spread out on the white pillow casing, her little face was pale except for the two bright red patches of color in her cheeks.

Slowly he ran the damp cloth down over her cheeks and to the hollow of her throat. Sleeping, Amanda lay perfectly still for his ministrations, and Kincaid found himself wishing she was wide awake and throwing a tantrum.

Memories of Mary Alice crowded his brain, and he couldn't help wondering if Amanda had survived that outbreak of diphtheria only to die later of some unknown fever. Immediately after that sobering thought entered his mind, he cursed himself silently for even entertaining such a notion. He sat back in his chair at Amanda's bedside and told himself that sitting alone in your child's sickroom gave rise to all manner of wild imaginings.

The door behind him opened quietly, and he turned to see Faith enter the small bedroom.

"How is she?"

He glanced back at his daughter. "I don't know. The same, I guess. She's sleeping." He turned quickly. "Is that good?"

"I'm sure it's fine, Kincaid."

She looked so composed. So sure of herself. He latched on to her statement and held it to him desperately. "I don't understand this, Faith. She was fine earlier. What is it? What's happened to her?"

"Kincaid . . ." Faith's voice was gentle as she stepped up behind him and lay one hand on his shoulder. "It's only a fever. It doesn't mean anything. Children sometimes get fevers for no apparent reason."

"No." He shook his head. "There's a reason. She's sick. Just like—" He broke off and changed the subject. "Why the hell don't we have a doctor here, anyway? What kind of town is this?"

"A very small town, Kincaid." Faith turned to Amanda and bent over her, straightening the bedclothes and smoothing back the black hair lying over one closed eye. "You have to calm down. Jane was here earlier, and she said—"

"Jane Carson's not a doctor."

"No, but she has uncommon good sense, and she's the closest we have to a doctor."

He grumbled something, but Faith ignored it.

"Jane agreed with Maisie, Minnie, and me that this is nothing to worry about. She probably just had too much sun is all."

"No." He ground his teeth together and shook his head. "It's more. It's a judgment."

"A judgment?" Faith asked. "From who?"

"God."

"What?"

"You heard me. It's a punishment on me for failing Mary Alice and for . . ." He stopped and looked at her briefly before letting his gaze slip back to his daughter.

"Kissing me?" she finished for him.

He didn't say a word.

"Kincaid, you're being ridiculous."

"This isn't ridiculous. Amanda's sick, isn't she?"

"You have to stop this."

He stood up abruptly and walked around the bed to the window facing Main Street. Soundlessly Faith walked up behind him and hesitantly reached for him. Instinctively he turned to her and pulled her into his embrace. Clutching her to him tightly, he buried his face in her hair and muttered thickly, "I don't know what I mean anymore, Faith. Hell, I hardly know what I'm doing half the time. It's just— seeing Amanda like this . . . so still . . . so quiet. It— terrifies me."

"I know," she murmured gently, her hands moving up and down his back with a calm, steady rhythm. "But she'll be all right, Kincaid. I promise you. By morning she'll probably be feeling like her old self again."

"Do you really believe that?"

She pulled back a bit and looked him squarely in the eye. "Yes, I do." Smiling, she added, "You forget. I'm the oldest of seven children. Childhood fevers are nothing new to me."

Slowly an uncertain smile twitched at his lips.

Deliberately then, Faith reached up and cupped his cheeks with her hands. "This is *nothing* like diphtheria." He tried to look away, but she held him fast, her eyes demanding his attention. "And Amanda is *not* Mary Alice. She's going to be fine. I promise."

After a long breathless moment Kincaid nodded, then pulled her close again. Resting his chin on top of her head, he watched his little girl with hopeful eyes. Savoring the feel of Faith's arms around him, he gave silent thanks that he wasn't alone anymore.

*   *   *

"You're sure about this, Maisie?"

"Hell, yes, I'm sure!" The older woman wrapped a skein of yarn around Amanda's upheld hands. Deftly Maisie began winding the lemon yellow wool into a ball. "You can see for yourself that Amanda's just as pert as ever! Aren't you, child?"

"I feel good, Papa. Honest."

Kincaid stared down at her face, holding her chin between his fingers. Carefully he checked her eyes, then ran one hand up to her forehead and paused there.

"Did Faith tell you about the puppies, Papa?" Amanda said brightly. "Sarah says I can have one all for my own self. And I get to pick him out myself, too."

"Puppies?" Maisie raised one gray eyebrow and looked at the girl. "You want to bring some flea-bitten little slipper chewer into my house?"

Amanda bit her lip and nodded.

"Uh, Amanda," Kincaid said, a wary eye on Maisie, "Maybe it'd be better if we waited until—"

"Well," Maisie interrupted, "I suppose we *could* use a good watchdog around here."

Amanda grinned and looked at her father.

Watching his daughter, Kincaid knew in that moment that he'd give her whatever she wanted if she just promised to never get sick again. "If you're very good for Maisie and Minnie today while Faith and I are gone, you can have a pup."

Amanda inhaled sharply. "Oh, *thank you*, Papa. I'll be good. Really. I can help Maisie, and then I'll help Minnie and be really quiet and not bother anybody at all, honest I won't."

"Heaven's sake, child!" Maisie admonished, a grin twitching at the corners of her mouth. "Hush now or you'll get my wool all in a snarl." Tossing a glance at her nephew, she added, "And don't you worry about a thing. Amanda isn't stirring one foot outa this bed until church tomorrow."

Amanda frowned, but kept quiet, eager to start being good.

"All right," Kincaid said finally. "If I could get a hold of that fella I'm supposed to meet today, I'd change the time until next week. But—"

"Oh, just git," Maisie told him. "If you're gonna start givin' my place some healthy competition with that hotel of yours, you'd best get busy buildin' it."

He grinned, bent to kiss Amanda, and walked around the bed. After planting a quick kiss on Maisie's lined cheek, he hurried out the door before the older woman's well-aimed swat could connect.

"And, Kincaid," Maisie hollered out, "you and Faith mind the sky! There's a storm comin' sure as you're born!"

As if to prove Maisie wrong, the sky was a deeper blue than usual with only a few scattered white clouds marring its perfect surface. Faith tipped her head back and stared at the wide expanse of it all. A smile touching her lips, she realized that she was very glad she'd agreed to accompany Kincaid.

It felt good to be riding in the buggy beside him, the sleek chestnut horse in the traces trotting easily along the rutted road. Straightening, she glanced out of the corner of her eye at Kincaid's hands. His long fingers held the reins loosely, easily. As his thumbs moved over the leather strips, her breath caught, remembering the night that same gentle touch had moved over her breasts.

A curl of warmth spread through her stomach and lower, until sitting on the thinly padded bench seat

was uncomfortable. She shifted uneasily and vowed
to keep her mind away from such remembrances.

"Almost there now," Kincaid said.

She looked over at him.

"I really appreciate your coming along with me,
Faith."

"I'm enjoying myself," she answered.

"Good." He nodded and breathed deeply, keeping
his eyes fixed on the road ahead, then added, "And
I appreciate what you did last night, too."

"I didn't do anything."

"Yes, you did." He tossed her a quick glance. "You
stayed with me. Kept me from losing my mind."
Smiling, he continued, "You helped a lot. Just knowing that you cared about Amanda as much as I did
helped."

"I'm glad."

Several long, quiet minutes passed, the only sound
that of the horse's hooves on the dirt.

"You know, if there's enough furnishings in this
old hotel, I could really get started quick."

"What about the lumber?"

"That's already ordered. It's coming in on Monday's train. With any luck, in a month or so the hotel
will be open for business."

And you'll be moving out of the boardinghouse,
Faith added silently. A tight, lonely feeling swept her,
and she fought to push it aside. It wasn't as if he
were leaving town, she reminded herself.

But, her brain prodded, he won't be just across the
hall from you anymore, either. No more bumping
into him in the halls. No more sitting at the same
dinner and breakfast table. No more listening for the
sounds of his bootsteps on the stairs.

"Faith? Did you hear me?"

"Hmm?"

He grinned excitedly and pointed. "There it is!"

Faith looked into the distance and saw the old hotel. Briefly she wondered how the place had lasted as long as it had. Off the main road to Ellsworth, there couldn't have been many passersby. Why would anyone have built such a place in the middle of nowhere?

As they came closer, she studied the three-story wood building. Shutters hung askew at the windows, raggedy curtains, pulled by the wind through broken panes of glass, fluttered in the suddenly cool wind, and even the small barn off to one side of the place looked desolate. Forgotten.

Faith shivered slightly, not sure if it was because of the breeze or if it was a reaction to the loneliness of the structure looming closer.

Kincaid pulled at the reins, bringing the horse to a stop.

"What are you doing?" she asked, her arms crossed in front of her.

"You're cold." He shrugged out of his black coat and draped it over her shoulders. The back of his hand brushed against her breast, and Faith swallowed heavily.

"Look there," Kincaid ordered and stared at the far horizon.

Faith followed his gaze and noticed for the first time a bank of sullen gray and black clouds huddled together as if gathering strength before an attack.

"Guess Maisie was right about the storm." Picking up the reins again, he snapped them against the horse's back, urging the animal into a faster trot. As they clattered across the old bridge that spanned the Smoky Hill River, Faith heard him say, "We'd better hurry up. Don't want to get caught out here in a storm."

*   *   *

The inside of the hotel was no more welcoming than the outside. Cobwebs hung from every corner, sometimes stretching from one side of the room to another. Old brass wall sconces, badly tarnished and most of their chimneys missing, lined the long hallway that led down the center of the building. Kincaid and Faith moved slowly from room to room, their footsteps echoing in the silence.

In the kitchen they found a monstrosity of a stove and a treasure trove of pots, pans, and dishes. As Kincaid went into the parlor, Faith climbed the stairs, one hand gripping the wobbly banister tightly.

Ahead of her she heard a soft scuttling sound and knew that prairie mice had made a home of the old place. She frowned but kept on. Belowstairs, she heard the unmistakable sound of glass breaking and called down, "Are you all right?"

"Yeah!" Kincaid's excited voice yelled back. "I broke a glass. But, Faith, wait'll you see what I found! A *wine* cellar! At least fifty bottles of good wine down here, and that's not even counting the brandy and whiskey!"

She rolled her eyes and muttered to herself that he'd be better served inspecting the place for furniture than planning a well-stocked bar. Shaking her head, Faith opened the first door she saw.

A bedroom. A massive four-poster bed stood in the middle of the room with a chest, a table, and a torn-up chair in the far corner. If all the rooms were like this, she told herself with a sudden burst of excitement, Kincaid would be able to furnish his whole hotel from this place. All he'd need to do was arrange for new mattresses for the beds and—she wrinkled her nose delicately—have everything else cleaned.

A far-off rumble of noise whispered through the empty room, and Faith cocked her head, listening. She waited another moment or two, and when it came again, she recognized it. Thunder.

Stepping into the hallway, she leaned over the banister and called out, "Did you hear that?"

He walked out of the parlor and looked up. "Yeah. Thunder?"

"I think so."

Nodding, Kincaid made for the stairs and took them two at a time. As he passed her, he said quickly, "You finish checking these rooms, and I'll look around upstairs real fast. Then we'd better get moving. If we hurry, we may be able to beat the storm back to Harmony."

Nodding, she hurried off, going into first one room, then another. Even as she mentally made notes of the things she found, a part of her brain registered every clap of thunder and realized it was getting closer. Fast.

At the end of the hall Faith stopped at an oval-shaped window. Rubbing at the encrusted dirt with her sleeve, she peered out at the prairie and the darkening sky above. The storm clouds seemed to be racing across the heavens. Dark and heavy with rain, they bumped and jostled each other for position as they crowded closer and closer.

Kincaid came downstairs and stopped directly behind her. He cursed quietly at first sight of the nearing storm. Laying one hand on her shoulder, he said firmly, "Let's go, Faith. If we hurry, we may still make it."

From the tone of his voice, Faith knew that even *he* didn't believe it. No sooner had they turned for the staircase than the heavens burst apart with a splintering crash, and wave after wave of rain hit the old building.

Running down the stairs, dragging Faith behind him, Kincaid made for the front door and yanked it open. From just behind his shoulder, Faith peered outside. Her jaw dropped. She'd never seen it rain like that. It was as if God had upended a bucket. She could hardly see their horse and buggy, just beyond the porch.

Thunder rattled the windows, and Faith thought she saw the shadow of their horse, rearing up in fear.

"I'll put him up in the barn!" Kincaid shouted to be heard over the deluge.

Faith nodded, but he didn't see her as he plunged into the torrent of water. A sudden gust of wind swept the rain directly at her, and she hurriedly closed the door. She leaned back against it for a moment, her brain racing.

There would be no going back to Harmony. At least not for a while. The two of them were well and truly *stuck* in the lonely old hotel. Her gaze flicked quickly over the inside of the forgotten building. A twilight dusk, created by the storm, seemed to disguise the signs of neglect. Cobwebs disappeared in the shadows, and layers of grime faded until they became one with the old, dark wood.

A half smile touched her lips as she realized that their long days of forced, cool courtesy and finding varied ways of avoiding being alone together had come to a crashing halt. For whatever reason, and by Whomever's intervention, she and Kincaid were alone. For who knew how long.

Tiny spirals of excitement spread through her body, quickly squelching any feelings of nervousness. Filled with sudden determination, Faith took a deep breath, shook her still-wet hands, and pushed strands of damp hair out of her eyes. With hurried steps, she walked to the parlor.

Going directly to the fireplace, she crouched down, looked up the chimney to check for obstructions, then grabbed for the nearby wood. Thankfully, someone had left a pile of firewood stacked beside the fireplace. Either the last owner or, more than likely, some passing stranger who'd used the place for shelter and left it ready for the next poor soul who wandered in. But whoever it was, Faith thanked them silently as she lay down kindling.

Looking around, she spotted a brass box on the mantel and hopefully opened it. She grinned her relief at the matches inside. Crouching down again, she held the tiny flame to the dry kindling and smiled as the flames grew and fed on the wood.

For a brief moment she held her hands, palms out, toward the fire, drinking in the luxurious warmth against her chilled skin. Then she pushed herself to her feet and turned around to look the room over carefully. As long as they would be staying right where they were for a while, she told herself, she might as well do everything she could to make them as comfortable as possible while they waited out the storm.

Kincaid was drenched. Head to toe, he looked as though he'd stumbled into the river. Standing just inside the barn, he glanced back at the horse he'd tied in a nearby stall. At least *he* was happy. With plenty of straw and a roof overhead, the horse would be content to stay put forever.

Kincaid looked down sadly at the picnic basket in his hands. The fresh dishtowel Faith had covered their lunch with so carefully was soaking wet, hiding equally wet food. The only things edible in the whole damn basket were the apples and a tin of peaches Maisie had tossed in at the last minute.

Shaking his head, he looked back out toward the house. He'd been hoping to stand in the barn until the rain eased up a bit, but it didn't look as if that was going to happen any time soon.

Hell, he told himself silently. The rain wasn't what was keeping him in the barn. It was just *safer* out here. Inside that house, Faith waited.

No doubt, he thought, she was scared, hungry, and cold. She'd be looking to him for help. For comfort. It would be just the two of them. Alone in that house. Maybe for hours. They couldn't very well try to travel in a storm like this. They'd have to wait it out.

And he had to wonder if his own "noble" resolves could stand up to such torture.

But thoughts of Faith sitting alone in the sudden darkness, shivering with cold and fear, prodded him into action. He ducked his head and raced across the yard to the front porch. He would just have to remember that she would be vulnerable right now. He would have to be strong. For both of them.

Once on the wide porch Kincaid tried to shake off the excess water but realized it was hopeless. Besides, his wet clothes weren't all that important right now. Comforting Faith was.

Deliberately he squared his shoulders, marched across the porch, opened the heavy front door, and stepped inside. Closing the door behind him, Kincaid stopped dead and sniffed the air.

Wood smoke. Confused, he walked to the parlor doorway and looked inside.

Faith had been busy. A blazing fire in the hearth

cast dancing shadows on the nearby walls. She had a cooking pot on the cast-iron arm over the flames and a blanket spread out on the floor in front of the fire.

"Kincaid?" she called from far off.

Shaking his head, he turned toward the sound of her voice. "Where are you?"

"In the kitchen," she called back. "I found a tin of tea, and now I'm looking for more. You just never know what folks might leave behind!"

He snorted and turned back to look at the fire. The crackle and hiss of dried wood filled the still air, and he felt himself drawn to the warmth of the little haven she'd created.

Faith would be scared? he asked himself. Cold? Hungry? He peeked into the cooking pot to find water on the boil for tea.

A slow smile spread across his face. Setting the sodden picnic basket down by the hearth, he bent over in front of the flames, warming his backside and watching the door for Faith's return.

Her quick, light step heralded her approach, and she tossed him a brief smile when she saw him. Then she effectively stopped anything he might have said when she told him, "You'd better get out of those wet clothes, Kincaid. You'll catch your death!"

His eyebrows rose questioningly, and he cocked his head at her as she crossed the wide room.

Seeing his expression, Faith grinned and stepped up beside him, reaching for the swing arm over the fire. With her skirt-wrapped hand, she pulled the iron hook out and sprinkled some aged-looking tea leaves into the boiling water to steep. Then she looked at him over her shoulder.

"Don't look so scared, Kincaid," she said with a

smirk. "I'm not going to seduce you. I'm just trying to keep you from getting pneumonia."

Their eyes met and held. He looked deeply into the soft hazel depths and read only amusement and a hint of excitement. Clearly, she was enjoying their adventure.

"You amaze me," he finally whispered.

"Why?"

"Well"—he spread his arms out, including the fire, the blanket, and the pot of tea in the gesture—"all of this, for one thing. I expected to find you huddled in the dark, shaking with cold, waiting for me to rescue you."

She stood up straight and looked him in the eye. Her soft smile slowly faded as she asked quietly, "Is that what Mary Alice would have done?"

Kincaid stared at her. He hadn't thought about it before, but now that she brought it up, he supposed that that was *exactly* why he'd expected such a reaction. It was just what Mary Alice would have done. Nodding, he admitted, "Yeah. She would have. And she would have had a few things to say to me about getting her into such a situation in the first place, too."

"You're hardly responsible for the rain, Kincaid."

"I could have paid more attention to the coming storm."

"So could I." She shrugged. "And as for the rest . . . as I've told you before, Kincaid. I'm *not* Mary Alice."

He looked down at her, noting the defiant tilt of her chin and the confident set of her shoulders. "No, Faith. I guess you're not, at that."

"Good." She grinned again and pointed toward a pile of dusty-looking blankets. "Now, take off your clothes, grab one of those quilts, shake it out good, and wrap it around you, while I dish up the tea."

She turned her back to him as she sniffed at the steeping brew. Kincaid smiled and murmured, "Yes, ma'am."

CHAPTER

FOURTEEN

Rain pounded at the windows with an insistent fury, as though it were a living creature demanding to be let inside.

Faith sat by the fire, determinedly keeping her gaze locked on the dancing flames. Though the sound of the falling rain was deafening, Faith imagined she could actually hear Kincaid's sodden clothing as he dropped it, piece by piece, to the dusty floor.

Just knowing that he was somewhere in the shadows, wrapping a blanket around his naked flesh, brought a shiver to her body that had nothing to do with the cold.

"Looks like you could use some of that tea, too," he said softly as he stepped up beside her.

"What?" Her voice was strained, her throat tight. Her eager, adventurous thoughts of only a few moments ago slipped away suddenly, leaving her just a bit uneasy.

"I saw you shivering, Faith." He leaned on the mantel and looked down at her. "You don't have to pretend that you're not cold, you know."

"I know." She had to look at him, or he would soon guess that she was more nervous than she'd claimed to be. Dragging her gaze away from the flames, she turned to him.

He had a faded yellow and red Wedding Ring quilt wrapped around his waist and legs. His chest was bare, and a few droplets of water clung to the dark, curly hairs sprinkled across his bronzed flesh. Every breath he took seemed to make the edges of the quilt dip dangerously. She swallowed heavily and forced herself to meet his gaze.

"The tea's ready, I think," she muttered thickly.

"Good." He squatted down beside her and reached for one of the cracked cups she'd set on the hearth. Turning it in one hand, he smiled crookedly. "The pots and pans and even that monster of a stove will work well in the new hotel. But I think we'd better invest in some new crockery."

"Uh-huh." She dared not look directly into his eyes again, she thought wildly. The firelight reflected in the green depths dazzled like fireworks and made thinking rationally difficult. Grabbing the steaming pot of tea with the edges of her skirt, Faith poured them each a full cup, then set the pan back near the fire to keep hot.

Kincaid lifted the cup to his mouth, took a sip, and grimaced. "Lord! Are you sure that's tea?"

"Of course I'm sure," she countered and took a sip herself. As soon as the bitter brew hit her tongue, Faith gasped and shook her head.

Laughing, he set his cup down and challenged, "Not so sure now, are you?"

Faith wiped her fingers across her mouth as if she could rub away the taste. Still frowning, she said, "Oh, I'm sure it's tea. I'm just not sure what century it's from." Sighing with disgust, she said, "I guess we'll have to settle for hot water." Then she added with a more hopeful note, "At least we have some apples and that tin of peaches for dessert."

He nodded and pushed himself to his feet. "And I

have something more tasty than hot water in mind to warm us up."

With long strides, quilt flapping about his legs, he left the room and walked down the hall. Faith heard him rummaging around in another room, and in only minutes he was back, holding two bottles in one hand and two dusty glasses in the other.

Seating himself opposite her on the pale green quilt, he set the bottles down and blew at the dust in the glasses. Then, using one edge of his covering, he wiped them clean and offered one to Faith.

Firelight played across his features, and the smile he gave her had less heaven than hell in it.

"What have you got?" she asked warily, empty glass in her lap.

"Well . . ." He lifted a bottle in each hand and studied the dirty labels. "Most of the writing is French, so I can't be sure. But I think this one"—he held out his right hand—"is Napolean brandy, and the other one is champagne." Cocking his head and wiggling his eyebrows at her, he asked, "Which will it be?"

"Oh, I don't—"

"I know, you don't drink. But this is for medicinal purposes. You have to keep warm."

"I didn't get wet," she reminded him.

"I saw you shiver," he shot back.

Well, she couldn't very well tell him she was shivering because he looked so good in a quilt, could she? Trapped, she held out her glass. "I'll trust you to choose."

"All right," he said with a brief nod. "I think we'll start with . . . a little brandy." After setting the other bottle down, he opened the brandy bottle and poured each of them a splash of the amber liquid.

Faith took hers hesitantly and sniffed at it. Wrinkling her nose, she shook her head. "I don't think I'll like this, Kincaid. Even the *smell* is too strong."

"Hmmm . . ." He thought for a moment, then grabbed the tin of peaches. "Perhaps straight brandy *might* be too potent for your very first drink. But," he continued as he opened the tin, "a brandy-soaked peach should be just the thing."

He reached across and dropped a slice of peach into her drink. "Don't be shy, Faith. Use your fingers. I won't tell Maisie."

Surprised by his suddenly light and easy bantering, Faith kept one eye on him as she dipped her fingers into her glass and pulled the peach out of the brandy. Tentatively she touched her tongue to the peach. Droplets of mingled juice and brandy began to roll down her hand, so she quickly sucked the sliver of fruit into her mouth. Chuckling softly, she caught Kincaid's eye as one by one, she licked the brandied peach juice from her fingers.

He cleared his throat and tugged his quilt more firmly about him.

As the liquor and fruit juice ran down her throat, filling her with a sweet warmth, Faith slowly chewed the slice of peach and swallowed it. She couldn't remember ever tasting anything so wonderful. Sweet and strong, it sent liquid fire to every part of her body.

Daringly she lifted her glass to her lips and tipped the amber liquid down her throat. She shuddered delicately at the immediate heat coursing through her veins, but then held her empty glass out to him.

His eyebrows shot up. "Good?"

"Delicious. And so warm." She shifted position on the blanket, making herself more comfortable. When Kincaid dropped another peach into her freshly poured brandy, she swirled the fruit around in the liquid for a bit before lifting the glass to her lips. With one challenging look at Kincaid, Faith tipped the glass, letting the brandy slide down her throat while enjoying the peach a moment longer. She shifted position again, this time stretching her legs out in front of her. Leaning back on her elbows, she cocked her head at him and said softly, "It tastes *wonderful*, Kincaid."

Kincaid studied her for the space of a single heartbeat. Her tongue darted out and licked a drop of peach juice from her bottom lip. She sighed, tilted her head back, and stared up at the ceiling. When she pulled in a deep breath, straining the buttons lining the front of her shirt, Kincaid groaned quietly.

Then he poured another inch or so of brandy into his own glass and drained it. The instant fire in his blood made the gleam in her eye even harder to ignore. There was a flush in her cheeks, and her breathing was faster, more ragged.

"It's a little warm in here, isn't it?" Faith said more to herself than to him, and undid the top button of her plain white shirt.

"Maybe you should move back from the fire, Faith."

"Oh, no, I'll be fine." She nodded sharply. "Besides, I love to sit beside a fire. I've always thought it was so . . . romantic. Don't you?"

An ice cave would be romantic, he told himself, if *she* were in it.

"Kincaid," she asked slowly, "what does champagne taste like? Is it as good as Brandy?"

"Yes, it's good, Faith. But," he said and reached for the basket, "I think you should maybe eat an apple before you try it. Get something on your stomach."

"But I'm not the least bit hungry, Kincaid." She lowered her head and stared up at him through her lashes. A small smile teased her lips. "Besides, I'm eating peaches. Please?"

He cursed silently. But then he told himself maybe it would be better to just give it to her. What with not eating and all, maybe she'd pass out, and he wouldn't be so damned tempted by her.

With that thought in mind, he opened the champagne bottle and smiled when she jumped and squealed as the cork shot out of the bottle.

A shower of foam erupted from the dusty bottle, and Kincaid caught what he could of it in the glasses. Even so, Faith's skirt and much of their quilt was soaked with wine.

"What makes it bubble up like that?" She laughed and brushed ineffectually at her stained gray skirt.

"Have no idea," he answered and quickly tossed his glass of wine down his throat.

She shook her head slowly and held her glass up to the firelight. "Look at all those bubbles," she mumbled and took a sip. Wrinkling her nose slightly, she turned to Kincaid. "Could I have another of those peaches, do you think?"

As Faith sat silhouetted against the fire, soft yellow lights from the flames shot through her hair like golden arrows. Kincaid could only nod. He didn't trust himself to speak. After he dropped the peach slice into her wine, he watched as she sipped at the liquid and nibbled delicately at the piece of fruit.

Suddenly she chuckled. "You know, I never really liked peaches much before this."

He set the champagne bottle down and poured himself another shot of brandy. To get through this time together without taking advantage of her was going to require some *serious* drinking. Hell, he told himself, maybe *he's* the one who should pass out!

"It really is *hot*!" she said with a frown and slipped

another button free. Then she rolled her sleeves up past her elbows. Shooting him a quick glance, she asked, "Aren't *you* hot?"

Hot didn't begin to cover what he was feeling, he told himself. Instead of saying so, though, he muttered, "No."

"S'funny," Faith replied, waving her hand in front of her face. "You should be hot, too. Maybe another peach would help." Holding out her empty glass, she looked at him.

"I think you've had enough, Faith."

She frowned slightly, set her glass down on the quilt, and scooted closer to him. Leaning toward him, she whispered in a low, clear voice, "I know you think I'm drunk, Kincaid, but . . ." She poked his bare chest with her index finger, then grazed her touch across his flesh gently. "I'm not really, y'know. I'm just . . . warm."

"Uh-huh," he muttered, holding his breath.

"Kincaid." She leaned even closer, and he felt her breath on his cheek. The flat of her hand caressed his chest, and he had to concentrate just to listen to her voice. "It's just the two of us here now. . . ."

"Yes?"

"And it's raining—that man you're supposed to meet won't be coming in this storm. . . ."

"Probably not." He sucked in a gulp of air when her fingernail scraped over his flat nipple.

"The fire is so nice, don't you think?"

"Yeah. Nice." The curve of her breast brushed against his arm, and he jumped.

"And we can't go anywhere at all, can we?"

"Not, uh . . . not for a while, no," he answered with a groan as her lips touched his shoulder.

"Kincaid?"

"*What*, Faith?" Jesus, he screamed silently, make her move away!

"Remember when I said I wasn't trying to seduce you?"

"Yeah."

She looked up into his eyes. Her fingers trailed up his chest, over his shoulders to thread through his thick, dark hair. He swallowed heavily and stared down at her. Her eyes glazed with passion, he felt his own surrender to the inevitable begin with her words.

"Well, I'm trying *now*."

"Faith."

"Don't say no yet," she whispered quickly and laid her fingers across his lips. "We're alone. No one would know but us."

He shook his head slowly, fighting for the last shreds of control.

"Kincaid," she murmured and kissed his throat briefly. "Today you gave me my first taste of champagne. Not too long ago you gave me a taste of what can happen between a man and a woman." Moving slightly, she raised herself up and slanted a soft kiss across his lips. Cupping his cheek tenderly, she added, "I want you to be the first to show me the rest. If nothing else ever happens between us, Kincaid, I want to always know that *you* were the first man I lay with."

Her soft hazel eyes locked on his, Kincaid knew he was losing himself in their gentle depths. The few remaining threads of his control snapped. This is crazy! his brain screamed. You can't do this. She's had too much liquor and not enough food. And yet, he thought as he looked at her, there was no hint in her eyes that it was merely the drink talking. She knew exactly what she was saying.

Her beauty, her courage, her touch came together in his mind and body, and he knew he couldn't turn away.

The thought of any other man holding her, touching her, was enough to choke him. Merely being the first would never be enough for him, he knew. But for now, this moment was all that mattered.

"Dear God," he muttered thickly and reached for her. She went into his arms eagerly, molding herself against him, running her hands up and down his back. Kincaid's mouth closed over hers hungrily, and in an instant her lips parted for him. His tongue dipped into her sweetness, and when she returned his caresses, he groaned and clutched her even tighter.

Holding her across his lap, Kincaid tore his lips from hers and lifting her slightly, let his mouth trail down her throat. Gratefully he inhaled the soft fragrance of her, and felt her pulse pounding furiously beneath his lips.

His fingers slipped to the remaining buttons on her shirtfront. Deftly he pushed the tiny pearl studs through their tinier holes until she lay beneath his hungry stare, covered only by the whisper-soft fabric of her chemise. Carefully he tugged at the ribbon closure, his eyes never leaving hers.

She reached up to run her fingers down his jaw, and her movement brought her bottom down hard against his swollen body. He groaned softly and slipped his hand beneath her chemise to cup her breast.

Faith gasped and closed her eyes. His long fingers teased at her nipple until it stood hard and erect, demanding his kiss. She opened her eyes again to watch him lower his head and take her nipple into his mouth.

No matter what happens, she told herself in a haze of passion, this time with him would be worth it. It had taken every ounce of nerve she had to ask him to make love to her. But with his first touch, her last niggling doubts and anxieties vanished. She sighed and gave herself over to the sensations coursing through her.

Slowly, carefully, his tongue traced damp circles around the hardened pink bud of her breast until she thought she would lose her mind. Her fingernails dug into his bare back, and she arched higher still, trying to tell him, without words, to take more of her. When the edges of his teeth scraped across the sensitive tip of her nipple, she bit down hard on her bottom lip and tried to swallow a groan of pleasure that shook her entire body. Then his lips closed around her, and he began to suckle at her flesh as if greedy for the taste of her.

"Kincaid," she whispered on a sigh and held his head to her breast firmly. Breathless, she looked at his mouth on her and felt another quake of desire rocket through her.

A spiral of delight arched through her body, centering itself between her thighs. Her hips moved in anticipation, and beneath her she felt the hardness of him pressing against her.

"Ah, Faith," he murmured gently as he pulled away slightly.

"Don't stop, Kincaid. Please don't stop." She reached for him, but he caught her hands in his. Placing a kiss on each palm, he shook his head.

"I won't stop, Faith." He lifted her easily and laid her down in the center of the old green quilt. "I only want to be able to see you. All of you."

Gingerly he pushed her shirt down over her arms. Her gaze locked with his, she vaguely heard the rain still pounding against the windows and saw the fire-light reflected in Kincaid's passion-filled eyes.

A thrill of excitement shot through her, and she slowly, teasingly, lowered the straps of her chemise. Her breath came faster, and she couldn't seem to swallow.

The cool air of the empty room touched her breasts, but Kincaid's gaze warmed her through. Tenderly he laid her back on the quilt and, with a few quick motions, had her skirt and pantaloons off and tossed aside. She lay naked on the cool fabric and never considered trying to cover herself.

Rising to his knees beside her, he tugged at the blanket still wrapped around his middle and let it fall to the floor.

Cautiously Faith lowered her gaze and felt a small tremor of nervousness wash over her. He seemed to understand her hesitation, though, and stretched out beside her on the quilt. Though she felt his hard body pressing against her hip, all anxiety fled as his hands began to move over her flesh.

Licking her lips, Faith closed her eyes and let everything but his touch fade from her mind. Everywhere his fingers moved, she felt new warmth rush over her. Aching to recapture the incredible explosion of feeling he'd shown her once before, she arched her hips slightly, hoping he would understand her need and answer it.

Instead, he levered himself up on one elbow and looked down into her face. "Faith," he whispered, and she smiled as his breath fell across her cheek.

Tentatively she opened her eyes and met his gaze. His fingers trailed down low over her abdomen, and she arched again, helplessly.

"Faith, tell me what you want," he said softly and kissed one corner of her mouth.

"You know," she whispered back and moaned as his fingertips grazed across the triangle of curly golden hair.

He traced his tongue over her lips, then bent and left a quick kiss at each of her breasts. His left hand smoothed over her thigh, her belly, and down her other thigh.

Faith frowned and closed her eyes. He touched every part of her except the center of her need. "Kincaid," she murmured and lifted her hips again. She stopped moving, though, when his hand slipped down to cup her warmth.

"Open your eyes, Faith," he coaxed.

When she did, he urged her again, "Tell me what you want, Faith. Tell me."

Staring up into his dark green eyes, Faith finally whispered, "Touch me, Kincaid. I want to feel you inside me again."

Even before she finished speaking, Kincaid's fingers dipped into the warm heart of her. Faith groaned and lifted her hips to welcome him deeper inside. His thumb rubbed gently over the hardened bud of her sex, and he lowered his head to caress her nipples once more.

Faith's head tilted back against the hard wooden floor, and she stared up at the dark ceiling. So many sensations coursed through her at once, she could hardly breathe. So much heat, she thought wildly, and gasped as his fingers slid to her bottom.

He raised up and moved to kneel between her thighs. Through slitted eyes, Faith watched him. His right hand caressed the damp warmth of her while his left stroked and teased her from behind. She twisted in his hands, unsure, yet hungry for more.

"Kincaid," she cried softly and reached her arms out to him. She wanted to feel his flesh against her own. To know how it felt to have his hard weight pressing down on her.

Slowly he shook his head and smiled softly, "Not yet, Faith. Not yet."

Astonished, Faith watched him as he easily lifted her hips off the floor. Her legs hung helplessly in the air, her thighs wide apart. His gaze on hers, Kincaid lowered his head to her body and, incredibly, *kissed* the juncture of her thighs. "Kincaid!" She jerked back, but he held her still, his hands clasped tightly on her legs.

"Trust me, Faith," he whispered.

She gasped and clenched her fists around the quilt. Never, never had she expected to feel anything like this. Any embarrassment quickly died under the new onslaught of sensations.

Instinctively she arched her back, moving against him as the first, trembling signs of delight began to snake through her body.

Only once before had she known this quiet building of tension. That night beside the river when his fingers first taught her what a *feeling* really was. But even *that* could not have prepared her for this. Tremors shook her body even as she strained and waited for more.

As the terrible need increased, Faith reached for him blindly. Opening her eyes, she watched him as he loved her, and the sight pushed her nearer the edge of completion.

She clutched at his hair as the first shudders racked her body. And while she trembled, he laid her down gently and plunged into her body. One sharp, short burst of surprise more than pain, and then he moved inside her, filling her until she wasn't sure where she ended and he began.

The hard, muscled expanse of his chest covered

hers, and she ran her hands along his back, trailing her nails over his rib cage.

And all at once, spasms of pleasure shot through her body, and she called his name, clinging to his shoulders desperately. Kincaid moved against her one last time, entering her deeper than before, and she felt his body's release even as he groaned her name.

CHAPTER

✳

FIFTEEN

KINCAID ROLLED to one side and drew her up close. He wasn't surprised to see that even his hands were trembling.

Faith cuddled up next to him, and as his arms enfolded her, he stared up at the fire-cast shadows on the ceiling. His heart pounding in his chest, he admitted silently that he'd never before experienced anything like what had just happened.

He'd been a married man. And after Mary Alice's death, Lord knew he'd tried to drown himself in a sea of willing women. But Faith Lind touched something in him he hadn't known existed.

This wasn't merely a physical release. It was more of a joining. Somehow, he felt sure that he and Faith had come together in a far more important way than simply a merging of bodies.

Closing his eyes, he sighed and let his hand trail down the smooth skin of her back and over the curve of her hip.

In the dark hush of the stormy afternoon, he could almost fool himself into believing that what they'd shared could continue. As that thought entered his brain, his eyes flew open and he stared blankly at the ceiling. Dammit, even *he* was getting swept away by the force of their attraction.

But Lord knew, he should know better than most

that a marriage was more than just sharing a bed! There was the day-to-day struggle to be faced. It was working through good times and bad, clinging to each other, helping each other. And he simply didn't dare to risk it again.

It didn't even matter if Faith was right when she'd said he hadn't failed Mary Alice. In his heart he felt he had. Casting a quick downward glance at the woman in his arms, he knew he couldn't take the chance of letting her down, too.

Sighing quietly, he tried to prepare himself for what Faith would undoubtedly have to say. He dreaded hurting her any more than he already had, but it would be best for both of them to face the hard facts right away.

"Kincaid," she said softly.

He tensed and held his breath.

"Kincaid, is there any champagne left?"

Surprised, he pulled his head back and looked down at her. She smiled softly and shrugged. "I'm terribly thirsty. Aren't you?"

He nodded and reached blindly behind him for the champagne bottle. When his fingers closed around it, he sat up and drew her up with him. Handing her the bottle, he reached for a glass, but she stopped him.

"It's all right." Tossing him a quick grin, she confided, "I've always wanted to do this." Lifting the bottle to her lips, she tipped it up, took a few swallows, and lowered it again. "Want some?" she asked.

He grasped the bottle and took one quick gulp.

Faith smiled and crossed her legs Indian style. Whether it was the intimacy of the storm or the liquor, or a combination of both, she seemed to have lost all her inhibitions concerning her own nudity.

Reaching for the bottle again, she took a few more

healthy drinks, then wiped her mouth with the back of her hand. She turned her head slightly to stare into the fire, and Kincaid found himself studying her profile.

Faith did *nothing* as he expected her to. Any other woman, he thought, would either be cowed by regrets or pleading with him to marry her. At the very least, he'd assumed that she would tell him how much she loved him.

He *knew* she did. A woman like Faith didn't give herself to *any* man lightly. Only love would guide her, and he'd come to realize over the last few weeks that even *loving* alone wouldn't be enough for her to lay with a man who wasn't her husband.

He cursed himself silently, viciously. She probably considered them engaged now.

A soft smile curved her lips, and he felt even worse. Firelight cast an ivory glow on her skin, and it was all he he could do to keep from reaching out to touch her again. To feel the fire in her burning beneath him once more.

Damn, he was some kind of bastard.

"Funny, isn't it?" she said suddenly, her voice low and dreamy.

"What?" he ground out.

She glanced at him quickly, then turned back to the fire. "All the time we've spent in the last few weeks trying to avoid each other only to arrive here."

"Yeah." So much for his fine, noble plan of friendship. He chanced a quick look at her. No hint of reproach or sadness colored her voice, and her features were calm, composed.

"I suppose it's not *really* funny, Kincaid," she went on. "It's only that, we'd finally reached a compromise. Agreed to be *friends*." She chuckled and looked at him. "I've never had a friend quite like this before . . . have you?"

I've never known *anyone* like you, he wanted to say. Instead, he simply said, "No."

She nodded, turned toward the window, and asked, "How long do you suppose it will rain?"

"No telling." He pulled in a deep, shaky breath. "But with the way it's coming down now, chances are good that the bridge won't be crossable even if it stopped this minute."

"I thought so." Faith nodded. Quietly she asked, "We'll be spending the night here, then?"

"Probably."

She lifted the champagne bottle once more and took another swallow. When she set it down, she turned to Kincaid. "Then I'd like to ask you something."

He raised himself up on one elbow and looked into her eyes. Desperately he wanted to say he'd promise her anything. But he couldn't. He couldn't give her any more than this empty room. And yet, Kincaid reached up and brushed away a long strand of sunshine-colored hair from her naked shoulder, leaving her breast open to his gaze. He pulled in a long breath, met her eyes, and asked, "What, Faith?"

Getting onto her knees, she inched closer to him. "While we're here"—she looked around the big room, then back to him—"in *this* hotel, at *this* time . . ." She laid her hand on his shoulder and let it glide slowly down his forearm.

"What?" He couldn't breathe again. He was surrounded by her scent, her touch.

"Don't think, Kincaid." She leaned over him and brushed her lips across his gently. "I'd like both of us to pretend, just for a while, that *nothing* outside this hotel exists."

"Faith, you don't know what you're asking." He tried to read her expression, but all he saw in her eyes was a quiet appeal.

"Yes, I do." Her hands cupped his face tenderly. "I'm asking that we forget who we are. Forget that we have lives beyond this place. Forget everything except what it is that lies between us."

"And what is that?" he asked huskily, his hand moving slowly up her thigh.

She smiled and shook her head. "I'm not sure. But"—Faith pulled in a deep breath—"there *is* something, Kincaid. And even if we never allow it life again, I think we *have* to now."

His gaze moved over her wonderingly. Knowing deep inside himself that he would probably regret this decision in the morning, Kincaid reached for her. There would be a lifetime for regrets and recriminations.

Faith sighed and leaned into him. He rolled onto his back, and she stretched out atop him, loving the feel of his hard strength. Slowly, delicately, she bent and kissed his flat nipples. Then, levering herself up, she moved up his chest, leaving a trail of damp kisses on his throat, his jaw.

Just as she'd told him, she refused to think about tomorrow. For now, she only wanted his arms around her. She wanted to be a part of him.

His hands moved over her back, pressing her to him. The calluses on his palms brought shivers to her skin. She smiled when he cupped her bottom firmly, squeezing her soft flesh with a tender strength. She slanted her lips over his, plunging her tongue inside his mouth with all the hunger that had gripped her before.

He groaned from deep in his throat and moved to roll her beneath him, but she broke away, breathless from his kiss. This time *she* would bring him to the brink of madness. Slowly, determinedly, she straddled his body and moved down the length of him, brushing his flesh with her warmth.

He watched her through hooded eyes, and Faith tossed her hair back over her shoulders and straightened up before him proudly.

"Faith . . ." He groaned and ran his hands up the outsides of her thighs.

On her knees she rocked from side to side, staying just inches away from his hard body. He swallowed heavily, and Faith knew the power she had over him. She placed her hands on his chest and leaned down, covering his mouth with her own. She wiggled her hips again, and he clamped his lips together tightly. Arching beneath her, he growled, and she smiled teasingly.

"Not yet, Kincaid," she said, throwing his own earlier words back at him. "Not yet."

"Playing, Faith?" he asked with a tight smile.

Then his fingers snaked around her thigh and slid inside her. She gasped, her body jerked in response, and she bent to kiss him again. His free hand held her close while his tongue teased hers. Faith's groans mingled with Kincaid's as the fires between them grew into a raging fury.

Finally, when she couldn't stand the wait any longer, Faith pushed herself up onto her knees. Locking her gaze with his, she lowered herself onto his body with slow deliberation.

When his shaft had barely entered her passage, she stopped and pulled away again. Ignoring his impatient groan, she continued her taunting dance, wanting to prolong the sensations as long as possible. Skin brushed against skin, warmth against warmth. The pulsing need of his body stroked her own desire until she sighed heavily and took him completely into her body.

"Jesus, Faith," he whispered and clutched her hips tightly.

Hands at his waist, Faith threw her head back and ground her hips against him. A lazy smile curved her lips. He was buried so deeply inside her, she felt that he was touching her soul.

His fingers moved to caress the bud of her sex, and she began to move over him, haltingly at first until she found the rhythm they both needed. Looking down, to the joining of their flesh, Faith watched as her body accepted his. Then she turned her gaze on him and knew he'd been watching, too.

As the now familiar tightening crept over her, Faith kept her eyes open and locked with his. When her body at last convulsed around him, she saw the tenderness in his eyes and didn't look away until his body exploded into hers.

Sunshine poked through the dirty, rain-streaked windowpanes and lay across Faith's face with hesitant light. She stirred, and Kincaid reluctantly pushed himself to his feet. Stepping softly, he walked across the room and stared out at the bright morning.

But for the mud, he told himself, he would never have believed that a storm had passed through such a short time ago. One hand on either side of the window, he leaned his weight against the wall and shook his head wearily.

Their time together was nearly over. The new day and the rest of the world waited just outside this room. A hollow ache filled him as he realized just how much he dreaded Faith's waking. Despite her brave words the night before, he knew she'd be feeling regrets in the light of day. And somehow, he had to find the right words to help her deal with what they'd done.

His hands balled into fists, his jaw clenched, he spun around to stare at the sleeping woman behind him.

Shit! *Faith's* regrets? Hell, what about his own? He'd deflowered the *schoolmarm*, for God's sake! And no matter what she'd said the night before, this little secret would not stay between the two of them. It was impossible.

By now, he thought disgustedly, Maisie and Minnie will have the entire countryside out looking for them. Everyone for miles around will know that they'd spent the night together.

Everyone. His head dropped. Chin on his chest, Kincaid stifled a groan.

Jesus, her parents. Frowning, he tried to get a clear picture in his mind of Mr. and Mrs. Lind. Inga Lind, he remembered, was much like Faith in size and coloring. But *Tom Lind* was a big, burly man who no doubt owned several guns.

When word of this escapade got around, Kincaid told himself, it was a sure thing that Tom Lind would be looking for him.

And who the hell would blame him? His fist smacked into the splintering wood with a satisfying crack. Dammit, he thought, if some man ruined *Amanda's* good name like he had Faith's . . . well. God help him.

Disgusted with himself, he sighed and remembered his vow never to let another woman into his life. Where had all his firm resolve and determination gone? He snorted derisively. It was too damned late for trying to keep her out of his life, and they both knew it. Even if they *didn't* marry, Faith Lind was so far into his life, he'd never be free of her.

Well, his brain taunted, do you *want* to be free of her?

I don't *know*! he silently shouted back.

Hell, he hardly knew his own name anymore.

The small part of his mind that was still rational told him that his time was running short. He'd have to decide soon. Before she woke up. He had to know what he was going to say when he faced her for the first time.

Turning away from the window, he walked back to her side and crouched down. Golden hair tangled and wild about her head, she lay on her side, one hand tucked under her cheek. Such a tiny, delicate-looking woman, he thought absently, and then grinned at his own thoughts. She might *look* dainty and delicate, but there was nothing fragile about her in bed. She looked so . . . different from the tidy, efficient schoolteacher.

But she wasn't the only one who seemed different. No matter what happened from here on out, Kincaid knew that he would never be the same man he once was. In her own gentle way she'd changed something deep inside him.

If only his mind were as at peace as his body.

Her eyelids fluttered, then opened. She stared right up at him and smiled, her eyes soft with pleasure.

"Good morning," he offered.

"Good morning." She stretched luxuriously, then sat up, pulling the quilt high over her breasts.

Kincaid sighed regretfully. The night was truly over.

"What time is it?" Faith said and pushed her hair out of her eyes.

"Don't know for sure." Shrugging, he added, "Can't be long after dawn."

She nodded briefly, then reached for her clothes,

stacked neatly beside the hearth. "If you'll hitch up the buggy, Kincaid, I'll be dressed in just a shake."

He stood up, took a half step, then turned back to her. "Faith, I—"

Her finger at her lips, she shook her head. "Don't say anything, Kincaid. Not now. Please?"

Drawing in a gulp of air, he jerked her a nod and turned for the door. Maybe she was right. After all, they had plenty of time on the ride home to talk everything out.

He closed the door behind him without another glance, so he didn't see the solitary tear roll down Faith's cheek.

Only an hour or less from Harmony and they'd hardly spoken a word. Every time he tried to talk about what had happened between them, Faith cut him off.

This wasn't going at all how he'd expected it to go. He'd been prepared to comfort her. To reassure her. He *hadn't* been prepared to be ignored! And dammit, he *had* to talk to her before they got back to town. Once in Harmony, they'd be surrounded by people! And knowing Maisie, Kincaid doubted that he and Faith would even be left alone in the dining room after this!

Without a word of warning, he jerked back on the reins, bringing their horse to an abrupt stop. Faith grabbed at the side of the buggy, but when he put out one hand to grab her, she managed to avoid his touch.

"What are you doing, Kincaid?"

"We have to talk, Faith," he answered and wrapped the reins tightly around the brake handle.

"I'd rather not."

"Faith, I know how you feel, but—"

"No, you don't."

"Don't what?" he asked, confused.

"Don't know how I feel."

He inhaled sharply and exhaled in a rush. "Then *tell* me. *Talk* to me."

She flicked him a glance, then turned her gaze back to the road stretching out in front of them. "I did all my talking last night, Kincaid. Don't you remember?"

"What? You mean about pretending that nothing else existed except that damn hotel?"

"Exactly."

He rubbed one hand across his jaw and looked at her. Lips clamped together, her chin had that too-familiar stubborn tilt to it. Her hands clasped tightly in her lap, shoulders rigid, she obviously didn't want to talk to him.

But she was *going* to.

"Fine," he said, mentally fighting down his temper. "We pretended. But that was last night. This is today. We can't pretend away the rest of the world forever. And we have to go on from here."

She heaved a sigh and turned her head slightly to look at him. "Don't you understand, Kincaid? We don't go anywhere from here."

"What are you talking about?"

"Last night was last night." She cleared her throat and let her gaze slide away from his. "Don't misunderstand me. I knew exactly what I was doing, and the . . . champagne had nothing to do with my decision."

"But—"

"And it *was* my decision, Kincaid. I wanted to . . . be with you." She turned and looked at him again. "But I knew that it was only for last night. And yes, we *do* have to pretend again. Pretend nothing happened between us."

"Faith, I . . ." He didn't know what to say. For the first time, he'd come across someone with a will as strong as his own, and he had no idea how to fight it. In fact, the only thing he was sure of was that hearing her say she planned to forget their night together cut at him like a knife.

"It's the only way, don't you see?" She stared down at her hands. "You don't want a wife, Kincaid. You've made that perfectly clear. And there's Amanda to consider."

"Faith, I don't know what to say."

"Don't worry, Kincaid." She forced a smile, and it nearly undid him when he saw her lip tremble. "I don't consider myself 'ruined' in any way."

He reached out one hand to her, but she pulled back.

"And since I *do* plan to marry someday, it would be better for me *and* my future husband if we just leave last night where it belongs. In the past."

Her future husband? A swell of jealous anger swept through him, directed at a man that neither of them knew yet.

"Can we go now, Kincaid? I really think we ought to get back. Folks will be worried about us."

Silently he unwound the reins and snapped them over the horse's back. As the buggy began rolling again, Kincaid told himself that it was all for the best. Like she said, there was Amanda. He and his daughter would build a life together, and Faith would find happiness with someone else.

Maybe, he snarled inwardly, with Danny Vega.

Shaking his head to clear *that* thought away, he tried to convince himself just how lucky he really was.

But he didn't feel lucky. Just lonely.

Less than half an hour later a single rider appeared in the distance. Faith straightened perceptibly and cast a wary glance at Kincaid from the corner of her eye.

His features still frozen in a silent mask, she looked away again quickly. Anger fairly simmered in the air around him, but she knew she'd done the right thing.

As soon as she woke to find him staring down at her with an apology shining in his eyes, her mind was made up. He'd evidently been expecting tears and anxious regrets over the night they'd spent together. No doubt that's just how his late wife would have behaved. Well, she told herself firmly, she was *not* Mary Alice Hutton, and it was high time he realized that.

She wouldn't give him the satisfaction of being proven right about her and women in general. Even though her heart felt as though it would break when she told him that she planned to forget last night ever happened.

As if she could.

Just thinking about the time spent in his arms was enough to set her blood boiling and her heart pounding. And if she was honest with herself, she would admit that yes, she *had* hoped he would realize how good they were together. Although she'd been completely prepared to settle for one night of loving and being loved, she wasn't able to completely squelch the notion that perhaps he would come to his senses and proclaim his love for her.

Faith's lips twisted mutinously. But he hadn't. So she'd been left with only one option. To turn the tables on him. Finally *she* would be the one to hold *him* at arm's length. To tell *him* that nothing could come of their being together. That one night of loving didn't mean a promise of tomorrow.

"C'mon, horse!" he shouted. "Get moving!"

She hid a weak smile. It was small consolation indeed that he wasn't very happy.

They met the rider less than ten miles from Harmony. Travis Miller pulled his horse to a stop and grinned as the buggy rolled up alongside him.

"Glad to see you folks!" He pulled his hat off and wiped his forehead with his sleeve. "Maisie was after me till late last night to set out lookin'. But had to wait for the storm to blow over." He stopped talking suddenly and looked at the two people in the buggy curiously. "You two all right?"

"Fine, Travis," Faith answered in a clear, strong voice. "It was good of you to come looking, but we were safe."

"Uh-huh." The sheriff nodded at her and glanced at Kincaid. "Where'd you two hole up?"

"At that abandoned hotel this side of Ellsworth," Faith said when it became apparent that Kincaid wasn't going to say a word. "The river overflowed the bridge, so we had to sit it out."

The sheriff nodded slowly as if he understood everything all too well. Deliberately Faith let her gaze slip away from his sharp eyes.

"Kincaid?" Travis asked, "Everything all right?"

"Fine, Travis." Kincaid shot an angry glare at the sheriff, whose eyebrows quirked in surprise. "Can we get moving? I'd like to see my daughter."

With a flick of his wrist, the reins snapped over the horse's back with a loud crack, and the buggy leapt ahead.

Travis Miller sat atop his horse, watching the couple heading for town. "Y'know, fella," he mumbled to the chestnut stallion, "I'd give twenty bucks to know what happened at that hotel last night." Then thoughtfully he rubbed his chin. Recalling the look on Kincaid's face and the pain in Faith's eyes, he told himself that maybe he was better off *not* knowing.

"Whatever went on, though," he said aloud, "looks like things are gonna be real interesting for a while."

Then, whistling under his breath, he turned his animal toward home.

CHAPTER

SIXTEEN

"You feel like talkin' about what happened last night?"

Faith's breath caught. Maisie was altogether too observant for her own good. Ever since they'd arrived back at the boardinghouse, the older woman's searching gaze had been concentrated on Faith.

Sighing, she shook her head and pulled the last remaining pin out of her hair. As she dragged a brush through the tangles, Faith tried to hide behind the fall of blond curls. She needed time to think.

Everything had happened so quickly. At least, it seemed that way to her. The buggy had hardly stopped rolling when Amanda'd raced out of the boardinghouse and thrown herself at the returning couple. After receiving her share of hugs and a tearful welcome, Faith watched Kincaid with his daughter.

Though he gave his attention to Amanda, Kincaid's still-angry eyes locked onto Faith until she'd had to look away or be burned by the fiery glints aimed at her.

But, she told herself, better anger than sympathy. She'd made a mistake the night before, though she wouldn't admit that to anyone but herself. Briefly her eyes squeezed shut against the pain. She'd been so *sure*. So positive that Kincaid loved her. *How* could she have been so wrong?

And why had she put herself in the position of being turned down again? Lord knew, in the last couple of weeks, Kincaid had kissed her, then pushed her away often enough to teach even the most thick-headed woman in the world to stop. To give up.

Her brush hit a particularly stubborn tangle, and she pulled at it viciously, glad of a *real* pain to focus on. Tears welled in her eyes as she told herself what a fool she'd been to hope that one night of physical love would be enough to convince Kincaid that he couldn't live without her.

Well! She grabbed up her hair in both hands, gave it a twist and balled it up into the familiar knot at her nape. Jamming the hairpins home, she reminded herself that at least one good thing had come of the night spent in Kincaid's arms. She was through fooling herself.

If he didn't love her, that was fine. He certainly had the right to choose the woman he wanted to love. *But*. Faith, too, had the right to choose. And she chose not to accept his pity. Heaven knew, she hadn't left herself with *much* pride. But she would hang on to all she had left with every ounce of her strength.

"Faith?" Maisie spoke up again and moved closer to her.

Their eyes met in the mirror.

"Something happened last night, didn't it?"

"No, Maisie. Nothing," Faith lied, proud that she didn't even flinch. "It was just the storm. Nothing more."

The older woman's eyes narrowed thoughtfully. "Kincaid seems almighty upset."

Forcing a smile, Faith managed a shrug. "Kincaid

Hutton has been 'upset' since the day he arrived in Harmony."

"True, all the same . . ." Maisie tapped her index finger against her chin. "I'd kinda hoped that, well . . ."

"Didn't you say something about a big breakfast, Maisie?" Faith interrupted and turned away from the mirror. Quickly she walked to the door, keeping her back to the woman who noticed far too much.

"Huh? Oh!" Waving her hands in the air, Maisie spun about, crossed the room, and stepped out into the hall. "Of course. You must be starvin'!" In the hallway she stopped suddenly, grabbed Faith's forearm, and said, "Why don't you just step over and tell Kincaid to come on down to eat? I'll go start the coffee."

Faith lifted her chin and shook her head. Somehow, she managed to keep from glancing at Kincaid's closed door. The one thing she didn't need was more time alone with him. "*I'll* start the coffee, Maisie. Why don't *you* fetch Kincaid and Amanda?"

She practically ran down the staircase, leaving Maisie at the landing alone. Slowly the older woman turned and looked down the hall toward Kincaid's room.

"A damn shame," she mumbled. She had a feeling that that nephew of hers had gone and done something stupid. Of course, she told herself, it was bound to happen. He was, after all, just a man. Her breath left her on a long sigh. And she'd so hoped for something special to sprout up between the two young people.

She could talk to Kincaid, but she sensed that she'd get even less information out of him than she had from Faith.

Still, she thought with a half smile, the game ain't

over till the last card's been played. *Now* was no time to leave the table!

Whistling softly, she walked to Kincaid's door and knocked.

"And, Lord," Maisie continued briskly, "we'd like to thank you for bringin' home our lost sheep." She slanted a glance at the two of them and was pleased to see them shift uncomfortably. "Of course, we have faith that You know best, so I figure that whatever happened last night to hold them up was *Your* doin'." She almost smiled. Faith was blushing. "Us poor miserable creatures just got to go along with Your plan. Amen."

"Amen," the boarders echoed.

"Don't know why you got to say grace again," Minnie muttered. "It was *my* turn!"

"Hush up, Min," Maisie countered. Passing a plate of fried potatoes to Kincaid, she said, "So. When do you start buildin' that hotel of yours?"

"Tomorrow. As soon as the lumber arrives."

Maisie swallowed her chuckle. His eyes had *definitely* slipped to Faith. "So it's for sure, then? You're really stayin' on in Harmony?"

"Yes."

"Yay!" Amanda hollered, then said gleefully, "Faith! You get to keep being my teacher! Aren't you glad?"

Maisie turned her sharp gaze on the young woman and waited. Sure enough, Faith's eyes flew to Kincaid quickly, then lowered again.

"That's wonderful, Amanda. Of course I'm glad."

"Me, too," Amanda continued and tugged at her father's jacket sleeve. "Papa, aren't you glad?"

Maisie propped her chin on one hand and looked at her idiot nephew.

Kincaid's lips twisted into a mockery of a smile, but his voice was gentle when he spoke to the happy little girl.

"Yes, honey. I'm glad, too."

Uh-huh, Maisie told herself. And if she had anything to do with it, he was gonna be a helluva lot *gladder* before she was through!

By Wednesday Kincaid's nerves were stretched to the breaking point.

He'd lived that one night over and over again in his mind. Every word, every touch was ingrained in him so deeply he doubted that he would ever be free of it.

Even watching the framework of his new hotel going up wasn't enough to distract him. And though he'd gotten in touch with the man from Ellsworth and purchased the furnishings from the abandoned hotel, he didn't know how in the hell he was going to live surrounded by reminders of that night.

He knew that every time he used the stove or sat in a chair or drank a glass of brandy, that stormy night with Faith would come rushing back into his brain.

Faith. He sat down on the schoolhouse steps, rested his forearms on his knees, and stared down into the dirt. He *still* didn't know what to make of her. Who would have expected a woman like her to breezily brush aside a night of explosive passion by saying "It was my decision. Don't concern yourself with it"?

He snorted and moved his foot out of the path of a hardworking ant. Staring at the insect, Kincaid asked himself why the hell was he so upset? Hell, he *should* be pleased! The scene he'd dreaded facing Sunday morning never happened. There were no hysterics from Faith. No declarations of love. There was . . . *nothing*.

Dammit, that's exactly why he was upset! The thing he couldn't figure out was why she *wasn't*!

What was she thinking? Hadn't she considered the possibility that she might even now be *pregnant*? He shook his head. Probably not. Hell, it hadn't even occurred to *him* until that morning.

But now that it had, he was determined to talk to her. He only hoped he could hold on to his temper if she tried to ignore him.

The doors behind him burst open, and a small herd of children raced down the steps and scampered off in all directions. Amanda, though, stopped when she saw her father.

"Papa? What are you doing here?"

He reached out and tweaked her nose gently. "I have to talk to Faith, sweetheart."

"Oh." Amanda bit at her lip, looked from the schoolhouse door to her father again, and said, "Faith's not very happy anymore, Papa."

"Hmmm?"

Tugging at her hair, the little girl added, "She doesn't smile like she used to."

His daughter's small features twisted into lines of worry, confusion. It wasn't so long ago, Kincaid told himself, that she wore that expression all the time. Seeing it again now bothered him more than he could say. The *one* thing he *didn't* want to happen was for Amanda to slide back into her world of imagination. Somehow, he had to make sure that her newfound confidence wasn't shattered.

A spearhead of guilt slashed through him, and he almost welcomed it. At least he was *used* to guilt. He knew how to live with that. "I know, hon."

"Why, Papa? Don't she like us anymore?" Amanda

leaned against his upraised knee and watched her father's face through wide, serious eyes.

"Sure she does, Amanda. She likes all of you children. Very much."

"Then why is she unhappy?" Her head cocked at an angle, her teeth bit at her bottom lip.

He inhaled sharply and tried to find the words to answer her. There weren't any.

Suddenly Amanda smiled and patted his knee. "She likes you, too, Papa. You could make her smile, I bet."

"I'll try, Amanda." Though inwardly he admitted his chances for success were few.

"Promise?"

"Promise."

She grinned, satisfied, and turned away to skip back to the boardinghouse. Over her shoulder she called out, "Maybe you should give her a hug, Papa. Hugs help a lot."

Kincaid nodded and waved to her. A hug. Shaking his head, he pushed himself to his feet. Hell. Hugging is one of the things that brought them to this situation in the first place.

Taking a long, deep breath, he climbed the steps and walked into the now quiet school.

Faith gripped the old rag tightly and rubbed it across the chalkboard. As the day's lessons disappeared, she told herself that it would be lovely if she could simply wipe away her troubling thoughts as easily.

The last few days had passed unbearably slowly. She'd never noticed before just how often she and Kincaid Hutton crossed paths. It seemed they were forever meeting on the staircase, the kitchen, the dining room.

Her arm dropped to her side, and she leaned her head against the cool black slate. She hadn't even been able to take a walk in the evening for fear of running into him outside. Alone. The safest thing for her to do, she knew, was to make sure they always had people around them.

She just didn't know if she could stand being alone with him. Not after sharing what they had and knowing that he didn't want her.

"Faith."

She gasped and spun around so quickly, she had to grab at the edge of her desk to keep from falling off the platform. "Kincaid."

He walked toward her, his boots almost soundless on the wooden floor. She looked as though she hadn't been getting much sleep lately. Her usually smiling hazel eyes seemed somehow flat, lusterless. She even looked a little pale, he told himself worriedly.

It was ridiculous. This campaign of cool, polite behavior was as wearing for her as it was for him. Despite his best intentions, Kincaid's temper began to rise. Couldn't she see that this nonsense was getting them nowhere?

"Stop looking at me like that," he said stiffly.

"Like what?" She gripped the rag in her hands as if it were a lifeline.

"Like you reached for a stick and discovered too late it was a snake!"

"Go away, Kincaid," she said and turned back to cleaning her chalkboard.

"No." He stepped up on the platform and walked to her side. Grabbing the rag out of her hands, he added, "Not until we've talked."

"There's nothing to say."

"*I* think there is." He fought to keep his voice low,

controlled. But she would hardly *look* at him! "Why the hell have you been treating me like the village half-wit?"

"What?" Her gaze flicked up to his, and for a moment he saw a flash of anger.

"You heard me." He leaned down toward her, but she didn't back up a bit. "*When* you speak to me, your voice is so cold, it's harder than a lake in winter. Most of the time, you look *through* me, not at me."

She pushed past him. "It's easier for both of us."

"Not likely, or I wouldn't be here complaining." He grabbed her forearm and spun her around. "*And* you wouldn't look like you haven't had sleep in days."

Faith pulled her arm free and glared at him. Her breathing fast and furious, she opened her mouth to speak, but Kincaid cut her off.

"And what about Amanda?"

Her brow furrowed in confusion, she stared at him.

Jesus! He even hated himself for dragging his own child into this. But he was getting desperate. Hell, she *still* wouldn't talk to him.

"What about Amanda? She seems fine to me."

"Well, she's not." All right, he told himself grudgingly, maybe he was exaggerating a bit. But who knew how long the little girl would be all right if he and Faith couldn't resolve their differences?

Faith shrugged slightly. "I haven't treated her any differently than before. She seems all right. At least, I haven't seen any sign of Boom's return."

"Well, just a few minutes ago she told me that you weren't happy anymore." There. The truth.

"She did?" Faith frowned slightly. Obviously she was more concerned with Amanda's feelings than his.

"Yes. She even made me promise to make you happy again."

Faith chuckled, but there was no humor in the sound. "Poor Kincaid. Isn't that a little like trying to put out a fire by throwing kerosene on it?"

"Faith . . ."

"No." She shook her head and looked up at him. "I'm sorry Amanda's been worried. But she'll be fine. Don't worry."

"Amanda's a smart kid, Faith. She *knows* something is wrong."

"Fine." Faith sighed and crossed her arms over her chest. "I'll try to smile more when I'm around her. Lord knows, I don't want her bothered by any of this. Will that satisfy you?"

Kincaid wanted to shout at her. This damn calm acceptance of hers was making him crazy. He was much more used to a stubborn Faith. A woman too sure of herself to allow *any* man to dictate to her.

He pushed both hands through his hair and clenched his fingers. In the distance he heard the sounds of hammers pounding. His hotel was going up quickly. He'd made a commitment to stay in Harmony. To raise his child in Harmony.

But if he wanted to have *any* kind of peace in his life, he had to find a way to reach a resolution with Faith. Neither one of them could spend the next several years avoiding each other. Harmony was too damn small for that. He had to keep trying.

"How long are you going to keep this up?" he finally asked, leaning back against the chalkboard.

"What?" she asked quietly, her gaze only flashing to him for an instant. "Our 'friendship'?"

He winced.

"As long as necessary," she continued on a sigh.

"I've already told you, Kincaid. Don't feel responsible for me."

"How can I not?" He pushed away from the wall, took two steps, and grabbed her upper arms. "You might be *pregnant*!"

Her jaw dropped. Eyes wide, she stared up at him, shaking her head. "I hadn't even considered that," she admitted slowly. "How stupid of me."

Finally! Kincaid swallowed his pleased smile. He'd said something at last that'd caught her attention. *Now* maybe she'd start talking to him. "What if you are, Faith? What then? We have to talk about this."

He could almost *see* the thoughts racing through her brain. Biting at her lip, Faith took several deep breaths as if to steady herself before saying softly, "*If* that happens ..."

"Yes?" he whispered.

"I'll ... *move*," she finished.

"*What?*" Kincaid let go of her abruptly. Snorting his disbelief, he stepped off the platform and began to pace furiously. Muttering incoherently and shaking his head, he only stopped when she spoke again.

"I've told you, Kincaid. I take full responsibility for my own actions. If the worst happens, I'll handle that as well."

"Sure." He turned slowly around to face her. "You'll move. Where?" Kincaid stomped across the floor to stand directly in front of her. The platform she stood on put them at eye level with each other. Staring straight into her eyes, he went on. "Alone? Unmarried? No money? No job? With a child? *My* child?" He inhaled sharply and exhaled again just as quickly. "Don't be a fool!"

"Kincaid," she said, and he heard the note of temper in her tone.

"Just wait a damned minute," he went on, his

hand held up for her silence. "You really expect to tell me that you'll just disappear with *my* child, and that I won't do a thing to stop you?"

"Kincaid, we don't even know that I *am* pregnant!"

"That's beside the point, dammit!" He'd never been so furious in his life. Did she really think so little of him? Had he really been such a complete bastard? "The point is, we have to accept the possibilities and *plan* for them!"

"What are you talking about?"

Crossing his arms over his chest, Kincaid took a deep, shuddering breath and blurted out, "All right, Faith, I'm willing to marry you."

Faith stared at him, stunned into silence. By the look on his face, she guessed that he was every bit as surprised as she was by his offer. Obviously, it wasn't a planned proposal. *No one* would bungle a rehearsed marriage proposal that badly.

No, it was a spur-of-the-moment decision, she told herself. No doubt, born of his own frustrations. Well, she thought as her own temper caught fire, if he thought she would actually *accept* him, he was in for yet another surprise!

Just how many times did he think she would allow him to step on her pride? Her fingers curled into fists at her sides, she looked into his dark green eyes, and all she wanted to do was blacken one of them for him! Imagine! He wouldn't marry her for love! But he *would* be willing to sacrifice himself for the sake of a child he wasn't sure existed!

Forcing a calm she didn't feel, Faith finally spoke into the lingering silence. "I'd like to thank you Kincaid for such a *gracious* proposal."

At least, she told herself, he had the decency to look abashed.

"But," she went on, "I'm afraid the answer is no."

"What?" His rigid posture drooped suddenly, and he stared at her as if she'd just spoken to him in Greek. "What do you mean, no?"

"Just what I said."

"But I want to *marry* you, dammit!"

A tiny corner of her heart began to crumble slightly. How she would have loved to hear him say that last Sunday morning. How eagerly she'd have accepted him.

How happy they could have been.

She blinked quickly, determined to keep the tears she felt building behind her eyes from falling.

"Faith!"

She didn't flinch at his shout. Instead, she bent to her desk and picked up the stack of papers waiting for her. When she turned back to face him, she said slowly, "You don't want to marry me, Kincaid. You just want to stop feeling guilty."

Clutching her things to her chest, Faith stepped off the platform and walked quickly to the door. Before she left, though, she chanced one look behind her. Through her unshed tears, she saw him, standing alone in a dying patch of sunlight.

CHAPTER

SEVENTEEN

FAITH THREW her head back and laughed, delighted at something her sister Zan whispered in her ear. Across the room Kincaid frowned, crossed his arms over his chest, and propped himself up against the rear wall of the schoolhouse.

He shouldn't have come, he told himself grimly. In fact, he couldn't imagine *why* he had. But with his very next breath he silently admitted the reason. He simply couldn't seem to stay away from Faith. Kincaid snorted. It certainly wasn't because he had a deep interest in the outcome of the spelling bee. Although it seemed everyone else for miles around did.

Shaking his head slightly, he looked out over the crowded room. Everywhere he looked, he saw people laughing, talking, joking with each other. Even his daughter was having the time of her life!

By lifting his chin a bit, Kincaid was able to see the top of Amanda's head. Seated in the front row of desks, she and Sarah Lind were sharing a bag of rock candy and giggling over some secret only little girls could appreciate.

A smile tugged at his lips. At least, he thought, *Amanda* was all right. *She* hadn't been bothered by what was happening between him and Faith. Not yet, anyway. But how long could *that* last? he wondered silently. Sooner or later the girl was going to notice the tension between her father and the school-teacher. Then what? Would she revert to her fantasies? Or would her new confidence be strong enough to help her when he and Faith grew further and further apart?

Damn Faith anyway. And damn him, too, for making such a complete botch of everything!

He straightened slowly as a tall man pushed through the front of the crowd and stepped up to the teacher's platform. Kincaid tensed when Edward Winchester approached Faith and her sister. Then the Englishman spoke to Zan, and Kincaid relaxed again.

Lord, he was in a bad way.

Faith checked her pendant watch. The contest had been going heatedly for over twenty minutes already without a mistake on either side. She tossed quick glances at first one team, then the other. Minnie and Maisie both wore proud, almost cocky grins and took turns preening for the audience.

With a false air of calm, Faith let her gaze drift out over the crowd until she found Kincaid. He was staring at her. Even from across the room—she felt as if he'd touched her. Her chest tight, she swallowed past the lump in her throat and tried to breathe normally. Deliberately she looked away again and turned her gaze back to the list of spelling words in her hand.

"Minnie," she said, hoping her voice wasn't quavering, "it's your team's turn."

Minnie gave her a firm nod and straightened her shoulders as if preparing for battle.

"The word is—*chrysanthemum*."

Someone in the mob gasped worriedly.

Maisie snickered.

Minnie lifted her chin and turned to face her team.

They were all staring at Zeke. "C'mon now, Zeke," Minnie encouraged. "You show 'em."

Zeke took a deep breath, inflating his already sizable chest. Slowly he began. "Chrysanthemum." Brow wrinkled, eyes squeezed shut, he said, "K-r-i-"

Minnie groaned, and Faith spoke up quickly.

"I'm sorry, Zeke, that's wrong."

The big barber's face fell, then he took a seat.

Facing Maisie now, Faith said, "All right, Maisie. If your team spells this right, you win. *Chrysanthemum.*"

Tossing a victorious glance at her sister, Maisie looked at the Reverend Johnson. "All right, Abe. It's up to you, now."

The thin man stepped forward, his wife Rachel's hand on his shoulder supportively. Sweeping his sandy-blond hair back from his forehead, Reverend Johnson said, "*Chrysanthemum.* C-h-r-s-a-"

Rachel groaned softly and patted his back.

Maisie muttered under her breath, and Faith spoke up over the rumbling crowd.

"I'm sorry, Reverend. That's wrong, too."

"I forgot the *y*, didn't I?" he asked quickly. "Could I start again?"

"That wouldn't be fair, Faith!" Minnie shouted out.

"You leave him be, Sister. Ain't you ever heard of turnin' the other cheek?"

"Not in spelling bees!"

Faith clapped her hands until everyone was quiet and watching her.

"I'm afraid we'll have to call this bee a tie, too."

"What?" Maisie and Minnie screeched together.

Shaking her head, Faith said adamantly, "It's the only fair thing to do, ladies." Neither one of them looked happy. But, Faith thought, at least the contest was over. Forcing a smile, she looked out at the gath-

ered people. "There are refreshments in the back, everybody. Help yourselves."

Maisie and Minnie were still hurling insults at each
other as the audience began to stand up and move
toward the food.

Faith sighed her relief. Her mind wasn't on the
match anyway. And pretending to be interested was
getting harder by the minute. How could she be expected to keep her mind on spelling words with
Kincaid's heated gaze locked on her?

All she wanted to do now was get back to the
boardinghouse. Maybe if she slipped out the back
door, no one would notice. And if she didn't leave
soon, she had the distinct feeling that Kincaid would
be seeking her out. Oh, she told herself, not because
he *loved* her. Because he couldn't believe his sacrifice
had been turned down.

Cold chills swept over her with the memory of his
indifferent, offhanded proposal. Had he *really* expected her to swoon in gratitude? To accept such an
obviously reluctant offer of marriage?

Lord, she was tired. Tired of wanting him. Tired of
fighting him. She just wanted to go home. She
wanted to sleep without seeing his face in her
dreams.

Risking one last glance at Kincaid, Faith saw
Maisie making her way toward him. Sadly she told
herself now was the time to leave. While he was distracted by his aunt.

She headed for the back door but hadn't taken
more than a step when Travis Miller stopped her.

"Well, now," Maisie taunted, "how come you're
lookin' like a man down to his last bullet in an Indian war?

"What?" Kincaid turned to his aunt, then looked

back at Faith. He didn't like the way Miller was looking at her. Worse, he didn't like the smile Faith was
giving the other man.

Maisie followed his gaze. A half smile curving her
lips, she looked back at her nephew. "What seems to
be the matter tonight, Kincaid? Can't be Amanda."
She pointed at the little girl, now getting a cup of
punch off the table. "She's havin' a fine time!"

"Yeah. Yeah, she is," Kincaid muttered and looked
back at Faith and Miller.

"Then what is it, Nephew?" She shot a glare at
Fred Winchester when he bumped into her.

"Nothing, Maisie." His face grim, he inhaled
sharply. "Nothing's wrong."

"Hmmm. Thought this might have somethin' to do
with Faith."

"What?" Eyes narrowed, he stared at her.

"Oh, I just had the idea you was a little interested
in her, is all."

Kincaid snorted. "Did you?"

"Then you're not?"

"Maisie"—he sighed—"this isn't exactly the place
for a heart-to-heart talk, is it?"

She shrugged and spoke up over the noise of the
crowd. "Maybe not. But you haven't been real easy
to talk to lately, have you?"

"Guess not," he admitted. "All right, Maisie.
Maybe I *was* interested. But"—he jerked his head toward Faith—"*she's* not."

"And you're sure about that?"

"As sure as I can be! I told her just this morning
that I'd be willing to marry her, and she—"

Maisie swatted his arm. "You didn't say it like that,
did ya?"

He didn't answer.

"You did." The older woman shook her head disbelievingly. "You beat everything, Kincaid. You know that?"

"She knew what I meant," he threw in defensively.

"Did she?" Maisie took a deep breath, grabbed the edges of her crocheted forest-green shawl, and pulled it tight across her breasts. "You men are a breed apart. You say some of the damnedest things and then claim us women got nothin' but cotton wool in our heads!"

Several people nearby shifted as Maisie's voice got louder. Inching closer, they were obviously listening, and Kincaid had the insane desire to gag his aunt.

"What did you think a fine woman like Faith would say to somethin' like that?"

"Maisie . . ." he grumbled.

"I swear, Kincaid . . . if you weren't my own nephew . . ."

Noticing the eavesdroppers, Maisie's tirade faded off. She frowned at them all fiercely until they slowly drifted away again.

"Maisie, can we talk about this later?" he said, bending down close to her ear.

"You bet we can. And *will*." Frowning, she turned around to face the crowd, and a hurried movement caught the corner of her eye. Squinting into the mob, she began to smile again. She jabbed her elbow into Kincaid's ribs and said sweetly, "Isn't that nice? Danny Vega's back in town, and he's come callin' on Faith!"

Kincaid stiffened. Straightening up to his full height, he watched over the heads of the crowd as Danny moved unerringly toward Faith. When the younger man reached the platform, Travis Miller moved off with a smile, and Danny stepped up beside her.

Teeth clenched, his stomach in knots, Kincaid

couldn't seem to tear his gaze from the couple a room's length away. And he didn't care a *bit* for the way the handsome young cowboy was looming over Faith like a vulture over dinner!

"My, don't they make a handsome couple, though?" Maisie crooned.

Kincaid growled something unintelligible and pushed away from the wall.

She couldn't seem to get out of the schoolhouse. Faith smiled up at Danny and tried to listen to what he was saying, but her heart wasn't in it. In her mind's eye she saw not Danny's soft brown eyes, but the sharp green of Kincaid's. And even as that thought entered her mind, she told herself to stop it. She had to quit thinking about Kincaid for her own peace of mind.

Determinedly she focused on Danny and concentrated.

"So anyways," he continued, a grin on his face, "I hear that Mr. and Mrs. Taylor are thinkin' of throwin' a dance here in town next week."

"A dance? Why?"

He shrugged. "Who knows? Maybe Lillie just feels like dancin'."

Faith chuckled softly. That *did* sound like Lillie.

"So," Danny asked, "you wanna go with me?"

She opened her mouth to speak, but Kincaid's deep voice interrupted her.

"Faith, I'll see you home now." He grabbed her upper arm and began to tug at her.

Immediately Faith dug in her heels and pulled free. Staring up at him as if he'd lost his mind, she said firmly, "I'm not going home yet, thank you."

"Who's this?" Danny stepped closer to her protectively.

Kincaid's teeth ground together and he sucked in a great gulp of air. He wanted to grab the cowboy and toss him across the room. Instead, he waited for Faith to tell the boy to go away.

"It's all right, Danny," Faith finally said, frowning at Kincaid. "This is Kincaid Hutton. He's the father of one of my students."

Danny stuck one hand out, waiting for the other man to grab it. "Pleased to meet you, mister."

Kincaid nodded absently, his gaze fixed on Faith. He shook the young man's hand, all the time asking himself if that's all Faith *really* felt about him anymore. Just as Amanda's father?

Draping one arm around Faith's shoulders, Danny grinned. "You don't have to worry, Mr. Hutton. *I'll* see she gets home safe."

He stared at the too friendly arm, then shifted his furious gaze to the cowboy's cheerful features. Damn the man! Since when did the cowboy feel so free to put his arms around Faith? And why the hell wasn't she complaining?

Kincaid struggled for air, and the noise of the crowded room disappeared under the roaring sound filling his ears. His heart pounding, blood racing, he swallowed back the shouts he wanted to hurl at the younger man. Then he noted in a still rational corner of his brain that Faith had slipped out from under Danny's protective arm. It wasn't enough.

He wanted her out of there. Away from the handsome cowboy. Away from the crowd surrounding them. He wanted her alone. His arms around her. Just the two of them.

Deliberately he grabbed Faith's hand and held it firmly. His teeth clenched, voice tight, he said, "That won't be necessary, Danny. Miss Lind and I have a few things we have to discuss."

"Huh?" Danny frowned uncertainly and looked from Faith to Kincaid and back again.

"It's all right, Danny." Faith smiled at him over her shoulder as Kincaid pulled her through the crowd toward the front door.

Once outside, Kincaid kept walking until they were clear of the lamp-thrown patches of light.

Finally Faith jerked her arm free and faced him. He stared down into her eyes, and even in the dark he could see the daggers she was shooting at him. And a part of him didn't blame her.

Hell, he could hardly understand himself! All he knew was that he hadn't been able to stand the sight of Danny Vega's arm around her.

"Just what do you think you're doing, Kincaid Hutton?" Hands at her hips, she bent toward him, fury written all over her face.

"How could you see him after—"

"After what, Kincaid?" She cocked her head. "Nothing happened between us. Remember? Didn't you say that would be best? If we just pretended that night never happened?"

"Forget what I said!" Dammit, this wasn't going well at all. He pushed one hand through his hair and tried to figure out when he'd lost control of everything.

"I don't think so." Faith sighed suddenly and spoke more softly. "You were right all along, Kincaid. It's best for both of us if we just stay clear of each other."

"I just wanted to talk to you and—"

"Be *friends*?" She snorted a laugh. "No. I believe we already failed miserably at that."

He winced at her scathing tone. She was right. Friendship would never be enough. Not between them. Still, he had to try. Had to say *something*.

"Faith, we—"

"No!" She breathed deeply, then exhaled in a rush. "There is no 'we.' We have no claims on each other, Kincaid. So please." She looked up at him. "Just leave me alone."

"What do you mean, no claims?" He grabbed her arms and pulled her close. "No matter what we pretend, Faith, there is something between us."

She ran one small hand over his shirtfront for a too brief moment. "No, Kincaid. You said all along that you didn't want another wife." A bitter smile curved her lips as she added, "I thought I knew better."

"You *did*! I asked you to marry me, didn't I?"

A sad chuckle escaped her. "And a handsome offer it was. But I already told you. The answer's no."

"And what if you're pregnant?"

She cocked her head to one side. "If I am— well . . ." Inhaling sharply, she exhaled just as quickly, saying, "There's no point worrying about that *yet*. I might not be, you know." Faith looked up at him, her features blank. "We'll know in a couple of weeks. Depending on what happens, *I'll* decide what to do."

Kincaid clenched his jaw as he stared down into those determined hazel eyes. In his imagination, he saw her small form rounded with his child. And with the image came a fierce wish that it be true.

"Faith," he started and looked down into her face. The features that had haunted him for weeks. He saw the pain in her eyes and knew that he'd caused it and knew also that she wasn't bluffing. She really didn't want him.

And suddenly he saw his own future laid out before him. The long, lonely years without her. His mind created lightning quick images of Faith walking with another man, surrounded by her children.

Children that could have been his. And he saw himself. Alone.

With a quiet groan he bent his head and covered her mouth with his. Desperation colored the kiss, and for one brief moment he felt her response. Then she went limp in his arms, and he broke away.

The glimmer of tears shining in her eyes, she looked at him one last time and said harshly, "Please, Kincaid. Leave me alone!"

Then she lifted the hem of her skirt and started running. He watched her disappear into the darkness, and from a distance he heard the door of the boardinghouse slam shut.

"Papa?"

He jumped, startled, then turned to face his daughter.

"Was that Faith?"

"Yes, Amanda."

"She still doesn't look very happy."

No, she didn't, he agreed silently. Then he reminded himself of her momentary response to his kiss and began to smile. It didn't matter that she insisted there was nothing between them. The truth was in the fire that ignited whenever they touched. She couldn't hide that. And she couldn't deny it. Not forever.

A fierce rush of hope filled him, and he said firmly, "No, she's not, Amanda. But she *will* be." He heard the determined note in his own voice and solemnly promised himself he would keep that vow.

"Papa?"

"What?"

Amanda looked down at the toes of her shoes, then peeked up at her father. "Are we still going to supper at Faith's mama's house?" Then softer still, she added, "Do I still get my puppy?"

A slow smile touched Kincaid's lips. He'd forgotten all about the Linds' invitation. And he'd be willing to bet that Faith had, too. Quickly he began to think. This is Wednesday, he told himself. Supper is this coming Sunday.

His smile became a grin. *Anything* might happen at supper, he thought. At the very least, he'd have the chance to talk to Faith's folks.

"Yes, Amanda," he said, walking to his daughter's side. "Of course we're still going!"

She smiled up at him, and Kincaid's heart twisted in his chest. He owed Faith so much. And he'd given her so little.

"Hooray! And I get to have my puppy, too?"

"Sure you do, honey." He took her small hand in his and began to lead her across the dark yard toward the boardinghouse. "But let's not mention anything about this to Faith, all right?"

"Why not?"

"Well," he said, a teasing note in his voice, "I think Faith has forgotten all about it. Wouldn't you like to surprise her?"

"Oh, yes, Papa!" Amanda laughed delightedly at the prospect of surprising an adult. "Won't it be fun?"

CHAPTER

EIGHTEEN

"ALL RIGHT, Nephew," Maisie said as she entered the workshop and closed the door behind her. "I want to know what you're plannin' to do about Faith Lind."

"What?" Kincaid set his hammer down on the workbench and faced his aunt.

The older woman walked straight up to him and crossed her arms over her considerable bosom. "I told you Wednesday night that I wanted to talk to you." Her eyes narrowed. "Well, it's Friday now and I finally figured out that if I was going to give you a piece of my mind, I'd have to chase you down to do it."

He sighed and leaned his hip against the bench. It was true. He *had* been avoiding talking to her. Maisie meant a lot to him. And having yet one more female he cared about disgusted with him wasn't something Kincaid was looking forward to. But judging from the older woman's expression, there wouldn't be any ducking the conversation this time.

"Well?" she asked impatiently, her foot tapping against the sawdust-covered floor.

He almost said, "Well what?" But he knew stalling wouldn't do any good, either. "I don't know what you want to hear, Maisie."

"Fine. I'll tell you." She took a step closer.

"Kincaid, I've always been real fond of you. I sure don't want to think you're gonna disappoint me at this late date."

"What do you mean?"

"You know exactly what I mean." Wagging one finger at him, she warned, "You can't take a girl like Faith and treat her casual and get away with it, y'know."

"I know that."

"Oh." Frowning, she considered him through narrowed eyes for a moment. "Then what are you plannin' on doin' about it?"

Frustration boiled up in him suddenly, and he slapped his palm down onto the bench top. "I already asked her to marry me. . . . She said no thanks."

Smirking, Maisie said, "If you really asked her the off-hand way you told me about—son, you're lucky she didn't hit you with something."

"I know." Shaking his head, Kincaid stared up at the ceiling. A splotch of white paint was peeling off one of the beams, and he focused on it. "Hell, Maisie. I never planned on getting married again! Jesus, living through *one* marriage like the one I had was more than enough for any man." He darted a quick glance at the woman opposite him.

He'd done it again. Said something the wrong way. Mary Alice was Maisie's *niece*, for God's sake.

"I'm sorry," he said, disgusted with himself.

"Don't worry about my feelings for Mary Alice, Kincaid." Maisie shook her head slowly. "Oh, she was my man's niece. And I suppose I loved her . . . but I swear, Kincaid, there never lived a more *tryin'* woman."

He stared at her.

"Oh, hell, boy. Don't look so surprised. We all

knew what she was like." She snorted suddenly. "But this nonsense about you never wanting to get married again because of her . . . well. That's just about the *dumbest* thing I ever heard."

He stiffened slightly.

"Climb down off your high horse, Kincaid." Waving one hand at him, she leaned her backside against the bench and went on talking. "You ain't the first man to do something dumb, Lord knows. And human beings bein' what they are, you surely won't be the last."

"Maisie . . ."

"Just hush a minute. Now, first off. You sayin' you never want to get married again because of your first marriage—well, that's like sayin' since eatin' one apple made you sick, you'll never have another!" She looked up at him out of the corner of her eye. "Chances are, you just picked a bad apple the first time around. And you'll never know the sweetness of apple pie if you don't try one again."

"Apples and marriages aren't quite the same thing, Maisie."

"Not quite, but close enough." She took a deep breath and narrowed her eyes thoughtfully. "Your problem, Kincaid, is you keep lookin' at every woman like she was a Mary Alice underneath. Well, that's the wrong road to take."

"I know that," he said, trying to get a word in. She brushed right past him.

"Y'see, Faith is a woman with a brain and plenty of pride. When you stuck your foot in your mouth with that foolish proposal, you hurt her good."

Kincaid clenched his teeth. He *knew* he'd been an ass.

"If you really want her, Nephew, you're gonna

have to work hard at it. You're gonna have to find a way to prove to her that you really *do* want her."

"I know."

"Good." She nodded and pushed away from the workbench. "I'm glad we had this little talk, Kincaid." Moving slowly, she crossed the room to the door and pulled it open. Before she stepped through it, though, she glanced back at him. "You just remember one thing. If you trifle with that girl—don't you worry about Tom Lind comin' after you. You worry about *me*."

"Yes, ma'am," he said, smiling.

She lowered her right eyelid in a slow wink. "Good luck, boy."

The rich aroma of freshly baked bread filled the Lind kitchen. Faith wandered in, inhaled deeply, and glanced around the familiar place. A big room, its scrubbed, white pine table held enough food to feed an army. Grinning, she reminded herself that that's exactly what the Lind family was. A small army.

From the apple-red curtains at the windows to the faded rag rug on the shining wood floor, it was home. And she was glad to be there.

More than any other room in the house, the kitchen held memories of cold nights and warm smiles. How many times, she wondered idly, had the entire family sat at that very table late into the night, drinking hot milk and listening to their father's deep voice telling them stories of fair ladies, princes, and dragons?

She leaned back against the wood counter, rubbed smooth over the years by dozens of hands, and found herself almost wishing that she could become a child again. Then she could rest in her papa's arms and know that the world outside couldn't hurt her.

"Now," her mother said as she bustled into the room, "would you care to tell me the reason behind that heavy sigh?"

Faith smiled halfheartedly and took the basket of vegetables her mother carried. Silently she unloaded carrots, potatoes, and onions onto the table. Reaching for a knife, she told herself to speak up. She'd hoped to get a moment alone with her mother. Now, with the children and her father busy outside, this was her chance. And suddenly she had no idea what to say.

Inga Lind picked up the nearest potato and began to peel it. "Where's your young man and his daughter today?"

Faith dropped a carrot. "What?"

Smiling, Inga repeated, "Sarah's friend Amanda and her father? Your young man? They were invited to supper today."

"He's *not* my young man!" Faith's insides trembled, but she dutifully picked up the carrot again and began slicing it with vicious strokes. "Where on earth did you get such an idea?"

"At the church picnic."

Stifling a gasp, Faith gaped at her mother. Good Lord! The picnic! Had someone seen her and Kincaid together after all? Her heart thudded in her chest as she told herself no. No, if that were true, the whole town would have been gossiping by now. And her father would have made a call on Kincaid.

"Oh," Inga finally added slyly, "nothing was *said*. . . . But you both had that 'look' about you."

The relief shooting through Faith was almost painful. Still, she didn't dare look at her mother. Inga Lind had always noticed more about her children than they'd have liked.

Strange, she thought. She'd hoped to talk to her mother about Kincaid Hutton. Now that the subject had come up, she was doing everything she could to dismiss it. God, she was tired of having her brain in such a turmoil.

"I don't know what 'look' you're talking about, Mama," Faith said and felt a stab of guilt for the lie. "You must have been imagining things. Anyway, he's not coming today." She couldn't believe she'd forgotten that he'd been invited to Sunday supper. She hoped he'd forgotten as well.

"Well, now, that's a shame," Inga said and tossed the peeled potato into a pot. "He seems like a nice enough fellow. Widower, isn't he?"

"Yes."

"I thought I recalled Maisie saying that." Inga nodded slowly and continued talking as if to herself. "Well set up, too. I hear he's opening a hotel in town. The way folks are talking, it'll be ready to take in guests in no time at all!"

"Uh-huh . . ."

"Handsome, too, I thought." She smiled at her daughter. "Didn't you think so, dear?"

Faith swallowed and grabbed another carrot. "I suppose so."

"Nice little girl. Shame him havin' to raise her on his own." Inga tossed another potato into the pot and looked at her daughter meaningfully. "What she *needs* is a mother."

Faith dropped her knife on the tabletop and plopped down onto the nearest chair. She looked up into her mother's understanding eyes and knew the time for pretending was over. "Oh, Mama, I don't know what to do anymore."

Smiling, Inga took the chair opposite and reached for her daughter's hand. "You love him, don't you, honey?"

Faith's tear-filled gaze lifted to meet her mother's.

Staring into the soft blue eyes that had been known to spot a lie at ten feet, Faith slowly nodded. "At least I *did*. I do." Frowning, she added, "I'm so confused. I've only known him a few weeks. And you can't fall in love in such a short time. Not the lasting kind of love, I mean."

Inga's gentle laughter spilled into the room.

Surprised, Faith stared at her.

"Oh, honey," Inga said, shaking her head, "love's not on some schedule or other." She leaned forward and held both of Faith's hands in her own. "Sometimes it's slow—sneaks up on you—and sometimes . . ." She sighed and smiled. "Sometimes one look is all you need."

Frowning at her daughter's troubled expression, Inga said, "I never told you about how your papa and me met and married, did I?"

"No."

"Well, I guess it's time I did, then." Inga smiled, stood up, and walked around the table to Faith's side. "Your papa was the cousin of a friend of mine. I met him at a church social when he was visiting his family." She stared out the window, a faraway smile on her face, and Faith knew she wasn't seeing the Lind farm, but her own memories.

"That first night, after we'd danced, your papa asked me to marry him."

"What?"

"That's right." Chuckling, Inga looked down at Faith. "Oh, at first I thought he didn't have all his logs in the fire," she admitted with a grin. "But it only took him five days to convince me that I was as crazy as he was! We got married on the sixth day, and just like the Lord, we *rested*"—she winked—"on the seventh."

"Mama!" Shocked, but somehow pleased that her

mother would confide in her, Faith looked at Inga
Lind as if for the first time. And indeed, it *was* the
first time she saw her as a woman, not just her
mother.

In a blinding flash of certainty, Faith knew that her
parents, too, had shared that incredible feeling that
she and Kincaid had experienced together.

"Honey," her mother said and pulled her to her
feet, "you're all grown up now. You have to know
that sometimes what's between a man and a woman
is so strong—it just can't wait for *any* schedule!"
Wrapping her plump arms around Faith, Inga
hugged her tightly and added, "It's a darn good
thing we got married when we did, too. You came
along almost nine months to the day after that wedding!"

Her hands on Faith's shoulders, Inga stepped back
a pace and looked deeply into her daughter's eyes.
Something was troubling her, that was clear. A
woman in love shouldn't have so many shadows in
her eyes.

For a moment all Inga wanted to do was find
Kincaid Hutton and take a horsewhip to him for
hurting her daughter. But she couldn't do it.

Faith was a grown woman. She had a good head
on her shoulders and could make her own decisions.
Like any other woman, some would be good, some
bad.

Sighing gently, she lifted one hand to cup her oldest child's cheek. It had to happen this way, she
knew. Ever since Faith was a youngster, she'd felt
things deeper, stronger, than anyone else. The older
woman wished heartily that there was something she
could say to make these painful, beautiful new emotions easier to bear, but she knew there was nothing.

Faith would have to find her way on her own.

"I won't say another word after this," she finally whispered. Her gaze locked with her daughter's, she went on: "I don't know what passed between you two—and I don't *want* to know. But there's no 'sin' in loving." Faith blinked and Inga knew she'd guessed right. "Others might see these things different than I do, but I believe the only 'sin' is turning your back on love. Out of hurt, or spite, or foolish pride. You must live with your own heart, Faith. Only you can decide what your life will be." She leaned forward and kissed the girl's cheek. "Just make sure that when you ask yourself what it is you want . . . you answer that question honestly."

"Mama, I—"

"It's all right, dear." She smiled gently. "I *do* understand. Now, I'm not saying your papa would, so we'll just keep this talk to ourselves, shall we?"

Faith nodded, wrapped her arms around her mother, and hugged her tight.

A flash of movement caught Inga's eye, and she turned her head to look out the window. A slow grin curved her lips. Patting Faith's back, she said lightly, "Well! It appears your young man could make it after all!"

"What?" Faith gasped, pulling away.

"Look." Chuckling, Inga pointed at the buggy just pulling into the yard.

Faith stared, her mouth agape as Kincaid set the brake, lifted Amanda down from the buggy, then turned to shake hands with Tom Lind. As the two men started talking, panic swept through her. Good Lord, she asked herself wildly, what was Kincaid telling her father?

Without a word to her mother, Faith left the kitchen, raced through the great room, and ran out the front door. When it slammed behind her, the two men in the yard turned to look at her.

Her heart pounding in her chest, she stepped off the front porch and walked to join the two men she loved best in the world.

"Faith honey," her father called out. "I was just telling your young man here how pleased we are that he could come to supper."

Kincaid grinned. His features were so stiff it was a wonder he could breathe.

She stepped up to her father's side, and when the big man's heavy arm dropped around her shoulders, she shot Kincaid a glare that *dared* him to say anything.

"I was telling your father about Amanda's fever and how we didn't know if she'd be well enough to come today," he said, knowing she wouldn't contradict him in front of her parents.

"Feeling better, is she?" Faith ground out, her eyes still spitting at him.

"Oh, yes." Kincaid forced a laugh and looked up at Tom Lind. "She wouldn't let a little thing like a fever keep her from picking out her new puppy!"

Tom cast a quick glance over his shoulder at the barn. "Speaking of puppies, I think I'll go look in on those two girls. See how Amanda's selection's coming along." He gave his oldest daughter a squeeze, then released her. "When you two have finished your hellos, Faith, you send him on in to me." Glancing up at Kincaid, he added with a wink, "I hear you've got a hotel about to open up. And I'm just the man to supply your kitchen with all the vegetables and eggs you're going to need."

"Sounds good," Kincaid said, his eyes never leaving Faith.

Tom snorted good-naturedly. "Like I said, when

you're ready to talk, you just come on out to the barn."

The moment Tom Lind stepped into the shadowy barn, Faith turned on Kincaid.

"What are you doing here?" she snapped, her voice low, furious.

He sucked in a deep gulp of air. He'd known this wouldn't be easy. "We were invited to supper."

"Papa! Papa!" Amanda's excited shout from inside the barn floated out to them. "Come see the puppies!"

Some of the anger left Faith's face, and her shoulders drooped a bit.

Smiling, Kincaid said quietly, "How could I *not* bring her? All she's talked about is the puppy your sister is giving her."

Faith's gaze flicked toward the barn and back to him again. She wasn't holding herself quite as rigidly, but her voice when she spoke held no welcome.

"I don't want you here."

"Your mother and father do."

Afternoon sunshine glittered in her hair. A soft wind lifted tendrils of her hair around her face, and when she reached up to smooth them back, it was all Kincaid could do to keep from grabbing her hand.

He waited what seemed an eternity before she raised her gaze to his again. When she did, he saw that the fire and anger were gone, replaced by a sad resignation.

Damn, he asked himself, how had he managed to wreck everything between them? And how could he get it back again?

"All right, Kincaid," she said softly. "You're here now. You might as well stay." A reluctant smile curved her lips when she heard Amanda break into loud giggles. "Amanda deserves her puppy. And I don't want to hurt her, anyway."

"Faith—" he started and moved to hold her.

"Don't." Faith stepped back and dipped her head. "I can't stand much more of this, Kincaid." He heard her voice tremble and cursed himself for a bastard. "Just . . . have supper with my family, then"—she looked up at him through watery eyes—"*please* leave me alone."

He watched her lift the hem of her skirt and dash for the huge, three-storied farmhouse. His fingers curled around the edge of the buggy seat as he stared at the closed front door.

Maybe this was a bad idea, he told himself angrily. Maybe he should give her the time alone that she keeps claiming she needs. His grip on the hot metal rail tightened. No. No, he couldn't risk that. He *had* to be around her. Force her to look at him. Listen to him.

She still loved him, he could *feel* it. If she didn't, his presence wouldn't bother her a bit.

"Papa!" Amanda called again, and he glanced over his shoulder toward the barn, then back to the farmhouse again.

He could hardly understand what was going on himself. Ever since he'd asked her to marry him, though, he hadn't been able to stop thinking about her.

A thoughtful smile softened his features. It was amazing, he realized. It was as though the minute the words had left his mouth, he'd known it was the right thing to do. Known it was the *only* thing he wanted to do.

Oh, he snorted derisively, he'd said it badly, he *knew* that. But then, he hadn't *planned* on saying it at all! But somehow, Faith Lind had crept past all the barriers he'd erected around his heart.

Without even trying, she'd taught him what *real* love was, and he didn't intend to lose it now.

The only problem still facing him now was getting Faith to *talk* to him!

CHAPTER

NINETEEN

A QUARTER moon was just climbing over the tree-tops when they left the Lind farm for the ride back to Harmony. Faith's horse tied to the rear of the buggy, she and Kincaid sat side by side on the bench seat. Snuggled between them, leaning into Faith's side, Amanda slept, cuddling her new puppy.

"She had a full day," Kincaid said softly.

"Yes," Faith answered, smoothing back the little girl's hair from her forehead. "It was good of you to let her have the puppy."

He shrugged and glanced at her. "Every child should have a puppy of his own. Just as every child should have a mother."

"Kincaid . . ."

"I enjoyed talking to your father, Faith," he tossed in quickly.

She cocked her head and looked at him curiously. He and her father had been thicker than hair on a dog all day. In fact, Faith admitted silently, Kincaid had gotten along very well with her entire family.

Between flattering Inga, playing with the kids, and talking fishing with Tom Lind, Kincaid Hutton had succeeded in charming *all* of them. But somehow, Faith knew which conversation with her father Kincaid was talking about now. She'd noticed the two of them together just after supper. And she knew the sly looks her father had given her as he'd kissed her goodbye had *something* to do with that whispered chat.

"What were you two talking about anyway?"

His fingers tightened on the reins, and he flashed her a quick glance. "I told him I loved his daughter."

"What?"

Amanda stirred restlessly against her, and Faith lowered her voice a bit. "You *lied* to my father?"

"No," he said patiently. "It wasn't a lie."

Faith sighed, pulled Amanda closer, and looked out into the dark countryside.

Kincaid's voice came again, lower, rushed, as if he was hurrying to tell her all he had to say before she could stop him. "Before—when I blundered that proposal . . . Look, I *know* I did that badly."

She stiffened at the mention of that humiliating scene.

"But, Faith, I *do* love you. I know it's taken me forever to realize that. And I'm sorrier than you know that I was such an ass!"

Faith bit down on her bottom lip to still its trembling. She'd wanted to hear all this from him, true. But how could she believe it now that he was finally saying it? He'd told her already of the sense of guilt and responsibility he'd felt for Mary Alice. Why should she believe he felt any different about her? Besides, he was probably only saying all this because he was afraid she might be pregnant. She took a deep breath and lifted her chin slightly. At least, Faith told herself, she could take *that* worry away.

"Kincaid, you don't have to be so concerned. I, uh"—she dipped her head a bit—"found out this morning. I'm not going to have a baby." Inhaling sharply, she looked at him from the corner of her eye.

"So you see, there's no reason for you to have to marry me!"

As quietly as possible, Kincaid drew the horse to a stop. Wrapping the reins around the buggy's brake handle, he turned toward her.

"Would you like to try again?"

"What?" She stared at him, but in the darkness it was hard to see his features clearly.

"I said, would you like to try for a baby again? Marry me, Faith. I *do* love you."

As he leaned closer, Faith felt his breath warm on her face. His deep voice filled her ears. Amanda shifted position again, moving into Faith's warmth. Instinctively she wrapped her arm around the little girl and pulled her closer.

"Amanda loves you, too," he said softly, then took her face between his hands and touched his lips to hers tenderly.

Faith's heart pounded in her chest. Was it true? Did she dare to believe him? She felt as though she couldn't breathe. His touch, his voice, the loving things she'd longed to hear from him. She loved him so much, did she really want to send him away?

"Marry me, Faith. Please."

Her throat tight, she tried desperately to think rationally. But with his fingers smoothing over her cheeks it was impossible.

Then Faith remembered her mother's advice: Ask yourself what it is you want, and be honest about the answer. Well, she wanted Kincaid. And Amanda, too. She always had. But to have them and the life she wanted, she had to take a chance. She might never know for sure if guilt or pity had prompted Kincaid's proposal.

But what was it Inga Lind had said? That it was a sin to turn your back on love for spite or pride?

She looked into Kincaid's eyes and made her decision. She loved him. So she had to believe that at least in some small corner of his heart, he loved her, too.

"All right, Kincaid," Faith finally said in a whisper. "I'll marry you."

His breath left him in a rush, and when he pulled her into his arms, Faith tried to dismiss the last lingering doubt niggling at her brain.

"Ow!" Amanda cried out at the same time her puppy squealed a protest. She shoved at her father's chest. "You're smashing me, Papa."

Faith heard him laugh and smiled herself at Amanda's indignant voice.

"I'm sorry, sweetheart. I was hugging Faith."

"You were?" The little girl's voice was hushed.

"Yes, I was." Kincaid bent low and kissed the top of his daughter's head.

"Why?"

"Because, Amanda."

Faith heard the pleased tone of his voice and smiled again.

"Faith has just said that she'd marry me."

Amanda gasped. Turning in Faith's arms, she looked up at her and asked, "Does that mean you're going to be my mama now?"

"If you want me to," came the answer.

"Oh, yes!" the little girl crowed. "Will that mean that Sarah's my sister now, too?"

Faith laughed and hugged the child tightly. "I think that would be fine, honey."

"Did you hear that, Boom?" Amanda asked her puppy.

"Boom?" her father asked hesitantly.

"Uh-huh. He's my friend, too. Just like Boom was before."

Kincaid groaned softly, and Faith chuckled, but Amanda went on talking to her puppy. "I get a new mama and a sister. But I don't want Gary to be my brother. He pulls my hair."

"Well," her father said, laughing, "why don't your mama and I see what we can do about getting you a *new* brother?" He picked up the reins, snapped them over the horse's back, and started the buggy for town again.

Over Amanda's happy chattering and the pounding of the horses' hooves, Faith tried to calm her racing mind. She'd done the right thing. She was sure of it.

He *did* love her.

She *had* to believe that.

"A weddin'!" Maisie chortled delightedly for the fiftieth time that afternoon. "It's so excitin'. But why in the devil can't you wait a while? Why's it have to be next Sunday?"

Faith shrugged, felt a dozen pins poke into her flesh, and stood completely still again. "Kincaid says he doesn't want to wait." She looked down at Maisie. "And I guess I don't, either."

"Well," Minnie said as she entered the front parlor, "all I can say is, four days don't give us much time to do things proper. And your poor mother, Faith!" She clucked her tongue sympathetically. "What with you havin' to stay in town all week because of teachin', Inga's hardly gettin' a sayso in this wedding."

"I know, Minnie. But it couldn't be helped." Faith sighed and shifted position. It felt as though she'd been standing on that stool for days. But Maisie had insisted that *she* be the one to make her wedding dress. Even though one of the best seamstresses in the state lived directly across the street.

But to the older woman it was more than just sewing a dress, Faith knew. It was her way of welcoming Faith into the family. Glancing down at the pale blue gown, she silently acknowledged that it was beautiful material, and to give Maisie her due, she was doing a lovely job.

"Now, Sister"—Maisie moved a cluster of pins to one side of her mouth so she could talk—"Inga and Zan are doin' all the food for the to-do, so don't you worry about Inga's feelings in all this. That woman can cook like nobody's business. And if I know her, we'll have enough food for *two* weddin's."

"True." Minnie sighed and lifted a teacup to her lips. Before she took a drink, though, she said, "Aren't you tired, Sister? Why don't you stop for a bit and have some of this nice tea?"

Faith shot Minnie a grateful look. Though her wedding dress was lovely, standing still for hours to have it fitted was very tiring.

Maisie sat back on her heels and looked up at Faith. Smiling around the pins between her lips, she nodded, satisfied. "This is comin' along fine. And thank you, Sister," she finally said. "I believe I'll do just that."

Faith stepped down off the stool and reached around to the pin at the back of her collar.

"Don't you take that off, missy!" Maisie warned as she shoved herself to her feet. "We ain't finished by a long shot, yet."

Faith's shoulders slumped tiredly.

"Now, don't give me that long face, neither. You can go on and give yourself a little rest, but don't you take that dress off, y'hear? Soon's I finish my tea, we'll get back at it."

"But, Maisie—"

"You want a wedding in one week, you got to put up with a little trial and tribulation, Faith." Maisie took the last pins from between her lips, walked over to her chair by the hearth, and dropped down into it. She groaned quietly and reached for the teacup Minnie held out to her. "Now, you go on outside. Get some fresh air into ya. That'll wake ya up some."

As Faith started for the door, Maisie called out, "I'll call ya as soon as I'm ready to go again, dear."

Faith wandered down the hall to the back door. She just wanted to get away by herself for a minute or two.

Ever since she and Kincaid had broken the news about their upcoming wedding, she hadn't had a moment alone. She was either teaching school, talking to Kincaid and Amanda, or listening to more plans about the wedding.

Smiling, she went through the kitchen, opened the back door, and stepped outside. She couldn't even go out onto Main Street. If she did, she knew that she'd be quickly surrounded by Samantha, Lillie Taylor, Rachel Johnson, and anyone else nearby.

Trailing her fingers over the porch railing, she glanced at the closed workshop. Kincaid wasn't there, she knew. He'd been spending every waking moment over at the site of the new hotel. Except for the time he spent with her.

Faith sighed and stepped off the porch into the late afternoon sunshine. She didn't regret agreeing to marry him. It was right. She knew it. Everything in her told her that was true. It was only that . . . oh, she shook her head and told herself that she was being ridiculous. If she spent the rest of her life doubting Kincaid's feelings for her, what kind of marriage would they have?

She had to trust him. She had to *believe* him.

Suddenly her brain dredged up the memory of the night before. When they'd sat before the fire in the front parlor until all hours of the night, talking, laughing, kissing. If she closed her eyes, she could still feel his lips on hers. Still feel his warm breath tickling the back of her neck.

In his arms her doubts fled. While he held her, she felt secure in his love. If only that belief was with her always.

She shook her head abruptly, clearing her mind of memories. She *would* believe. And she, Kincaid, and Amanda would be happy.

A flutter of excitement curled in the pit of her stomach as she realized that in less than a week she'd be Mrs. Kincaid Hutton. How strange, she thought idly, to no longer be "one of the Lind girls." Her lips curved slightly as she pictured her own children, years from now, hearing themselves described as "the Hutton kids." Or "one of Faith's brood."

Carefully lifting the pinned-up hem of her new dress, Faith walked past the workroom and the newspaper office, headed for the churchyard. Once out of the shadows of the buildings, she looked to her right and saw Kincaid, high up in the almost finished framework of the new hotel.

Her heartbeat staggered, and she pulled in a deep breath of the hot, late April air. He waved one arm at her, and she knew without seeing his face that he was grinning. He'd been doing a lot of that since she'd accepted him. It was only one of the reasons, she told herself, that she should believe in his love.

She'd tried to watch him carefully for signs of guilt or resignation ... but there weren't any. And when he kissed her, Faith *knew* deep in her soul that he couldn't be pretending that much tenderness. Smiling to herself, she put her head down again and continued on. As she neared the front of the church, she heard voices from inside.

Stopping, she cocked her head to listen. Lillie Taylor and Rachel Johnson. From the sound of it, Faith guessed that they were having a difference of opinion as to the decorating of the church for the wedding. Gathering up her dress, Faith quickly sidestepped to the side of the church.

Obviously, she thought, she wouldn't be finding any peace in there! Instead, she slipped around to the back of the building and leaned carefully against the plank wall. Staring out at the surrounding prairie, she took several deep breaths and enjoyed the relative quiet. Though the voices from the church and the hammers from the men working on the hotel were distracting . . . at least no one was talking to *her*.

Kincaid watched her until she disappeared behind the side of the church. His grin still in place, he turned back to the pine plank he'd been working on. With a few strokes of his hammer he pounded another nail into the nearly complete wall and reached for the next one.

He couldn't remember *ever* being this happy. He only wished he was as sure of Faith's feelings. Oh, he knew she loved him. It wasn't that. But sometimes he felt as though she still didn't believe that he loved *her*. Frowning, he swung his hammer back and brought it down hard on the nail head. It slipped off, smashing his thumb.

"Dammit!" he shouted and shook his hand violently.

"Uh-huh," a voice called out from the stairs.

He turned and watched Travis Miller carry up another load of wall planks.

"Just as I always thought," the sheriff said with a smirk. "Wedding bells ring and a man loses all sense."

Holding on to his still-throbbing thumb, Kincaid smiled. "Did you come to work today, Travis? Or just to hear yourself talk?"

The sheriff lifted both hands in mock surrender. "I promised you two or three hours of hammer and nail time . . . and I'm here to deliver."

"Then get started, huh?"

"Yessir, boss." Travis grinned, carried the planks to the far side of the room, and set to work.

Kincaid pushed his worries about Faith aside. Everything would be all right. After all, he had the rest of their lives to convince her how much he loved her.

A flash of movement caught the corner of her eye, and Faith turned and looked over her left shoulder. She smiled and shook her head. Amanda and that puppy.

The two of them were racing across the open ground toward the schoolhouse. Amanda's delighted squeals were accented by the high-pitched barks of the tiny brown-and-white dog.

Faith watched as the little girl and her dog ran up the steps and disappeared inside the building. Frowning slightly, Faith told herself she should go and tell Amanda not to play in the schoolhouse. But surely it wouldn't do any harm, she thought, and she didn't really want to start off their new relationship by being a bossy stepmother.

Instead, she decided to keep her eye on the school. And if the girl and her puppy didn't leave soon, *then* she'd go over there and chase them out. Mother. A smile touched her lips as Faith remembered all the

times in the last couple of days that Amanda had
taken the opportunity to call her "Mama."

She'd even begun lording it over Gary and Ben just
a bit at school. After all, they were just the teacher's
brothers. *Amanda* would be the teacher's *daughter*.
Smiling softly, Faith leaned against the church and
watched the schoolhouse. She couldn't imagine why
Amanda had gone in there in the first place.

"C'mon, Boom," Amanda called and walked directly to her seat. "I left my present for Papa and
Mama in my desk," she said, more to herself than the
puppy. Glancing back at the little dog, happily sniffing his way around the empty schoolroom, she told
him, "I want to give it to 'em tonight after supper.
You don't think I have to wait till the wedding, do
ya?"

The puppy looked up at her, cocked his head, then
bent back to his sniffing.

Amanda laughed and dug through her papers
again. After a long moment, though, she slammed
down the lid of her desk, disgusted. "I can't find it,
Boom. I can't find it anywhere." One finger in her
mouth, she said thoughtfully, "I drew the picture,
and then I took it over by the light so I could see it
good." Her face lit up. "That's right. 'Cause when I
was lookin' at it, Sarah called me outside, and I just
put it down there next to the lamp."

Boom barked and wagged his tail.

Amanda walked to the sideboard where the day's
papers were stacked beside the now dark lamp. In
the indistinct light of late afternoon, the little girl
frowned and squinted at the pile of papers.

"It's awful dark in here, Boom," she mumbled and
glanced at the kerosene lamp. "If I had a light, I

could see a lot better and find my present even quicker."

The little dog barked and jumped sideways excitedly.

Smiling to herself, Amanda hurried to the teacher's desk, pulled open the top drawer, and took the box of wooden matches that Faith kept handy. At the sideboard she carefully lifted the glass chimney off its base, turned up the wick, and struck a match.

When the wavering light was burning, Amanda blew out the match and replaced the chimney.

"That's better, huh, Boom?"

The lamp sat on the corner of the stack of papers on the narrow bench top. Looking at the stack of schoolwork, the little girl realized that her drawing was probably on the bottom.

"I bet Faith—I mean Mama—didn't see it, either, Boom. I bet she just put down all her papers on top of it and never even saw it. Don't you? I bet it'll still be a surprise."

Boom barked again, jumped at Amanda's shoe, and started gnawing on the toe.

"Stop that, bad boy!" Amanda held on to the sideboard and gently shook her foot, trying to ease her puppy away. But Boom wouldn't be stopped. He leapt back at her shoe as if it were another puppy, wanting to play. Digging his tiny, sharp teeth into the leather, he growled ferociously.

"Durn you, Boom," Amanda said, her fingers sliding the stack of papers toward the edge. "Papa won't like it if you make a hole in my shoe!" Deliberately she gave him one last, good shove. The puppy scuttled back, she lost her balance, and started to fall.

Grasping for a handhold, her little fingers curled around the papers and tugged. The stack shifted, the kerosene lamp wobbled unsteadily for a long moment, then flipped over and crashed onto the wooden floor. In a heartbeat burning liquid raced across the bare planks, drawing a bright orange line of destruction.

Amanda stared at the quickly spreading flames and screamed.

A distant, muffled crash sounded out, and Faith frowned, trying to identify it. Then Amanda screamed.

Heart pounding, throat dry, Faith started running. Her long skirts tripped her up, but she jumped to her feet again quickly. Holding the dirty wedding gown high over her knees, she ran on toward the schoolhouse, aware now of Amanda's crying and the frantic yelping from the puppy.

It seemed to take forever to cover the few hundred feet of open ground. And as she got closer to the school, Faith heard something that chilled her to her soul.

The angry crackle and hiss of fast-moving flames.

The school was on fire.

With Amanda inside.

CHAPTER

TWENTY

HER HEART in her throat, Faith's feet felt as though they were made of lead. Her breath came in strangled gasps as she ran up the school steps, through the open door, and into a smoke-filled nightmare. As she came around the edge of the cloakroom wall, she hesitated for a heartbeat.

Thick black smoke hung from the ceiling like heavy storm clouds. Along the front wall and halfway down the side of the building, flames licked at the old dry wood hungrily. Blinking away the sting of smoke from her eyes, Faith looked frantically around the room.

Amanda let loose another piercing scream, and blindly Faith started for her. Tossing and shoving the neat rows of desks into a jumbled pile behind her, she took the fastest route possible to the terrified little girl.

"Amanda!" Faith yelled over the roar of the growing fire.

The little girl spun around, saw Faith, and ran into her waiting arms. Her chest tight, eyes streaming, Faith turned back toward the front of the building. She bent low, desperately trying to keep clear of the billowing smoke. With Amanda clutched to her chest, she dashed for the cloakroom wall and the door just beyond.

Outside the burning room, Faith heard the child's gasping and coughing and gave silent thanks for it. As she ran down the steps, she half expected the entire town to be on the run to help. But no one was there.

A quick glance behind her told her why. From the outside, the flames were still invisible. As she sucked in great gulps of cool air, she desperately tried to think what to do. In a few minutes she knew the entire schoolhouse would be an inferno, and if they didn't contain the fire, it could easily spread to the dry prairie grass and the town beyond.

Of course, she screamed inwardly as she suddenly remembered *exactly* what to do! The church bell— rung only on Sundays—and in emergencies.

But first, she had to assure herself of Amanda's safety. Peeling the child's arms from around her neck, Faith ran her hands over the girl's body surely, quickly, checking for injuries. Thankfully, she seemed unhurt except for the blind terror still causing her small body to tremble violently.

"Boom!" Amanda screamed suddenly and made a wild dash for the schoolhouse.

Faith grabbed her before she could take more than a few steps. "What are you doing?" she cried, holding tightly to the child.

"Mama! Boom's in there! I have to get him! He'll die!" Eyes wide with fright, Amanda stared up at Faith and screamed, "He can't die! I won't let him!"

Faith held her and looked at the open school door. Frantically she tried to remember the strength of the fire. It was mostly along the front wall, she knew. She told herself it would be foolish and dangerous to go back inside, but then she looked down at the little girl watching her trustingly.

Amanda had been through enough in her short

life. If there was a way to save her more pain, Faith would try.

"Where is Boom?" she demanded.

The little girl stared at her blankly as if she hadn't even heard the question.

"Amanda!" Faith shouted and gave the child a quick shake. "Where is Boom?"

"By your desk."

Nodding, she pushed Amanda back another step or two and shouted, "Go for help! Get your papa at the hotel!" When she didn't move, Faith yelled, "Run! Tell him to ring the bell!"

When the girl took off, Faith lifted the hem of her dress to cover her nose and mouth and ran back up the steps. Back to the fire.

The smoke seemed thicker. She squeezed her eyes into narrow slits and held her dress tighter over her nose. She'd never known before just how loud a fire was. The roaring and crackling filled the air with noise as dense as the smoke.

And as the gray, swirling clouds moved and danced along the walls and ceiling, Faith caught quick glimpses of the flames crawling over the wood.

Coughing, eyes streaming, she took a step and slammed into one of the children's desks. The pain in her shin seemed almost a comforting triviality as she stumbled blindly toward what she hoped was the front of the room.

Keeping low, Faith strained to hear the puppy's bark or whine. Anything to tell her she was near her goal. The heat gathered around her, pushing at her, taunting her for coming back to challenge the flames.

A splintering crack sounded nearby, and she looked to see the windowpanes shatter with the pressure of the fire. As the outside air slipped in through the cracked glass, the flames seemed to take a deep breath. In a blinding flash the line of fire raced up the walls with new energy, feeding on the air, and growing hungrier by the second.

Faith stumbled back, her bleary eyes on the wavering orange and yellow light as it crept ever nearer. Her foot came down on something soft, and the "yelp" she heard was the sweetest sound she could remember. Dropping to her knees, Faith swung her hands about the floor until she found the quivering puppy and picked him up.

Holding Boom tight, she stood to make a run for the front door. But the smoke was everywhere. Swirling, dipping, it blurred the walls, concealed the windows. Thicker and darker, it moved over everything, disguising it, hiding it, until Faith realized that she didn't know which way to go.

She was trapped in a blinding world of darkness where the only light meant death.

"Now, what d'you suppose *that's* all about?" Travis grinned and pointed out the second-story window toward the schoolhouse.

"Huh? What?" Kincaid walked over to join him and was in time to see Faith race up the steps and inside.

"You figure she got smart and she's tryin' to run away from the weddin'?"

Kincaid smirked at his friend. "Real funny, Travis." Turning his gaze back to the one-room building, he watched Faith come back outside, carrying Amanda. He straightened up quickly and was aware when his heart began to pound.

Was Amanda sick? Hurt? Dammit, he was too far way to see a damn thing. Turning on his heel, he started for the stairs, but the tone of Travis's voice called him back.

"Oh, Lordy . . ."

His fingers curled around the windowframe, Kincaid saw Faith give Amanda a shove toward the hotel and then dart back into the school. But it was the telltale curl of smoke lifting off the shingled roof of the bright yellow building that shot him into action.

His blood roaring in his ears, Kincaid took the steps two at a time in his race downstairs. Behind him, he heard Travis shout, "I'll ring the church bell for help!" and the man's running footsteps. But Kincaid wasn't waiting for help. He couldn't wait another moment. Faith was in that building.

And it was burning.

Jake Sutherland stood outside his livery stable, taking a momentary break from the fiery heat of his forge. Wiping his brow with his forearm, he looked off toward the end of the street to see Kincaid Hutton running like a madman.

Right behind him, Travis was sprinting for the church. Trouble. The big blacksmith didn't wait to hear the first peal of the church bell. He dropped his massive hammer into the dirt and started running after Kincaid.

James Taylor poured another scoop of flour into the scale and studied the dial carefully. Two pounds exactly, he told himself. But then, after twenty years, he *should* know how to measure out the right amount on the first try.

He lifted the metal measuring bowl and tipped the funnel end into a brown paper bag. As the flour slid into the sack, a flash of movement caught his eye. He looked up quickly and watched Jake Sutherland, still

in his heavy, black leather apron, running down the
street like the devil himself was chasing him.

A thread of uneasiness crawled through James,
and when he heard the church bell peal out its
"Disaster—Come Running" chimes, he was already
out the front door.

Jane Carson looked up at the peal of the clanging
church bell. Her forehead creased in lines of worry,
she dropped the pale green satin fabric onto the floor,
jumped to her feet, and ran out onto Main Street.

Zeke Gallagher threw open his barbershop door
and thundered out onto the porch. Swinging his
head first one way, then the other, he finally spotted
Travis Miller leaping off the church steps and running for the school. Without pausing to pull a shirt
on over his long johns, Zeke ran off after him.

When Alexander and Samantha Evans hurried out
of the newspaper office, they were almost run down
by the anxious citizens of Harmony. Every last soul
in town was answering the distress summons.

Cord Spencer and Charlie Thompson ran past
them without a backward glance. The girls from the
First Resort weren't far behind them, and they were
followed closely by Luscious Lottie herself. Dressed
only in her chemise and bloomers, the madam's
bright red silk wrapper flapped and fluttered behind
her like a giant set of wings.

Reverend Johnson and Rachel, with Lillie Taylor a
step behind, flew out of the church.

Maisie and Minnie slammed out the back door of
the boardinghouse, screaming like banshees.

*   *   *

Kincaid caught up to Amanda before she'd taken more than a few steps. One quick glance at the girl told him she was more frightened than hurt, so he didn't waste time he didn't have.

"Stay here, Amanda." He flicked a look over his shoulder and saw the whole town on the run. "Stay with Maisie and Minnie."

He ran past his daughter then, his gaze locked on the now obviously burning schoolhouse. Flames had licked through the ceiling and were beginning to consume the roof. In only a matter of minutes the fire would completely engulf the building.

He had to get Faith out of there.

"Sweet Jesus!" Maisie gasped.

Kincaid spun around, looking out over the crowd. Already, the people were forming a bucket line to carry water to the fire in the hopes of beating it before it spread.

Wildly his eyes moved over the scene. Finally, after what seemed hours, his gaze lit on a coil of rope near the boardinghouse workshop. Racing for it, he snatched it up, tied one end of the rope around his waist, and handed the other end to Jake Sutherland.

"What the hell you doin', Hutton?"

"I'm goin' in there. It'll probably be too smoky for me to find my way out, so you hold on to this rope good and tight," he warned.

"Are you crazy?" James Taylor shouted, still unaware that Faith was inside the building. "Nothin' in there worth dyin' for."

Then they heard it. A scream of pure terror, rising to an unbelievable pitch before fading away into silence.

Kincaid clenched his jaw. "Faith's in there."

He took a step, but someone pulled him back.

"You heard that. What if she's already dead? What will it serve, you dyin', too?"

Kincaid didn't even bother to look. He didn't want to *know* which of his friends and neighbors had suggested that Faith might be dead. Jerking his arm free, he ran for the steps and entered the building.

When he stepped around the cloakroom wall into yet another wall of waving black smoke, Kincaid was grateful he'd taken that extra moment to tie himself to a rope. Without it, he wouldn't have had a chance in hell of finding his way back out again.

Silently, frantically, he whispered a short, heartfelt prayer that he would find her in time.

The fire was all around him. Heat pressed down on him and his chest burned with the effort to breathe. Coughing and gasping, he tried desperately to see through the swirling clouds, straining to see just a hint of Faith's hair—a flash of color from her dress.

Dear God, he whispered again brokenly. Help me.

"Faith!" Smoke reached into his throat with his shout, and he gagged before calling her name out again, louder this time. "FAITH!"

A moment that lasted years passed. And in that tiny eternity Kincaid saw the long years ahead stretch out in all their lonely splendor. His heart breaking, he blinked back the tears in his eyes. No. He wouldn't lose her. Not now. Not after he'd finally found her.

Forcing himself to take a gulp of the hot, smoky air, he called to her again, *willing* her to be alive. To hear him.

When her unsteady voice answered, "Kincaid! Kincaid! Over here!" he felt his heart start beating again.

Crashing through the cluttered chaos of the room,

Kincaid moved through the smoke like a man possessed. His eyes watering, his breathing labored, he finally saw her, huddled into a ball on the floor near the far wall.

With prayers of gratitude echoing in his heart, he bent down and scooped her into his arms. She curled into him, keeping her arms tight against her body, the hem of her dress over her face.

He yanked at the rope, dipped his head, and hurriedly retraced his steps with his body curved over hers protectively. He felt a few, tiny sparks of fire fall onto his broad back, but he ignored them. And as he moved toward escape, his friends outside took up the slack in the rope, guiding him to safety.

He held her tightly, even after they were clear of the building. Shouts of relief and happiness fell around him, but he was deaf to them all. Instead, his ears strained, he listened to the strangled breathing from the woman in his arms.

He ran past everyone, only vaguely noticing Harmony's citizens diligently passing buckets of water to be tossed on the burning building. Intent only on getting Faith safely away from the flames, he hurried toward the boardinghouse.

With every gasp of breath Faith took, Kincaid felt his own body shudder. His whispered thanks continued as he realized how close he'd come to losing everything that mattered in his life.

His daughter. The woman he loved. A quiet groan ripped through him, accompanying one last prayer of thanksgiving.

"Papa!" Amanda yelled as he ran past her. "Papa, is Mama all right?"

Maisie grabbed the little girl when she would have followed her father. "Hush now, Amanda. I'm sure

Faith will be fine. Let your papa talk to her first, though, all right, sweetheart?"

Amanda's lower lip trembled and her big green eyes filled with tears. "She went into the fire to get Boom, Maisie. To get Boom for me. And she almost couldn't get back out again. And Boom died anyway."

"But she did come back, darlin'. Your papa got her out for us." Maisie wrapped her arms around the little girl. "No sense cryin' now. I'm sure sorry about Boom, sweetheart. Hush, hush . . . The older woman began to sway from side to side, rocking the little girl in comfort. While her hands patted and soothed the child, Maisie watched the burning schoolhouse roof crash down through the charred walls.

He couldn't bring himself to put her down yet. Sitting at the boardinghouse kitchen table, Kincaid held Faith on his lap, and in between breaths he again thanked God and everyone else who'd returned her to him.

"Faith?" he whispered, his hands moving over her as if he still couldn't believe that she was alive and in his arms. "Faith, are you hurt?"

He held a glass of water to her lips and waited while she sipped at it. Her face was smudged and sooty, the ends of her hair were singed, and her blue wedding dress was ripped, torn, and stained. Kincaid smiled, rested his chin on top of her head, and drew in a long shaky breath. He knew she would never look more beautiful to him than she did at that moment.

A tiny sneeze, a weak yelp, and insistent sniffling caught his attention, though, and he pulled back to stare down at Faith's lap. Astonished, Kincaid saw

Amanda's puppy wobbling unsteadily across Faith's thighs before bracing his front paws on her breasts.

When Boom barked and sneezed again, Faith grinned and looked up at Kincaid. "We have to tell Amanda," she said hoarsely and rubbed at her throat.

"Tell Amanda . . ." Kincaid echoed.

Faith nodded and took another sip of water. "Tell her that I found Boom for her."

"That's why you went back inside the school?" he ground out. "For a dog?"

"For Amanda's puppy." Faith nodded. She watched as his features hardened. His arms tightened around her until they felt like bands of iron.

"Do you realize you nearly *died*?"

"Yes," she answered and reached up to cup his cheek. "But I didn't. Because of you."

He flinched visibly, and his eyelids squeezed shut. Turning his face into her hand, he kissed the palm and said brokenly, "I could have lost you. Forever. Because of a puppy?"

Faith stared up at him. When his eyes opened again, she saw his unshed tears, and her breath caught in her throat.

For a moment she let herself remember the terror of the fire. The helplessness that gripped her. Until he came. Through the fire and the smoke, he'd found her and carried her to safety. Over her own labored breathing, she'd heard every one of his frantic prayers and knew that she would never doubt his love for her again.

Smoothing her palm over his cheek, she whispered gently, "You'll *never* lose me, Kincaid, never."

He covered her hand with one of his own and nodded slowly. Then, with infinite care, he bent low and grazed her lips with his own. When he pulled back, he let his gaze move lingeringly over her features before he bent once more and kissed her sooty forehead. "I love you, Faith. More than I ever thought possible."

"I love you, too." She smiled up at him and snuggled closer.

"And if you *ever* do anything that *stupid* again," he growled, "I'll . . ."

She reached up and pulled his face down to hers. Just before she kissed him, Faith whispered, "Lock me in my room?"

"Good idea," he admitted. "And I'll stay in there with you. To keep an eye on you."

"Mmmm . . . an even *better* idea," Faith agreed and smiled as his lips came down over hers.

"Papa?"

Kincaid groaned and straightened up. Looking at the door, he watched Amanda hesitantly enter the room.

"Papa?" his daughter said again, her eyes on the floor. "Is Mama all right? Did you tell her I'm sorry? I didn't mean to knock the lamp over. Honest I didn't. I was so scared, Papa. I didn't want her to get hurt!"

"Amanda . . ." Faith spoke up quietly, her voice still hoarse. "Come here, honey. I'm all right, really."

Head down, the little girl took a few shuffling steps before she heard Boom's tiny bark. Her head jerked up, and she looked at the dog in Faith's lap with astonished delight.

"Boom!" she yelled and ran the last few feet separating them.

The little dog jumped into Amanda's arms and licked her face enthusiastically.

"Mama, you *saved* him!" She giggled helplessly, then said, "Oh, thank you, Mama." Amanda reached for Faith's neck and hugged her tightly. "I love you." Laughing again as her puppy began barking excitedly, she added, "Don't feel bad, Boom. I love you, too."

Kincaid wrapped his arms around Faith and smiled. She leaned her head against his chest and listened to the steady beating of his heart as they watched their daughter.

Together.

"I now pronounce you man and wife," Reverend Johnson said and slapped his Bible shut. "Kincaid, you may kiss your bride."

Kincaid looked at the preacher and grinned. Then, cupping Faith's face tenderly, he bent down to give her a gentle kiss.

But his new wife pulled him close, wrapped her arms around his neck, and kissed him hungrily. Several long moments passed before Maisie called out, "Come up for air, you two! We got a party to get to!"

A burst of laughter shattered the quiet, and Kincaid and Faith broke apart to lead their guests out to the yard and the waiting reception.

Strolling through the crowd, the bride and groom heard snatches of conversations.

"Hell, we been needin' a new school for years."

"A school raising's just the thing to get it done, too."

Maisie's voice stood out over the others. "I say we raise some money by challenging River City to a spelling bee!"

"With *you* as captain, I'll wager!" Minnie yelled.

"Seems only fair," her sister shot back. "We oughta ask Faith . . ."

Kincaid grabbed his new bride's hand and raced around the edge of the building.

Laughing, Faith told him, "It's no good, y'know. They'll find us."

"Oh, no, they won't," he whispered and pulled her close. "We're goin' on a wedding trip."

"Wedding trip?" Faith pulled back and looked at him, surprise in her eyes. "To where? What about Amanda?"

"Amanda's staying with your folks." He grinned and kissed the tip of her nose. "It's all arranged."

"Kincaid . . . what are you up to?" She cocked her head and looked at him warily.

"Do you trust me, Mrs. Hutton?"

She sighed and smiled. "Absolutely, Mr. Hutton."

"Good. The buggy's loaded. We're ready to go."

"But go where?"

He ran one hand down her waist and over the curve of her hip. "I have reservations at a certain abandoned hotel near Ellsworth."

"What?" She gave him a slow grin as she began to understand.

"I've arranged everything with the owner. The place is ours for three whole days."

"And nights," Faith tossed in.

"And definitely nights," Kincaid agreed.

"What are we waiting for?"

Kincaid grinned, grabbed her hand again, and raced around the church toward their new hotel, where he'd left the horse and buggy early that morning. As he helped her up onto the bench seat, Faith glanced at a well-stocked basket in the back.

"It appears we won't be going hungry, Husband." She threaded her hand through the crook of his arm. "Looks like you've thought of everything."

"I have all the necessities." Looking down at her, he wiggled his eyebrows. "Brandy, champagne . . . and plenty of peaches!"

Faith laughed, delighted with this burst of romanticism. Reaching up, she kissed the corner of his mouth and whispered, "Then, Mr. Hutton, we have everything we could possibly need."

Kincaid took her in his arms and kissed her thoroughly. When he finally pulled away, he said softly, "I *know* we do, Mrs. Hutton."

Come take a walk down Harmony's Main
Street in 1874, and meet a different resident of
this colorful Kansas town each month.

A TOWN CALLED
❧ HARMONY ❧

__**KEEPING FAITH** by Kathleen Kane
0-7865-0016-6/$4.99

From the boardinghouse to the schoolhouse, love grows in the
heart of Harmony. And for pretty, young schoolteacher Faith
Lind, a lesson in love is about to begin.

__**TAKING CHANCES** by Rebecca Hagan Lee
0-7865-0022-2/$4.99 *(coming in August)*

All of Harmony is buzzing when they hear the blacksmith,
Jake Sutherland, is smitten. And no one is more surprised
than Jake himself, who doesn't know the first thing about
courting a woman.

__**CHASING RAINBOWS** by Linda Shertzer
0-7865-0041-7/$4.99 *(coming in September)*

Fashionable, Boston-educated Samantha Evans is the
outspoken columnist for her father's newspaper. But her
biggest story yet may be her own exclusive–with a most
unlikely man.